7-18-24

OAK CREST
TOWN CENTER
LIBRARY

MAN

OF

EXILE

by

Jeremy M. Wright

The characters and events in this book are fictitious. Any similarity to real persons, living or dead, is coincidental and not intended by the author.

Copyright © 2022, 2009 by Jeremy M. Wright

Cover design by Lance Buckley

All rights reserved. No part of this book may be reproduced in any form or by any electronic or mechanical means, including information storage and retrieval systems, without permission in writing from the publisher, except by reviewers, who may quote brief passages in a review.

First paperback edition by Stone Gateway Publishing April 2022

ISBN-13: 979-8-9855225-3-2

Printed in the United States of America.

For Gale Husk, who is somewhat mental, but not in that creepy way that makes one want to take off running the other way.

More than anything, thank you for the long, wonderfully bizarre conversations that have sparked major life into my novels!

"My hypocrisy goes only so far."

~ John "Doc" Holliday ~

Also by Jeremy M. Wright

Fiction

Chasing Daylight

From Shadowed Places:
13 Darkly Twisted Tales

Young Adult

The Good Ship

MAN

OF

EXILE

1

They had found him. The hunt had lasted three intensely long years, but now they finally had him.

Brandon Harris stood waist-deep in the breaking surf of the Indian Ocean. He held a surf rod and wore a white baseball cap to protect him from the blistering sun. He was thin and pale, and it surprised the men who watched him to find the young man fishing for sport. With his high intellect, they fully expected to find him in front of a computer planning his next strategic attack to cripple the empires of the criminal underground.

The rod gave two jerks as a fish tested the bait. The rod then bowed as the fish took the line. Brandon gave a tug to set the hook, and then cranked the reel, drawing the fish closer to shore. He moved up the shore as he pulled the fish from the water. It was a decent-sized black drummer. He smiled as he inspected the catch of the day.

"Nice fish," the man called the Tourist said.

Brandon was two hundred yards down the beach, and the Tourist could see him clearly through the binoculars. He didn't worry that the young man would spot him watching, because Brandon actually believed no one was looking for him anymore. He thought he was safe from the terrors of the world, but the terror had found him, regardless of his best efforts at escaping them.

Brandon gathered his gear and fresh catch and headed up the shore to his quaint beach house.

The Tourist opened his cell and made a call. "It's definitely him. We'll wait until nightfall and then we'll take him," he said with a subtle Russian accent.

"Understood. I've already left his house. There's an encrypted code on his computer. I won't be able to find what we need without that code. When we take him, I'll ask him politely if he'll decrypt the information for me," Mr. Smith said.

The Tourist laughed. In the three years he'd worked with Mr. Smith, the Tourist had never seen him work information from anyone politely. Promising someone a quick death was as polite as Mr. Smith could get.

"That sounds good to me. He's at the back door now," the Tourist said.

"I'm already in the clear. I'm heading toward you from the north."

Mr. Smith stepped from the tree line and headed down the beach. He was a brawny professional killer, with natural bronze skin and closely cropped black hair flecked with gray. Although he was handsome, there was a certain level of mischief in his eyes that made most people uncomfortable. He glanced at the laptop as he stopped beside the Tourist's beach chair.

"Is it done?" Mr. Smith asked.

"Yes, our comrades in the U.S. have done well. I received the video of Senator Ryan's home invasion. Our men have taken the senator's wife and son, and the senator received an ultimatum. I've sent two emails to the FBI. It should be interesting to see the extent of Special Agent Harper Caster's methods of execution. Of course, I could simply kill him outright, but what fun would that be for me? You know how much I want revenge for what he's done. I know the man is a gifted investigator, but he won't know which direction this challenge is coming from."

"Revenge can be a dangerous business, my friend," Mr. Smith said.

"Revenge is necessary to unbind the heart of pain."

Mr. Smith retrieved two bottles of German beer from the small cooler, removed the caps, and handed one to the Tourist. "Here's to our challenges ahead. May we succeed in the conquest to rule the laws of man."

"Here's a toast to Special Agent Harper Caster. I wish him a noble death on our road to greatness," the Tourist said.

They clanked bottles and drank in salute.

— —— —

It was just after one in the morning when the Tourist removed the lock picks from his pocket and in the sliver of moonlight made quick work of the deadbolt. They slipped inside the beach house in silence. Mr. Smith guided them to the main bedroom at the back of the house.

The Tourist approached the bed and watched the sleeping man. Brandon was lightly snoring. He was still completely unaware that he would soon face a series of hard times and much pain. The Tourist didn't even see a gun on the nightstand or in the drawer. He carefully slid his hand beneath the pillow and found no weapon within reach. Brandon must have truly believed that no one would ever find him.

A simple mistake that cost him everything, the Tourist thought.

He glanced over his shoulder, nodded to Mr. Smith, who then flipped on the bedroom light.

Brandon Harris's eyes shot open and then pinched shut in reflex from the overhead blinding light.

The Tourist viciously brought down the barrel of his gun on Brandon's left kneecap. There was a slight crunch, followed by a violent scream.

Brandon bolted upright and seized his injured knee with both hands.

"Oh, God! Oh, God!" he said. He rocked back and forth on the bed as the pain thundered up his entire leg.

"Shh, the screaming is unnecessary, Mr. Harris. I'm sure the pain is great, but you shouldn't worry, I was gentle enough not to break bones. I apologize that our introduction was a little more brazen than I typically desire. That's my associate Mr. Smith and I'm the Tourist. We're pleased to make your acquaintance after all these years. You're a rather difficult man to get in touch with, so to speak."

Through tear-filled eyes, Brandon looked up at the man with the Russian accent.

"This is my house. What do you think you're doing here?"

"Yes, we're well aware of our current location, Mr. Harris. As for the reason we are here, I'm surprised that you haven't already reached that conclusion. My employer wishes to speak to you. We're here to take you home," the Tourist said.

"Employer? Who do you work for? Is this about the money? Okay, okay, I'll give it all back. I swear it. Just help me get to my computer and I'll transfer all of it to any account you want. Then you can go. There's no need to hurt me anymore or take me anywhere. I can transfer the money from here."

"The money? Oh, I see. I'm afraid that your super computer of a mind has drawn the wrong conclusion. We're not employed with the Russian cartel that you swindled millions from. They're looking for you as well. It just so happens that we found you first. You've been very busy at upsetting many people. Last year, we almost had you in Panama, but you must have felt unsafe because you fled a few days before we arrived. We had lost your trail for some time and eventually discovered you were residing in South Africa, but someone must have informed you, or maybe intuition warned you, and you fled once again. Now, here along this majestic Australian coastline, we've finally dropped a net on you. I have a distinct feeling that you will not escape this time. We will bring you back to the United States. There's much work to be done," the Tourist said.

"I don't understand. If it isn't the money, then what is it you're after?"

The Tourist nodded again to Mr. Smith and the man quickly disappeared into the other room. He returned a moment later with Brandon's laptop and placed it on the bed.

"If you would be so kind to open your computer," Mr. Smith said.

Brandon slowly rotated on the bed and carefully let his legs hang over the edge. He gritted his teeth and released a grunt of pain as he picked up the computer and placed it on his lap.

As the computer booted up, the Tourist said, "I apologize for the pain. The act was to get your attention. I wanted you to understand how serious we are. Now, I need you to decrypt the file titled Blackstone."

Brandon's fingers paused on the keyboard. "The Blackstone file? That's what this is all about? So, your employer is—"

"It's irrelevant who my employer is. The file was not yours for the taking. You made a mistake three years ago by hacking the wrong computer. No one must see those files, and we're here to retrieve them. When we've acquired all the information you've stolen, the three of us will take a long plane ride," the Tourist said.

"Okay, okay, I think we can work out some kind of deal here."

"No deals."

"Look, how about if I give you the files and two million for your troubles? That's one million dollars for each of you. That's a pretty good deal, right?"

"No deals."

"The files and four million. Please?"

"No deals. Don't beg. It makes you more pathetic than you already are. Our employer hired us to recover the stolen files and bring you back to the states. We are men of action, and our word is a binding contract. Our employer expects this, and we always deliver as promised. Besides, I could easily turn you over to the Russians who have placed a five-million-dollar bounty on your head. Now open the file," the Tourist said calmly.

"The files and ten million. You couldn't possibly say no to that offer."

"Don't insult my intelligence. You don't have ten million to bargain with. The answer would be no, regardless. Don't make me tell you again to open the file."

"Okay. I'll give you what you want, just don't kill me." Brandon's fingers began working across the keyboard and within a minute he decrypted the Blackstone file, and all the information was now available.

The Tourist smiled. "Very good, Mr. Harris. Now pack your necessary belongings. It's time to go."

2

-----Original Message-----
From: thetourist@gmail.com
To: hcaster@fbi.gov
Sent: Sunday, August 30, 2020 8:34 PM
Subject: 5 mysterious people

Special Agent Harper Caster,

I have only one thing to claim to you in this email, and it's a claim you should take seriously. I would if I were you.

This is what I have to say to you:

I'm going to murder five people. Only five. I think that's the magic number. Who would miss five people in such a cluttered world? The answer is simple. These won't be ordinary lives. You'll care about these people. You'll want to take your full forces to solve these crimes. Your American government will be outraged by these five murders. The murders will plaster the headlines for months. This will bring chaos like you've never seen before. I promise.

It sounds all too crazy, doesn't it? But I assure you that I am in my right mind. I am of sound mind, of strong mind. Why else would I be sending this? Of course, I will not tell you who the five will be. That wouldn't be fair. I want you to understand that this isn't a game for me. I get no personal satisfaction being hunted by the FBI and other international government agencies. No doubt that from this email you believe I'm boasting, egging you on, so to speak. I assure you I am not. I don't wish to be captured and spend my remaining years in a facility for the criminally insane. That certainly doesn't sound very pleasing to the ears.

The magic number is five. I'll tell you why. With exquisite planning and caution, your authorities won't capture me. Five is the perfect number, not too few, and certainly not too many. I realize that a series of murders will bring the authorities closer to my true identity. Without more victims, without more bloodshed, the trail will grow cold. They will never find me as I disappear with my mission accomplished.

Five perfect murders. Jack the Ripper did it so long ago. I think it's time someone does it again. Unlike the Ripper, I don't have my sights on prostitutes. They're quite safe. I wouldn't waste my time planning such a worthy quest on the pitiful.

Just to give you a heads up, your American president is quite safe as well. Don't misunderstand, I could get him if I were so inclined, but he's doing such a wonderful job of corrupting the U.S. the way it is. Besides, he's on the fast track out the door.

That brings me to another point. I never said the five soon-to-be victims are Americans. You won't know which nationality they are until it's much too late. It may seem random to you, but it is goal seeking to me.

Not to confuse you, but I certainly don't place myself on the same pedestal as Jack the Ripper. In fact, I believe that my intellect and desire are well beyond his legend. It's not rage or curiosity or pleasure that drives me. It is purpose that is my motivation. In the end, you can rest assured that I'll do as the famed Mr. Ripper. I'll make history and then vanish without a trace. They'll even write books about me.

   Sincerely,
   The Tourist

3

The message I read simply seemed like a joke at first. I suspected someone at the FBI had internally emailed me from the Hoover Building. I thought it was probably just a few agents having a little fun with me. It's no secret around the office that I'm tightly wound up. I figured some of the other agents were trying to get me to loosen up a bit. After I read the email several times, I understood it wasn't my colleagues having fun with me. Aside from the obvious message of promising murder, there was a strong conviction within the writing.

I thought it was all a crazy joke until I opened the second email.

It had been a normal day until that point. I finally rolled out of bed a little later than usual. I spent the morning having breakfast with my wife and daughter. Then I pulled out of the driveway and headed for work nearly an hour later than my strict internal clock demanded. At noon, I enjoyed a laid-back lunch with a couple of friends I saw a few times a month. Things had been easy-going this fine summer Monday afternoon. In fact, things had been good for quite some time. I began finding myself in the steady rhythm of a somewhat normal life.

Returning to the office after lunch was my first mistake of the day. Turning on my computer was my second mistake. Opening the two unknown emails was my third and final mistake of the day.

I read the first email three times. It was short and to the point, but also downright baffling. Was someone actually planning on killing five people? What purpose did the sender have by bringing me into the investigation? Why would this person feel the need for a chase?

I was leaning back in my chair with my eyes glued to the screen. The video played for the third time in the last twenty minutes. I desperately tried to burn every terrifying image into my brain.

The video ended and I clicked the play button again.

"It's on, we're rolling. Action!" the unknown cameraman said.

The camera focused on a green door with dim lighting filtering through the frosted panes of glass. The camera turned to the brass numbers above the door. 12242. The camera then rotated in the darkness to a light pole thirty yards down the street. The view zoomed on the sign anchored to the pole. It was an awkward angle, but it was legible. Montgomery Street. The camera rotated back to the door. Someone's hands came into view as they pulled on latex gloves. A key was used to unlock the front door, and the cameraman rotated the knob and gently pushed the door open. Moving inside almost stealth-like, the camera focused on the security keypad on the wall. The cameraman punched in a code and the security system deactivated.

One figure came into view and then another. From what I could tell so far, there were three individuals inside the home. Two of the intruders were partially in view and one operated the camera. There were quick glimpses of the house's layout and the furnishings. By the look of the eccentric décor, the homeowner made a comfortable living.

Guided by the soft glow of plug-in night-lights, the three individuals moved up the staircase to the top floor. They went down a short hallway and through a partially closed bedroom door. A flashlight clicked on, revealing two people sleeping in a king-sized bed. Two of the assailants moved to the opposite sides of the bed. In the flashlight's beam, they removed a roll of duct tape from their coat pockets. With precise timing, they pulled a length of tape loose and wrapped it over the mouths of the two-sleeping people. Even in the shadows, I could tell there was a man and a woman in the bed.

They suddenly awoke and instant panic set in. They tried screaming, but the tape muffled their efforts. The two assailants violently tore the man and woman from the bed and slammed them to the floor. More tape was pulled from the roll and the intruders quickly bound the victims' wrists and ankles.

"It will be easier for you if you don't fight," the cameraman said.

I detected a slight Russian accent, purposely washed out, but it was there.

The restrained man on the floor disregarded the advice and fought harder. His taped legs thrashed out and caught one assailant squarely in the jaw and rocked the man from a squatted position to sprawled flat out on his back. The other assailant stepped forward and brought his hiking boot down hard on the man's left knee. The restrained man screamed behind the layer of tape.

"That was a warning. My assistant here would love to end this day by putting a large hole in your head. If you fight again, I'll grant him that request. Now be still and listen closely," the cameraman said.

The camera moved forward and then focused on the man and woman. They redirected both flashlights, and the faces of the victims became clear.

I leaned forward until my face was only inches from the screen. Even though I had watched the video three times, this part was the hardest to believe. I knew these faces very well. In fact, the entire country knew them.

The cameraman said, "I want you to take a deep breath through your nose and calm yourself. We won't kill you. Not if you do exactly what we ask. I promise. I'm going to ask you to do one simple thing. It's a very easy action for you to take. So that we're assured you follow our request, we're going to take your wife and son with us. Here's what I ask of you, Senator Ryan. Tomorrow, you'll make a televised announcement stating you're withdrawing from the presidential race. Are we understood? Then, and only then, you will receive your family back."

When the video went blank, I snatched the phone from the cradle and called FBI Director David Gill.

4

I forwarded both emails to Director Gill. Now I was in the director's office, sitting across from him as he intently studied the computer screen. I watched him closely. Director Gill remained expressionless as he read the first message and then viewed the five-minute video. The only minor reaction I noticed was a muscle spasm at the corner of his right eye when the video reached the part that revealed Senator Ryan's identity.

When the video ended, I half expected Director Gill to hit the ceiling with panic. In fact, I received the opposite reaction.

Director David Gill leaned back in his chair and rubbed his eyes. I wasn't sure if he had even blinked during the five minutes of playtime. Next, he leaned forward and casually brushed his thin black hair from his forehead as he collected himself before speaking.

"Are these emails connected?" he asked.

"I think so. The second email came from a separate address account two minutes after the first. Whoever the sender is, they have some computer skills. Not even the big brains of the FBI geek squad could trace them. Clearly, we're dealing with someone who has an unmerciful group of followers. As you can see from the video, there were three men in Senator Ryan's house. So, if there's a connection with these emails, then does it mean the senator's wife and son are two of the five victims?

But that would go against what the man in the video said. He told the senator his family would be unharmed if he withdrew from the presidential race today. Maybe they're not connected at all. Maybe they're two entirely different games this person wants to play. Either way, that means I'm going to have myself one hell of a busy week," I said and slumped in the chair.

"You should have called in sick. That's what you get for being a kiss-ass overachiever. I can tell you one thing, if these two emails are unrelated, then top priority is the senator and his family. This other email claiming five murders could be some kind of sick joke or maybe a diversion. As the sender points out, there's no way we can figure out who these five people will be. Whoever the person is, they obviously want you involved," Director Gill said.

"Maybe I could email back and ask him to hold off the killing until next week, when it would be a little more convenient for me. I'm sure the sender wiped the IP address from existence by now. I can turn a computer on and double click, but that's the extent of my intelligence on the matter," I said.

"We're obviously dealing with someone who has a brighter bulb than you. I'm going to get ahold of Senator Ryan and find out where he is. I can say that I honestly don't understand why they kidnapped his family to make him withdraw from the race. They've already gone through far more trouble than they needed to. Why wouldn't they just kill him? I'm glad they didn't, but wouldn't that be an easier route for men of that caliber?" Director Gill asked.

"Who can really summarize the justifications of madmen? I don't even understand the purpose of sending me the video email. Are they playing a game? Are they daring me to catch them? If Senator Ryan does as they demand and they release the wife and son, what's the main reason for bringing me in?"

"Answering those questions is how you're going to earn your pay for today. I'd like to know what the hell happened to Senator Ryan's Secret Service detail. The video didn't show a confrontation with the men stationed at the house. You saw the address in the video. I want you to take Molar and Briggs as backup and get to the senator's house as quick as possible. I hope I can get the senator on the phone and we won't have to create a big stir in front of his house. The media would go apeshit over this. Be extremely cautious when you get there. Try not to draw the attention of the neighbors. I want to keep a lid on this for now. We don't know what these men will do if we expose their operation. They probably told the senator that contacting the police will bring serious consequences. Of course, that doesn't explain the damn emails sent to you. I don't know what the hell is going on. Get going, Harper. Quietly lock down the senator's house and collect all potential evidence," Director Gill said.

"I'm on my way, sir," I said.

Director Gill was already on the phone with his assistant in the outer office.

"Jennie, I need you to get me Senator Andrew Ryan's home, cell, and office phone numbers as quick as possible, please."

5

Derek Molar and Malcolm Briggs sat perfectly still as I maneuvered through the D.C. streets and explained the headline events unraveling this afternoon. They watched me as if I were explaining an unexpected training procedure instead of genuine facts. This was such a wickedly crafted story that Derek and Malcolm hadn't yet committed themselves to buying my interpretation of the worst Monday afternoon in the last decade.

My cell rang when I turned the corner of Montgomery Street and coasted into the senator's driveway.

Director Gill said, "Harper, I got ahold of Senator Ryan. He's at his office. He actually seemed surprised when I asked him if he was all right. I asked about his wife and son. He told me that his wife was having a late lunch meeting with a few friends and that his son was, of course, at school. I checked with the elementary school Dillon attends, and his father called him in sick today. Also, I found out that the two Secret Service agents assigned to Senator Ryan last night were unaccounted for at the office this morning. Where are you guys now?"

"Sitting in his driveway acting inconspicuous. We're just three friendly FBI guys stopping by for a cup of coffee. I was about to approach the front door when you called."

"Okay, now we have a dilemma. Senator Ryan is safe. He claims that his wife and son are also safe, which is apparently a bold-faced lie. If you enter his home without his permission or a warrant, there could be a series of headaches coming my way if I tell you to enter the house. So, what I want you to do is have a look through the windows. If you see anything inside that might lead you to believe that someone invaded the home or someone is being held captive inside, I want you to use any means necessary to secure the residence. Please don't create a circus for the neighbors. I still want you to maintain extreme secrecy as long as possible," Director Gill said.

"I forgot my bullhorn at home, anyway."

"The three of you are on your own. Be careful. Call me the minute you find out anything."

"Will do." I turned off my phone and eyed the other agents. "Senator Ryan is okay. The wife and son are unknown. They could be held inside or even abducted, as the man in the video claimed. I think most of the neighbors should be at work but try not to act too obvious when you're peeking in the windows. Derek, you go around the south side of the house and Malcolm can take the north side. I'll take the front door. Look for anything out of the ordinary."

We stepped from the black sedan and headed in different directions. I hurried up the cobblestone steps to the front door, then leaned in close to the window and cupped my hands around my eyes. I couldn't see anyone inside, and nothing seemed disturbed. I tried the knob and found it locked.

"Harper," Derek said from the side of the house.

"Yeah? Did you find something?"

"Come and look."

I headed down the steps and rounded the house. I followed Derek to a rear window, popped up on my toes, and squinted as I looked inside. Studying the layout of the impressive kitchen, I saw what had grabbed Derek's attention on one of the marble countertops. There was a white towel or maybe a tee shirt soaked with red.

"I'll call that probable cause for entry. We're going in through the back," I said.

Malcolm met us at the back door. Unlike the front door, the back was unlocked, which gave me an instant, unsettling chill. Something felt terribly wrong. Why was the senator lying about everyone being safe? The video and the bloody towel on the counter debunked the senator's earlier claim to Director Gill. Someone was seriously injured inside the home. For whatever reason, Senator Ryan was concealing last night's assault.

With guns drawn, we carefully stepped inside and began a meticulous search throughout the house.

Derek took the upstairs and Malcolm went downstairs. I slowly moved through each room on the main floor. What seemed odd to me was that nothing was disturbed inside. If it hadn't been for the bloody towel on the kitchen counter, I wouldn't have believed a home invasion had actually occurred.

"Clear downstairs," Malcolm said as he entered the living room.

Derek came down the steps and holstered his gun. "I don't know what you saw in the video, but it definitely looks as if a struggle happened up there. The blankets and pillows in the master bedroom are on the floor. There's also a small pool of blood on the carpet at the end of the bed. The kid's bed wasn't made, and it looks like someone quickly grabbed clothes from his dresser. Other than that, everything looks in order."

"Senator Ryan didn't even lock the back door or set the alarm before leaving for work," I said.

"Why do you suppose he did that?" Derek asked.

I said, "Probably because he has nothing left to protect. All right, Malcolm, I want you to get the kit from the trunk of my car. You guys will have to collect all potential evidence. I know you're not a CSU team, so you'll have to fake it. We can't risk involving local police. There are too many potential leaks if we went that route. The press would no doubt have wind of this by the end of the day if we did. I'm going to take the car to Senator Ryan's office and find out exactly what the hell is going on."

6

I arrived at the Capitol Building just after three o'clock. My nerves were incredibly jumpy as I parked on a nearby street, put two quarters in the meter, and walked the short distance in the blistering heat. I had no clue what I was going to say to Senator Ryan.

Before I left the senator's house, I had looked at the master bedroom. As Derek explained, the sheets and pillows were on the floor and there was a pool of blood. It was definitely the same bedroom I saw in the video. There was no hoax about it. The senator and his family were in some serious trouble. He'd kept his mouth closed about the assault and was probably relying on the belief that if he did exactly as they asked, everything would turn out fine. There was no way the senator could trust armed assailants, but they gave him little choice.

I went up the stairs and into the welcoming air-conditioned office building. I stopped at the security station, showed my identification to the guards, and then went to the information board. Senator Ryan's office was 314 on the third floor. I took the elevator and quickly found the senator's office a few doors down the hallway.

Gina Weston, according to the nameplate on her desk, smiled politely as I entered the outer office. She was an attractive brunette in her mid-thirties and dressed in a blue blouse and black slacks. Even though her features were pleasant and innocent, I knew very well she could crank the grinding wheel when the pressure came down.

"May I help you, sir?"

I showed my identification and said, "I'm Special Agent Harper Caster with the FBI. I know that Senator Ryan is incredibly busy, especially with his presidential campaign and all, but I was wondering if I could steal a moment of his time."

She furrowed her brow at the mention of the FBI and then offered another smile.

"What would be the nature of the meeting, sir?"

"Well, it's a personal matter. Is he available?"

"He's down the hall speaking with Senator Cobbe in 322, and he has a press conference in twenty minutes. The senator has a booked schedule for the rest of his day. I can schedule an appointment for you tomorrow if you like."

"You said office 322?" I turned and headed out.

"Wait, you can't disturb him. Sir, just wait a minute," she called after me.

I didn't have the time or patience to wait. If Senator Ryan had a press conference in twenty minutes, then I already knew the subject of that meeting. Senator Ryan was going to announce his withdrawal from the presidential race, just as the intruders had instructed him. There wasn't any way I could change his mind on that matter. I wasn't even going to try. I simply needed the facts of the situation. He was a man standing alone and against an impossible obstacle. If it were possible, I thought he could use a friend, someone standing in his corner and keeping his secret.

Before I reached office 322, I saw Senator Ryan approach from down the hallway. He looked completely deflated. The attack at his house had happened around eleven o'clock last night. He'd probably had very little sleep before being abruptly awakened and threatened. I couldn't imagine the tormented images that must have gone through his mind after the assailants left the house with his wife and son as hostages. Those kinds of thoughts would nearly drive any man to a mental breaking point.

"Senator Ryan, I'm Special Agent Harper Caster with the FBI. Could I have a moment of your time?" I held out my hand, and we shook.

"Sorry? You're FBI?"

"Yes, sir."

"All right. What can I do for you, Agent Caster?"

"Just a private talk. I know you've got a lot to do today. I won't keep you any longer than necessary."

"I have a press conference that I need to prepare for. Whatever this is, it's going to have to wait. I apologize for the bluntness. Please, just make an appointment with my secretary," he said and walked to his office.

I tried to keep my voice at a level that wouldn't attract the attention of people passing us in the hallway.

"I received a video email this morning, senator. You and your wife are in that video."

He quickly stopped. I could see his slumped shoulders tense. He stood there for a moment, staring at the floor, frozen in time. When he finally turned around, I immediately noticed that his face had completely flushed. I thought he might actually faint from the shock of news I delivered.

"What are you talking about?" His eyes were bloodshot and rapidly switching from the passing faces to mine.

In a whisper, I said, "I know what happened to you and your family last night. I know about the men who entered your home. I even know what they want you to do at this press conference."

He straightened his posture, thrust his hands in his trouser pockets, and said, "Follow me."

As I trailed Senator Ryan down the hallway, I noticed a slight limp with each step he took. In the video, he had received a kick to the left kneecap. I could tell that he was trying to mask it as much as possible, but it was still evidently there. He stepped into the men's restroom. I followed several paces back after making sure the hallway was empty.

"I would prefer it if you didn't speak lies in the open like that. Reporters will do anything they can to get their hands on any rumors. You said you saw a video of my wife and me and men who entered our house? I'm not sure what exactly it is you're after, Agent Caster, but I have a lot on my plate and certainly no time for this," Senator Ryan said and walked to the restroom door.

"If you don't mind me asking, what happened to your leg?" I asked.

"A racket ball injury, if you must know," he said over his shoulder.

As he reached for the door, I said, "Did this injury of yours bleed?"

"Bleed? No. I just twisted it, that's all."

"Then whose blood is all over the towel on your kitchen counter?"

Senator Ryan quickly turned and charged toward me. I half expected him to strike out with a raging fist over the fact that I knew he was lying about last night. Instead, he stopped in front of me and pressed his face close to mine. The weariness that consumed him moments ago had given way to anger.

"You were at my house? You have no right, no authorization to be on my property. I'm going to have your ass in a sling for this. The one thing you never want to do is cross me, and now I know how much you've stepped over the line." He was shouting now, and I knew that everyone in the hallway and neighboring offices could hear the senator's threats.

"Sir, I want you to give me a second to explain my actions. I went to your house, and I entered through the unlocked rear door, but only because I saw the bloody towel and thought that someone inside needed help. As I told you before, the men who entered your home last night recorded the entire event. For whatever reason, they emailed the video to me. Did they tell you not to involve the authorities?"

Senator Ryan's sudden fear and anger subsided. He now returned to the worn-out man I had first encountered in the hallway. He looked as if the fight had completely left him.

"They said that if I involved the authorities or if I refused to withdraw from the presidential race, they would mail my wife and son to me in little pieces over the next year. Your reasons for coming here just killed my wife and son, Agent Caster. Those men will know you were here. They're going to cut them again. They promised they would. You saw my wife's blood, didn't you? They cut her last night to show me how serious they are. They cut her arm open, and the blood kept coming out. You can't imagine how much she screamed, and I couldn't do anything to help her."

Just then, the emotional events became overwhelming, and tears slipped free, slow at first, and then faster as his mind undoubtedly began flashing horrific images of his wife and son under the blade of sadistic madmen.

I thought about what he said. Someone could have easily followed me from the senator's house. The men would know that I spoke with the senator. The true reason for the email was confusing. Did those men send me the email of the assault as a way of getting Senator Ryan to break their rule unknowingly? If the first email claimed there would be five perfect murders connected to this case, then did it mean that the men strategically planned to fracture the rules by bringing me in, making the senator's wife and son the first two deaths out of five?

Senator Ryan stepped to the sink, ran cold water into his cupped hands, and splashed his face. He pulled a couple of paper towels from the dispenser and wiped his hands and face dry.

When he finished composing himself, he turned and said, "If you're looking for something good to do for the day, something that lightens your heart as a good deed fulfilled, then you'll listen to my request that you leave this office building. Get in your car and go back to work, delete that damn email and forget all about this day. I think that's the only way my wife and son have a chance of surviving this. I have to go. I have an important announcement to make in the next ten minutes. Good day, Agent Caster."

"I'm involved for whatever reasons they intended. I don't have a choice in the matter," I said.

Before he left the restroom, he offered a weak smile and said, "Neither do I, Agent Caster."

7

I remained behind as Senator Ryan left the restroom. Stepping up to the mirror, I caught the reflection of a man who seemed to have aged ten years since this morning. I couldn't believe how much this day had already beaten me down. I mimicked the senator and splashed cold water on my face. It offered a little revival, but it was short-lived.

I returned to Senator Ryan's office. The secretary claimed he had left for his press meeting being held in one of the first-floor conference rooms. I wondered if any of the attending reporters knew the shattering headline news the senator would deliver. What explanation he would concoct to avoid the truth behind his withdrawal from the presidential race.

A small list of potential suspects began filling inside my mind. I had immediately reached for the obvious at the start. Republican Senator Frost was a man who could gain it all with Senator Ryan removed from the picture. For all I knew, Senator Frost could be under the same circumstances, only to be revealed later today.

Truth be told, I wasn't here to save Senator Ryan's political career. I wasn't here to talk him out of giving into the demands of the unknown men. I was here to save the day by finding his wife and son alive, and possibly stopping five murders. It was too much stacked against me, but I took the challenge with a crazed hunger.

I wondered if these intruders and now kidnappers were working alone or maybe hired guns taking orders from an unknown instigator.

I flashed my badge to the security guards at the doors. I didn't have a press pass, but a government badge worked just as well. I followed a pack of reporters into the already cramped conference room. Cameras were positioned around the room, and reporters had recording devices at the ready. The media would capture every word the senator spoke and be eagerly ready to upload the announcement to vast national outlets. Only these reporters didn't know the magnitude of what they would witness. The press conference would soon spread across the world in a matter of minutes.

I shifted my way through the crowd to the far right wall and stayed near the back of the room. I curiously watched the camera crews and reporters, wondering if any of them might be one kidnapper playing a disguised role. I thought the men behind this might have very well desired a front row ticket to Senator Ryan's crumbling career.

Senator Ryan's campaign manager, Robert Norris, stepped to the podium and addressed the crowd.

"Ladies and gentleman, thank you for coming on such short notice. I'm sure that you're all curious about the subject of this last-minute announcement, but I urge you to hold all questions until Senator Ryan has finished his statement. Also, please hold your questions until Senator Ryan has pointed to you. This way everyone can hear the questions asked as well as the answers. We don't need one hundred people firing questions at the same time. Be patient and you'll get your turn. Thank you in advance for cooperating."

Robert Norris stepped aside and, a moment later, Senator Ryan walked through the door behind the podium. I could tell right away that he was nervous about the meeting and announcing his departure from the presidential race.

Whenever I'd caught a news blurb of Senator Ryan, he was always smiling and waving while carrying a relatively good-humored nature. Everyone in the room sensed that something was different about the man. His somber and worn features told an unexpected story. The reporters must have known at this point that bad news was rapidly on the way.

He stepped forward, tightly gripped the wood podium edges, and studied the still sea of bodies. His sight shifted from one lingering face to another. Even in the tightly packed crowd, Senator Ryan found me. His eyes locked on mine for a long, uncomfortable moment, and then he focused on his notes.

His hand slightly shook as he took a long drink of water. He actually looked as if he might get sick in front of hundreds of people.

"As Mr. Norris has said, I appreciate all of you coming on such short notice. I'm going to make this quick and as painless for me as possible. I've always enjoyed my life in the different government offices I've held over the years. I would love nothing more than to be your next president. I believe I could make significant changes that would benefit all Americans. Unfortunately, recent circumstances have arisen that will make that task impossible now. I've brought you together to make an official withdrawal from—"

Senator Ryan paused and referred to his notes again. He took another drink of water. His hand was shaking worse than before. He took a quick glance at Robert Norris and then back at the crowd. A small wave of murmurs passed over the room as the confused reporters tried anticipating where this announcement was heading.

Senator Ryan stepped from the podium and paced the platform. I couldn't imagine the inner conflicts he was battling. He was a man being ordered to step down from the presidential race and give up everything he'd worked so hard for. With his wife and son's life on the line, I didn't see how he could alter his decision without serious consequences.

I wasn't sure why he halted the speech, but I had an idea, and the idea wasn't sitting well in my stomach.

Finally, he returned to the podium and looked over the crowd with a more assured posture than he had held before. His voice was also stronger than before as it echoed clearly through the speakers.

"I had a perfectly planned speech ready for you this afternoon. Against better judgment, I won't deliver that speech. I was strictly ordered to give a special announcement, and my defiance could very well cost me more than I'm prepared to lose. The reason behind this meeting was to declare my withdrawal from the presidential race. In fact, I won't take this action. I don't feel a need to conceal the truth from the public any longer. I want everyone to know the forces of terror that I'm currently facing. Last night, three armed assailants entered my home, bound us, and ordered me to step down from this race. They took my wife, Katherine, and my son, Dillon, with them. I was told that if I refused to step down, they would kill my family."

The group of reporters suddenly got restless at this dramatic news and thundered out with a fury of questions. Cameras urgently flashed to capture Senator Ryan's every expression during this unexpected statement.

I tightly pinched my eyes shut, as I couldn't believe what he was doing. He was signing death warrants for his wife and son, and possibly himself as well.

Robert Norris held up his hands and shouted at the crowd. "Please settle down, ladies and gentlemen."

When the reporters finally responded to the request, Senator Ryan continued.

"There's no guarantee that if I meet their request and stand down that they'll return my wife and son unharmed. These are deviant men holding my family, and there isn't trust found in the word of these men. The reasons behind my refusal to agree with their orders are simple. The world is now aware that men have taken my family. These men holding them against their will are now hunted men. Not only will all available government agencies be chasing them, but I will as well. I will use all my power, all my connections to find out who these men are and bring my family home safe. Should these men decide to harm my family based on the action I've taken here, I can promise that there's no corner of the world where I won't find them. I will bring a thundering roar of justice down on them if they don't release my family right now."

I excused myself from the conference room. I wanted to get out of there before the mob of reporters completely lost their composure. There were a million questions that they wanted answered, but probably wouldn't get. Either way, I thought that each one of them had one hell of a story to write. Soon they would break through these doors and make a mad dash back to their home base to get the breaking story on a fierce roll. I didn't want to be around for that.

I had something more important to do. I had to find Senator Ryan's family before the kidnappers saw his wife and son as nothing more than a liability. The pressure would soon come down on these men, and I couldn't fully prepare myself for the actions they would take.

8

After I left the press conference, I went back to my office and locked myself away from the world. I spent over an hour reviewing both emails that got this hellish roller coaster spinning. I was desperately trying to uncover something that the home invaders may have overlooked before sending the material to me. There could have been something as simple as a tattoo, a birthmark, or even an unexpected facial reflection in a window.

One thing I was positive about was that the first email was a lie. Those emails, whether or not related, were a method of boasting and bringing forth a challenge of unprecedented strategy. The writer of the email wanted a battle of wits. He claimed he wouldn't inform me of who the five targets would be, but I was sure that he would have to in order to get the game moving. Somehow, everything would become links in a chain.

There would be no purpose, no motivation behind the first email if he had no intention of giving me a chance to win the game. Otherwise, the threat of the email would remain lifeless and certainly not a high-level priority for the FBI. There had to be a supportive backbone behind the emails, some kind of direction to get me started.

I was rounding out my second hour of staring unblinkingly at the video email when Malcolm and Derek came through my office door. Both of them looked like hell. I could tell they had something interesting to share.

"Well?" I asked. I leaned back in my chair and my spine cracked half a dozen hollow pops.

"Well, we tossed the senator's house, put everything back, and then tossed it again for the sheer hell of it. We actually had a little fun until Senator Ryan returned home and gave us an earful about fractured laws, job termination, and prison time," Derek said.

"Yeah, I suppose having your wife and child kidnapped can turn you into a party crasher quick as you like. Hell, when the press started setting up camp on his front lawn, I thought he was going to go nuclear," Malcolm said.

"I hope for the sake of his family that you found something extremely interesting before he got home," I asked.

"Not only that, but we also snuck it off the property without permission. I guess it's going to be your head on the chopping block should he figure it out, Harper," Derek said.

"Well, if it's my head, then I think I'd like to take a gander at this evidence."

Malcolm removed several clear plastic bags from the evidence kit and handed them to me.

"I figured it was only fair for you to see this, since the evidence has your name and face on it," Derek said.

I carefully laid the clear bags on my desk, leaned in close, and studied the contents. I couldn't believe what I was looking at. The evidence made the entire case even more baffling. Within the evidence, the mystery of whether the two emails, the two games, had a connection showed its face value.

Derek was right about the evidence. It had my name and my face on it. Concealed in the clear bags were two photographs and a single-page letter. The first photo showed me walking to my office desk. The photographer had taken the picture from an adjacent building on a level higher than my office on the third floor. Judging by my suit choice, I guessed the person had taken the photo last Friday.

The second photo was taken outside of a movie theater my family and I frequented. It was raining as my wife, Clara, my twelve-year-old daughter, Kaylee, and I ran for the cover of the theater. I knew when they took this photo as well. We had gone to see another Disney flick on Saturday night. They took the picture from a car across the lot.

I studied the printed page several times. It read:

Special Agent Caster,
I'm sure by now you've come upon more questions that outbalance the answers. I assure you that in due time, the answers will come, regardless of whether you desire them. I suppose you've established that I wasn't telling the entire truth in my first email. You'll have a chance at saving all five lives. The game has already begun and you're falling behind. I honestly don't believe you'll have the cunning to save them. It would be astounding for you to prove me wrong. Do you have the ambition to see the game to its destructive finale? I hope you do. In fact, I'm counting on it.

Sincerely,
The Tourist

"Have either of you heard of the Tourist?" I asked.

They shook their heads.

"Do you have any idea why this nutcase has singled you out? Why would someone purposely taunt an FBI agent? I wonder if he's begging to get caught, maybe subconsciously setting himself up for capture. Sometimes killers have a logical side to their personality that creates potential clues left behind, leading to an arrest. Some of them want to stop, only they can't do it themselves," Malcolm suggested.

"I have a hard time believing this guy is setting himself up. Whoever he is, he's not alone. There are at least two other men associated with this guy. He has an agenda crazy enough to cost five people their lives and a U.S. senator the chance to lose the presidency. I believe he really thinks he's going to pull this off and vanish. As for the reason behind involving me in the chase, I couldn't hazard a guess right now. Maybe he thinks the five murders are far too easy or beneath his level of expertise. He obviously wants to add something spectacular to this game he's playing. He's adding an extra thrill with the possibility of capture and a lifetime of imprisonment, maybe even death."

I slid the clear bags across the desk.

"They wrapped the photos and note up in that bloody towel we saw on the counter. We collected fingerprints from all around the house, a sample of the blood in the master bedroom, and hairs as well. I'll run all these down to the lab right now," Malcolm said.

I said, "Thanks. I wonder why he placed those photographs in a bloody towel. Maybe he's trying to tell me that the blood of the five victims will be on my hands."

9

The limited information about the Tourist wouldn't come from Director Gill. He had told me so. Since the information I needed was vital to the recovery of the senator's wife and child, he unofficially claimed that he would glance the other way if I took it upon myself to snoop through the top-level database. The opportunity was there, and I seized it.

Before I slipped from Director Gill's office, he threw me an unexpected curveball.

"Oh, I almost forgot, a higher power has made it clear that they're sending assistance your way. That's all I'll say for now," he said and smiled in a way that told me nothing good was on a fast approach.

The little shit loved to be coy, and his favorite pastime would always be messing with my head. I wasn't sure of what to expect, but I knew I'd probably have a hard time swallowing the bitter pill.

There were many levels of the FBI database. There was a level open to all agents that held the basics of nearly every wanted or captured person. There were both computer and paper files of unsolved and closed cases. There were endless files that offered criminal history, known associates, fingerprints, and DNA workups of millions of criminals worldwide.

The next level of the database was available to only a select few senior agents like me. The files in this area contained information that went much deeper into high-ranking criminal figures, current top-secret operations, known or suspected terrorists around the world, and many other twisted things that could make one's skin creep.

What I truly needed would lie beyond those levels. When I spoke with Director Gill after the evidence from Senator Ryan's home came to me, I made it very clear to him that the people behind the operation were threatening my family. I think he understood how much they intentionally pushed me into this case. Now it was evident how they'd placed my family in the crosshairs if I didn't bring these people down as quickly as possible.

There was a level deep in the bowels of the Hoover Building, and on that level was a large room packed with top-secret files. There were several computers linked directly to the FBI mainframe, containing every piece of information gathered long before the birth of the FBI. I could access the world's most sinister secrets from this room. There were only a handful of men in the Hoover Building who had authorized access to this room.

Actually, I was sort of one of those people. No one granted me authorization, but I had the code all the same. Don't ask me how, because it's classified.

I removed an access card from my wallet as I approached the thick metal door. I slid the card through the port and then entered an eight-digit code into the keypad. There was a quick chirp and then the hydraulic locking pistons retracted, and the heavy metal door rotated open.

I didn't worry about the half a dozen cameras throughout the corridor capturing my movement to the door. I was confident Director Gill would make certain the security records never saw the light of day.

I could not see the opposite end of the room from the entrance. There were rows of gray metal shelves containing boxes of evidence from some of the world's most notorious heists, kidnappings, political corruptions, and many other horrible crimes. There was only one thing in this room that could spark my interest above all others. I wanted to know about my competition. I wanted the file that told me all about the mysterious man who called himself the Tourist.

Even though I'd unofficially had access to this room for several years, I'd never dared to step so far. Whatever files there were on the Tourist, I could only find on this level of the database, and this was a move I had to make.

I passed a stack of cardboard boxes and took a seat at one of the six computers. I entered a pirated password and, just like that, I had access to all the hidden secrets in the database. It took only a matter of minutes to find exactly what I was looking for. I now had all the known information about the Tourist.

Unfortunately, the files were thin and bleak. Apparently, the sources for the FBI weren't as strong as I had hoped on this matter. In fact, in the files, there was a short list of names associated with the man calling himself the Tourist. There hadn't even been an actual birth name, or a country of origin discovered on the man. Within the material available, there were claims of ties to a Russian cartel dating back fifteen years. Also, the FBI linked the Tourist to mercenary activities in Egypt, South Africa, China, and a dozen other countries. There was speculation that he was still in connection with the Novilov cartel that dominated such cities as Moscow, St. Petersburg, and many other Russian cities.

To place a straighter line on the matter, the FBI was sure that all the attacks attributed to the Tourist were orders brought down by cartel leader Kiril Novilov. The reasons behind the attacks in several countries were unclear, but each target was a political figure.

Now the Tourist had come to the United States, and he'd set his sight on a presidential candidate. There was a deep agenda behind this attack. His methods had changed. None of the other case files spoke of corrupting a government by intimidation or the kidnapping of a government official's family. The targets were quickly and expertly wiped clean from the face of the planet. The Tourist had taken each of them out with either a strategically placed explosive or a high-powered, long-distance rifle shot.

There hadn't been games before. Why now? Why had the Tourist allowed Senator Ryan to live when a single bullet could have ended things at that moment in the bedroom? The Tourist had his chance for an execution of the family and could have moved on. There was something significant about this point I wasn't seeing yet.

Now Senator Ryan had refused to give into the demands of the kidnappers, and he'd complicated things even more. Would these men now execute the senator's family based on his rebellion against their commands? Would they come after the senator next? What could any of these men gain by denying the senator the presidency?

The biggest question of all raced to the front of my thoughts. What the hell did five unknown deaths have to do with this entire equation?

10

"Did you find what you were looking for?" a voice asked as I exited the restricted vault.

I was studying copies of the files I'd made and hadn't noticed someone had waited outside for me. My body momentarily chilled over as if I were a teenager caught with one of my dad's adult magazines. I stopped and glanced at the figure leaning against the corridor wall.

The woman was attractive, with long black hair pulled back in a ponytail and a pleasingly slim figure. Her skin glowed bronze against a cream pin-striped suit with a crimson blouse. Her eyes watched carefully, calculating everything.

"Excuse me? Do I know you?" I asked. I closed the file and held it at my side. I didn't have a clue who this woman was, but an uneasiness washed over me.

"No, we've never met. My name is Sara McNeal. I'm with DHS." She held out her hand, and I took it.

"The Department of Helter Skelter?"

"I wasn't told you have an incredible sense of humor, Agent Caster. The Department of Homeland Security, actually."

"I hate to be the bearer of bad news, but you took a wrong turn somewhere along the way. This is the Hoover Building. You're a couple of blocks off the mark. Which agency within the department are you employed with?"

"A department not readily found on the usual list. Director Gill informed me you'd be hiding out in the basement. I would have joined you inside that room, but I don't have proper clearance," she said.

"Neither do I," I said, and began walking down the hallway. Sara McNeal followed.

"You're not even curious why I'm here?"

"I'm curious about a lot of things in life, but that isn't one of them. I'm sorry, I've had an incredibly busy day so far and it doesn't look like it'll be slowing down anytime soon." I approached the elevator and pressed the call button.

"I also hate to be the bearer of bad news, Agent Caster, but whatever it is you're off and running to do, I guess my orders are that I have to tag along."

As I turned to her, everything finally clicked in place. Earlier, Director Gill claimed he had a little surprise for me later today. This young woman sent over from the DHS was it. I hadn't seen this one coming at me like a freight train with a howling whistle, even though I should have expected it. I had to unwillingly join forces with another government agency, a mysterious one at that.

"I get it. The DHS has assured themselves that the FBI, scratch that, a single agent within the FBI, couldn't handle this earth-shattering case by himself. Right?"

We stepped on the elevator, and I pressed the third floor button.

"Earth-shattering might be the understatement of the year, Agent Caster. A group of men are attempting to unweave the very fabric of our governmental structure. They're trying to destroy every red-blooded American's right to elect the candidate of their choice. If we give into this act of terror, then we might as well open the door for all those who oppose our way of life. We're not about to allow corrupted men to accomplish the purpose behind this unspeakable action against our nation."

"That was a glorious speech. Did you practice those lines all the way over here? You didn't even stumble once," I said.

"This is certainly no time for jokes, Agent Caster. We have serious issues that need immediate attention. The news stations are constantly replaying the press conference Senator Ryan held earlier. The men who are holding his family captive are currently weighing their options. They're going to execute his family if we don't nail them down as soon as possible. Maybe they already have. In either case, the DHS is sure that the senator's brazen actions will cause the death of his family. Whoever these men are, they mean business with no bullshit. They didn't get their demands met, so now they'll destroy the man who refused to give in. Besides, don't get so cocky about being a one-man team. I'm sure that you're aware the Secret Service, CIA, Homeland Security, and other agencies are all over this case."

"I'm fully aware of all that. Exactly what do you think I was doing in that room, Agent McNeal? Do you think I would jeopardize my employment by sneaking in there just to take an unauthorized coffee break? I'm trying to find these men before they kill the senator's wife and son. I'm searching for some kind of lead to run with. That's the way we do it here at the FBI."

"I'm sorry then for what I said. I know you were already aware of the circumstances. I have a tendency to state the obvious far too often. Not to mention that my personality is rather rough around the edges. By the way, I'm not exactly an official agent with DHS."

The elevator stopped on level three, and we headed for my office. I took a seat at my desk and motioned for her to sit in one of the empty chairs.

"What exactly does that mean? Are you actually an undercover agent with the KGB instead?"

"No. I do work within DHS as I recently finished my specialized training. This is my first field assignment."

I leaned back in the chair. I had just received a hard mental kick to the skull. Well, if that didn't beat all, they were teaming me up with a trainee.

11

I called Director Gill to verify that they were, in fact, teaming me up with a DHS rookie. For the briefest of moments, I hoped another agent was having a little fun with me. Unfortunately, that hadn't been the case. I thanked him for his truly twisted sense of humor and hung up.

"You realize that Director Gill had nothing to do with me being assigned to this case, right?" Sara said.

"I know. Director Gill can't hold a candle to the guys who are secretly commanding this wild card of a case. I imagine the order came directly from the president. What I'm still trying to figure out is how someone like you could maneuver yourself into something this sensational," I said. I wasn't trying to be rude, but it just came out that way.

"I could ask the same thing about you. Of course, I already know the details behind the emails, your so-called invitation. Let me just say that I didn't screw my way to this point, if that's your implication."

"I wasn't implying that at all. I was only saying that this is the most interesting case someone has ever shoved me into face-first. I've only had a few cases in my career that could moderately compare. Truthfully, I wouldn't touch this case if I could help it. I can feel it in every fiber of my being that this case is going to spiral downhill at a terrifyingly rapid pace. The man behind this operation has claimed that he's going to end five lives. The senator and his family are in the immediate crosshairs. Now it has become clear that my family and I may suffer the wrath of this maniac if the cards don't fall the way he has designed them to. In any case, I suppose I should catch you up on current events."

I turned on my computer and then opened my email. I needed to check to see if the mysterious man who called himself the Tourist had sent a follow-up letter in light of Senator Ryan's refusal to his demands. I had additional emails, but none of them were important to the case. I opened the letter for Sara McNeal to read. After she carefully read the email several times, she played the video.

I went to the window and opened the file I had taken from the database. I was desperately trying to find something that would allow me to figure out a clue behind the Tourist's identity. What the hell was this guy's motivation behind the removal of a presidential candidate?

When she finished watching the video for the third time, I handed her the file that I had unofficially retrieved.

"Now read this and tell me what you understand from it," I said.

Just like the emails, she reviewed the material several times with extreme focus.

"Is there anything in there that stands out to you?" I asked.

"Well, first of all, I find it hard to believe that a person with this type of criminal history spanning across the globe has only five confusing pages in his file. I would think the FBI or some other agency would have an entire book on this guy. He's into some serious stuff. They've linked him to high-profile assassinations worldwide.

There's not even a suspected true identity anywhere in this file. He's a total ghost," she said as she shuffled through the pages.

"Right, it's truly a flat-bottom basic file that gives us little to go on."

"It's almost as if the FBI were deliberately trying to avoid anyone discovering anything about this man. It could even be a woman. I don't want to assume the Tourist is a man, not until we know for sure," she said.

"Why would the FBI do something like that?" I asked as I casually watched her. I had my suspicions, but I wanted to test her ability to break down her own theory. If we were going to be pressed together in the vise of this mind-warped case, I needed to understand the different directions her mind could travel when we come face-to-face with a brick wall.

"If it had been intentional to keep important information from this file, then I could speculate that perhaps the Tourist had once worked for the U.S. government or maybe still does. He could be an operative of some sort. Although our upstanding government officials will never admit it, I'm sure there's trained military men who make a comfortable living taking care of people who need to be blinked away."

"Excellent. I like the way your mind works. So maybe this highly trained son of a bitch government assassin had decided that he no longer wanted to take orders and becomes a rogue killer. Maybe he has set his targets on the people behind the secret operation that made him into the man he is today. Or maybe he has chosen to destroy Senator Ryan's campaign as a way of receiving the national attention he feels he has always missed out on," I said.

"Yeah, I think we've figured it out. Should we take this to the press now?"

I laughed. "Sure, we could do that. Maybe we could guess what he looks like and have front-page news by morning. We could get lucky with a citizens' arrest. Case closed." Despite the situation, I felt myself warming up to Sara McNeal.

"So perhaps what's in this file is totally bogus, a clever ploy to confuse anyone brave enough to sneak into the restricted files," she said, and smiled.

"I wasn't there. I found those files on the floor in the bathroom."

"I guess it's a good thing that you found the files and not the janitor. Okay, so the million-dollar question remains. In what way has this information pushed us closer to the Tourist and finding the senator's wife and son before it's too late?" Sara asked.

I glanced at the clock. It was after eight. I had missed dinner for the first time in nearly a month. Clara was going to be pissed. At least with a case like this one, I had a pretty good excuse in my corner.

I then remembered the photos discovered at the senator's home. Whoever these people were, they had been watching my family. The thought certainly got my motivation on a roll to get home. Although I had called Clara earlier in the day to check in, I was a little worried about the actions the men would take next. Now Clara and Kaylee might have unwillingly become a part of this case.

I said, "Why don't we head home and chew on what we've uncovered so far? With the little we have to go on, there isn't any kind of move we can make right now. For the time being, the fate of the senator's wife and son is out of our hands. We'll figure out some kind of direction tomorrow."

12

I had worked myself into a frenzy over the safety of my girls. The stress of the situation was apparently uncalled for. As soon as I parted from Sara and left my office, I used my cell to call home. Clara answered and I could tell by her lofty tone that everything at home was good. I didn't want to let on that something was bothering me, but I think she detected an inflection in my voice that gave away my worry.

Things at home were the opposite of my expectations. Clara held our dinner in suspension until I arrived. She had prepared a tuna casserole, peas, rolls, and a cheesecake for dessert.

During the meal, Clara started a conversation related to the current events that plastered every newscast. I felt uneasy when she questioned whether I knew anything about the circumstances Senator Ryan currently faced. I shrugged and gave her a look she knew all too well. It was the type of look that told her I was unfortunately caught right in the middle of something unpleasant.

"They chose you?" Clara asked.

I shrugged again. "Director Gill didn't choose me, but someone else did. Just like usual, I'm right where I don't want to be. You know I can't talk about an ongoing case."

Usually, my wife would press even harder at this sudden revelation, but tonight I thought she could read the weariness on my features. The conversation traveled on to Clara's law office gossip that she was most famous for discussing. Working as a paralegal for one of the city's largest law firms, she had her fingers twirling in everyone's business.

Even though the day had ground me down, I stayed up until nearly one o'clock. Comfortable sleep rarely finds me, and when it does, it only stays briefly. My mind continued to journey back to the unexpected press conference. What Senator Ryan had done was incredibly defiant and outright careless. However, I understood things from his perspective. As Senator Ryan had claimed during the conference, withdrawing from the presidential race wasn't a guaranteed safe passage for his wife and son. On the other side of things, he was taking a giant risk by not giving in to the demand. Maybe he was relying on the authorities to take these men down and bring his family home unharmed.

The gates of Tuesday opened to a fury that swiftly took down the former contender known as Monday.

When my cell rang a little after six-thirty and the caller ID announced it was Director Gill, I knew that bad news was on a fast approach.

"Yeah?" I said in a sleep-deprived voice.

"Hey, I know it's early, and tell Clara that I'm sorry. This is the big one we weren't hoping to see, Harper. We have a body on the north side of Tranquility Park just off the bike path. It's Katherine Ryan. A couple of joggers found her a little over an hour ago. The local police have the area locked down. I need you and Ms. McNeal to get there immediately."

I pinched my eyes shut. I couldn't believe this was happening.

When I hung up, I immediately called Sara and gave her the location. She said she'd be on her way in a minute flat.

The crowded lot of Tranquility Park was nearly two hundred yards from the body of Katherine Ryan, so I parked on the grass next to a large elm. The media and curious pedestrians already overwhelmed the park. They restlessly watched from behind the crime scene tape and the battalion of added security. I hoped local law enforcement had been quick enough to hold everyone back and reduce the chance of someone destroying any kind of crime scene evidence. God forbid someone had already snapped a picture of the victim and uploaded it to social media.

The sun had barely broken the horizon an hour ago, but the heat of the morning was already making this awful experience even more unbearable.

Sara stood near the front of the crowd. I weaved my way next to her and flashed my ID to the patrolman at the barricade. We shouldered through the mob and quickly made our way toward the swarm of blue uniforms.

"When are you going to get an official DHS identification badge? I mean, other than the nifty one that says *trainee* on it," I said.

"I told you. I just finished my specialized training. They haven't issued me an official identification yet. Besides, I'm still learning the moves of flashing a badge by watching you," she said.

"I've got the moves," I agreed.

"I think we were both positive that the case would come down to this," Sara said.

"Yeah, I didn't think the kidnappers would take Senator Ryan's resistance very well. He was probably right. They might have killed her anyhow, but he should have taken different measures during his press conference. The way he spoke out seemed almost like a challenge to the kidnappers, almost taunting them. Hostile men like these don't take no for an answer. What I had been fearing all day Monday came true today."

"Right now, these men are probably calculating the methods they'll use to corrupt the man who stood against them. I don't doubt they're going to find another way to destroy the senator," Sara said. She removed sunglasses from her jacket pocket and put them on.

I showed my badge again, and the patrol crew allowed us to proceed down the bike path.

A three-man CSU team worked the body and the surrounding area. This would be the most important crime scene of their careers, and precision was an absolute must.

Katherine Ryan was still wearing a burgundy cotton nightgown. Her body was pale white, almost mannequin-like. Her head was sickly turned away from us, twisted in a direction that made me believe the kidnappers had sharply wrenched her head and quickly ended all of her fears. She had been an attractive middle-aged businesswoman, but now she was the definition of the downfall of humanity.

"Can I help you?" a crime scene tech asked.

"I'm Special Agent Caster with the FBI. This is Sara McNeal with some sort of position within the Department of Homeland Security. We're heading up the investigation."

We shook hands, and he said, "I'm Charlie King. I was told to expect you. Except for a couple of joggers that were standing near the body when we arrived, no one else has seen Mrs. Ryan. The husband and wife in the matching blue warm-up suits over there found her. We already took a statement from them." He pointed to a thirty-something couple who looked a bit nauseous from their morning discovery.

"You haven't found anyone else? No other bodies?" Sara asked.

"No, ma'am. I had my guys carefully search the area just before you arrived. It's just her, no one else. Is there supposed to be another body?"

"I'm sure you saw Senator Ryan's press conference. They took his wife and son at the same time. I guess we can consider not finding the boy's body a good sign. We can only hope the kidnappers will find no benefit behind the death of a ten-year-old child. Maybe they're holding the kid for additional leverage. If you ask me, they've made their statement clear enough already," I said.

I heard a startled yelling behind me. I spun around and couldn't believe what I saw. Senator Andrew Ryan was here. Worse than that, he had broken through the police barricade and was running toward us.

Cameramen from the local stations quickly turned to capture every grueling, heartbreaking detail of Senator Ryan's mental collapse. He was cutting across the grass in an awkward, stumbling run. Several patrolmen held out their hands as a simple gesture at calming a man who was bouncing on his remaining strand of sanity. He blazed by them with little regard. When his eyes fixed on the lifeless body of his wife in the sun-dried grass, his momentum kicked into overdrive. He shouldered through more of the men in blue who tried to restrain him.

"Hey, get control of him," I screamed to five patrolmen who stood watching the course of events play out. The men glanced at me and then jumped into action.

I was on the move and Sara had gained a lead on me as a horde of people intercepted Senator Ryan before he reached the body of his wife. He began shoving men to the side as a frantic attempt to break through. I stepped in front of him, wanting him to see a familiar face.

"Senator Ryan, I can understand your anger, but you need to stop this. You need to let these men do their job. There could be evidence here that will lead us to your son. Do you understand what I'm telling you?" My voice was firm, but I was also trying to be sincere in light of his loss.

"Tell them to let me go, Agent Caster. I swear to God that I'll have every one of you fired if you don't let me go right now." He charged forward again. At least a dozen hands held him back.

"Senator, I know you're angry. I know you're hurt but allowing you to enter the crime scene won't help matters. The only way you can help your wife now is by letting this team of men do what they need to do."

The fight left him as he pulled back from a struggling charge to an upright position. Everyone who had a hold of him released their grip. His hands went to his face and be began crying. He stood that way for a long time. When he collected himself, he pulled his hands away and angrily wiped at the tears.

Senator Ryan looked hopelessly at the body of his wife. As he swiped away spilling tears, his gaze then found me. "I'm going to destroy you for this, Agent Caster. I told you yesterday to let go of this case. If you had done that, she would still be alive. I don't care if they wanted you to get involved. You should have walked away when you had the chance. This is all on you, Agent Caster. You killed her. You've just kissed your FBI career goodbye."

"Sergeant, please escort Senator Ryan from the premises. He's not of stable mind right now and could very well ruin any evidence collected," I said.

I had felt a flash of anger score through me. I couldn't believe he was actually pointing blame at me.

Sergeant Wilkins looked uneasy as he took the arm of a man who could very well be the next United States president and walked him to the parking lot.

"Just let it go, Harper. He's upset, and he knows there's no reason to lay blame on you. He's done this to himself. It'll take a little time before he completely realizes that. You did the right thing by sending him away," Sara said.

"I think the news crews are going to love me for that one," I said.

13

I watched as officers escorted Senator Ryan back to his car. Cameras followed his every move and his heart-wrenching reaction. Senator Ryan's Secret Service detail kept the crowd at bay as he got in the back seat and closed the door. When the black sedan tore off down the road, the cameras shifted back toward us and the body of Katherine Ryan.

"Something was entirely off about his departure," Sara said.

"I'm glad you said that. I had the same thought, but I didn't want to appear as if I were lashing out at Senator Ryan for what he said."

"I think that if I were married and someone brutally murdered my spouse and ditched her in a park, I don't think any of those officers could have held me back. I would have leapt over their heads if necessary. Even if I knew that I could possibly damage a crime scene, I would be at her side," Sara offered.

"Yeah, I'd be out of my mind. I'd probably start swinging at the officers until they let me go or knocked me out. Do you know what the strangest thing about his departure was?"

"Well, I can't believe that he even didn't ask about his son," she said.

"Exactly. We know he received the news about his wife being here, but he couldn't have been positive that his son wasn't here as well until I said something about it. He didn't show the slightest concern about Dillon's whereabouts."

I dismissed the whole unsettling moment and did what I came to do. Sara and I crossed the bike path and stood a few feet from Katherine Ryan. I kneeled and looked closer at the body. Her nightgown was spotted and streaked with dirt. Her bare legs and knees had minor abrasions and were also coated with dirt. Wherever Katherine Ryan had spent the last day and a half, it hadn't been a luxury suite.

"Tell me what you see," I said to Sara.

"Well, first of all, I don't see any dirt patches in this area of the park. So, wherever she picked up all of that dirt, it probably wasn't from here. I can even see dirt beneath her fingernails, almost as if she had been digging. She could have been trying to burrow her way out of the place they held her captive. It seems like those wounds on her knees and shins had scabbed over before she died. So those injuries probably happened earlier yesterday and not in her final hours this morning."

"Good. What's your speculation about the cause of death?"

"If I had to predetermine the medical examiner's results, I'd have to say she suffered a broken neck. Aside from abrasions on her legs and the laceration on her arm, I don't see any blood. You already told me that Senator Ryan said they cut her arm during the abduction at the house to show their seriousness. I highly doubt they went by the means of poison or anything like that. These men are professional killers. I couldn't say for sure where they held her, but perhaps they didn't want to set off an alarm with gunfire. Using a knife is always too messy and very personal. Besides, stabbing someone to death seems to fall along the lines of a person who enjoys the kill. These men are different. I don't think this was a thrill for them. This was simply a job and nothing more. Professionals are really good at killing people with their bare hands."

"Your observation is insightful. I like the way you read into things. You might have outclassed me on that point. I was simply noticing the way they awkwardly twisted her neck out of place," I said and winked.

"Yeah, I caught that, too," Sara said, and winked back.

I circled the body. I hated this part of my job. I truly loathed viewing bodies and trying to determine the horrific events that led to that person's death. It sometimes made me think that one day I would lose a battle of wits and strength against one of the many villains of society. I wondered if men like these would be standing over me and pondering the same things I was. Maybe they'd be saying to themselves, *Poor bastard. Looks like this guy crossed paths with a pride of lions that thought Irish American meat was juicy and tender. Can you get me a coffee, Carl? I'll take it with lots of cream and sugar, thanks.*

I had an outlook on life. I suppose everyone did. My particular outlook was bleak and lacked a promise of mankind evolving much further than our current status. My line of work offered front row seats to the oncoming apocalypse. I think Charlton Heston had played it right more than he knew. Someday, mankind would eventually whittle away to a scarce minority, and apes would take control as the dominant species.

The crime scene men finished what they came to do. They were packing up evidence and their gear. Whatever evidence they collected would be reviewed later when we could focus on each item.

"So, tell me what it is you see, Harper. Let's reverse the role-playing. I want to be the FBI guy with a bad attitude and a receding hairline for the next couple of minutes," Sara said, and offered a playful smile.

I grinned back. "Cool, I get to be an attractive DHS rookie. I should be able to score a few numbers from all these good-looking men in blue."

"So, you think I'm attractive?"

I suddenly felt flustered. I hadn't meant it like that. It just came out that way. So, I did what I did best. I countered an unintentional compliment with an insult.

"Sure, I mean, for a swamp creature, you're not bad."

"You won't get phone numbers from these guys with that forked tongue."

"I think we should put the charm off to the side. We need to study the case at hand. Okay, I also noticed what you said earlier, but one thing I'm curious about is why they decided to dump the body here. They obviously wanted Mrs. Ryan to be discovered right away, but was there a reason they chose this particular site?" I asked.

"It's off the beaten path of residential neighborhoods and on the edge of downtown. There are no tire tracks going to or coming from the body. They must have carried her from their vehicle and dropped her here. There are no park lights in this area, so they wanted privacy. I can't imagine they chose this area because it was close to where they had been holding her captive."

"No, they would choose a place far from their safe house," I said.

"Maybe this park has significant meaning to the victim. Maybe she came to this park to get away or even walked the trails. Who could say for sure?" Sara said.

I was crouching next to Katherine Ryan again. I was staring into those once beautiful green eyes that were now void of all compassion. A man known as the Tourist took her from a place she once felt secure, held her hostage for over a day, and then brutally broke her neck and left her body here for all to view. I found myself making a promise to her, a promise that her son wouldn't suffer the same fate. We were going to find Dillon and bring him home alive.

When I stood, a brief flash ran through my mind. It was one of those flashes that may seem random at first, but your mind understands its significance and holds on to it. There was a newspaper article I had seen some time ago. I couldn't remember all the details, but I did remember the article spoke about this park soon after construction began.

"Let's allow the M.E. to finish up. I don't want her lying out here any longer. I think we should head back to the office. I have a muddled idea that needs some clarifying," I said.

14

It had taken a short amount of time to uncover the article I suspected would help me answer one confusing question. The local paper ran an article about Tranquility Park eighteen months ago. The article that stuck in my mind was one focusing on local real estate billionaire Lewis Rockwell. The article did a light touch-and-go on the property donated by Lewis Rockwell that would later become a park in a bustling section of downtown D.C.

After Sara and I left the scene at the park, we went back to my office to dig up any and all information about Lewis Rockwell. What intrigued me even more was the fact that Mr. Rockwell was a huge supporter and major contributor to Senator Ryan's presidential campaign.

I called ahead and spoke with his secretary. She assured me that he was in his office and probably would be there until after five o'clock as usual.

I took a left on Bancroft and parked in front of a meter across the street from Lewis Rockwell's office building.

"What I've got is a strange hunch about Lewis Rockwell's obscure connection to Katherine Ryan's crime scene. At least that's the lead I'm going with for the time being. I could actually be completely wasting our time," I said.

"I hope you were able to book an appointment with Mr. Rockwell or we could be in the waiting room for quite some time," Sara said.

"I think it will be in his best interest to make time for us."

We took the elevator to the sixteenth floor. Lewis Rockwell owned the entire building, but he dedicated one floor to himself and five of his closest associates. As we exited the elevator and headed down the hallway, I noticed a recreational room complete with a billiard table, pinball machines, a big-screen television, lounge chairs, and a well-stocked bar in the far corner. There was an assortment of snacks set out on the poker table. As we moved down the hallway, we passed an impressive gym.

"I wonder if this guy ever leaves the building. This place is nicer than The Waldorf-Astoria," Sara said.

"When you own most of downtown D.C., and large sections of other major cities, you can pretty much splurge on unnecessary luxuries. I think *People* magazine once said he was one of the few remaining wealthiest and most desirable bachelors in the U.S."

"Sounds like someone has a crush," Sara said.

We approached Mr. Rockwell's office, and I knocked on the doorjamb as we stepped inside. There was an attractive blond secretary sitting behind a large mahogany desk and plucking away at the keyboard. She glanced up and offered a smile that was most likely a routine gesture instead of an actual courtesy.

"May I help you?"

"I'm Special Agent Caster with the FBI and this is Sara McNeal with DHS. I called a little while ago. We need to steal a few minutes of Mr. Rockwell's time if it isn't too much trouble."

She offered us a puzzled look and said, "I'm afraid I don't understand. Is there some sort of problem?"

"You don't need to be alarmed. We just have a few questions for him."

"Oh, all right. Well, he's on a conference call right now and told me not to disturb him. If you'd like to wait, he'll be done in a little while." She motioned toward a row of chairs that appeared more like bizarre art sculptures than a place to plant your rear end.

Nearly a half hour went by as I tried keeping my irritated movements to a minimum. We had spent that time listening to Ms. Young clicking away at her computer and answering the phone in an obnoxious, flirty voice. Finally, when my ass fell asleep, I decided I wouldn't let him ignore us any longer.

"I think I'm just going to peek in his office and say hello," I said as I walked to the closed office door.

"Wait, he doesn't like it when people do that," she protested.

Sara was behind me as I opened the large wood door and stepped into the office. I was already holding my badge out as I approached the massive mahogany desk.

"Excuse me, I'm on an important call. Ms. Young?" he said.

"It's not her fault. I just don't have all day to devote my ass to a seriously uncomfortable chair," I said and introduced Sara and myself.

"I apologize, gentlemen, but something has come up and I'm going to have to call you back." He removed the earpiece and glared at us.

"I assure you this should only take a few minutes of your high-dollar time," I said. Maybe I was being a little rude, but men with this type of arrogance got under my skin in a big way.

"What is it I can do for the both of you?" he asked, and then took a long and lingering glance at Sara.

I snapped my fingers to get his attention back to me.

"Are you aware that we found Senator Ryan's wife Katherine murdered in Tranquility Park this morning?"

He gave a short, snorting laugh. "You must be kidding, man. This is my town, and nothing happens here that I don't know about. Yeah, I know someone kidnapped her and the kid and pitched her body in my park. But it's a public park and I don't have control over who passes through. If you're asking me who murdered her, then I guess you'd be expecting me to do your legwork. Look, I've got other problems at the moment," he said and picked up his phone earpiece.

I slapped it out of his hand. "I'm going to explain something to you, and it's in your best interest to pay attention. I have attained certain evidence that is making things evidently clear that you're a part of Katherine Ryan's murder, unless you quickly help us understand a few things. If you want, I could haul you in for questioning. How many millions do you think you'd lose during the time I have you detained?" I was bullshitting to the max, but I didn't like this guy and I thought he could use a serious reality check.

"My lawyers would have a field day with you guys. But since time is money and I really have nothing to hide, fire your questions quickly and then get the hell out of my building."

"All right. During my research on you, I noticed that you're one of the primary funding providers for Senator Ryan's campaign. Why is that?"

"He has a great personality and a nice smile."

I removed my handcuffs and stepped around the desk.

"All right, all right! Just relax. I help support a presidential candidate every election year. I fund a lot of different things that will help my enterprise grow one way or another. Have you asked yourself why I would donate millions to his campaign, then mastermind the kidnapping of his wife and kid, and then demand that he take a hike from the race? I'm not going to dig that deep into my pocket for someone, only to take it up the ass in the end and lose everything."

"Can you name anyone who would take those kinds of measures against Senator Ryan?" Sara asked.

"Honey, the list is long. If I were you, I'd be taking a long, hard look at his competition."

Sara placed her hand on the desk stapler and leaned forward. "If you call me *honey* again, I'm going to use this to staple your dick to your forehead."

Lewis Rockwell bellowed with laughter. "A chick with a badge and fierce as hell. I absolutely love this city."

Sara moved toward him, but I held her back with relative ease.

"So, you think that maybe Senator Frost might have something to do with the kidnapping and murder? Are you so obtuse that you didn't consider the fact that just maybe the FBI and DHS thought of that already?" Sara asked.

I could tell she was still harnessing the urge to step forward and knock him to the floor.

"It never really occurred to me. To be completely frank, nothing in the world will stop Senator Ryan now. He's got one hell of a sympathy card that he'll sure as shit use to gain even more favorable followers. The guy is going to be president. There isn't a single thing that can stop him now. Let that sink into your heads for a minute. After all that has happened, I'd say that I've found the right corner to stand in. Now, if you don't mind, I have some business to finish up," Lewis Rockwell said. He leaned back in his chair and laced his hands behind his head, and offered a sly, all-knowing wink.

"I have a distinct feeling we'll be speaking again soon, Mr. Rockwell," I said.

I firmly grabbed Sara's arm and ushered her from the office to the elevator. As we rode to the lobby, I pinched my eyes shut and began an uncontrollable laughter. It felt like an odd thing to do under the circumstances, but I couldn't help it.

"What's with you?" Sara asked. She was watching me as if I'd lost my mind.

"Staple his dick to his forehead?" I asked as I caught my breath.

Sara shrugged and said, "It seemed like a nice thing to say at the time."

15

When the garage security gate began rolling up several buildings down, the Tourist pressed a button on his watch and the face illuminated. It was a quarter after one o'clock at night. He turned his head and watched the silver Mercedes exit. The headlights carved a path along the dark road as it turned right onto Victor Street.

The reason he had picked this location was simple. Victor Street was one of the less used streets in the downtown area. When he calculated the fact that it was after one o'clock on a Tuesday night, the area would be barren. Even if someone were to witness the event, there would be absolutely nothing they could do about it. The only thing concerning him at this point was an unplanned and inconvenient drive-by of the local police.

The Tourist stood from the bus bench when Lewis Rockwell gunned the Mercedes engine and ripped down the street. The Tourist had previously calculated the distance from the garage door to the bus bench. He had also known the speed Lewis Rockwell typically reached in that distance without the factor of traffic. He was sure his timing would be impeccable.

Just before Lewis Rockwell reached the intersection with a green light in his favor, the Tourist heaved the bundle from his arms. The figure resembled a filthy street person dressed in ratty clothes. The decoy crunched against the grill, skidded up the silver hood, and slammed against the windshield, hitting hard enough to splinter the glass into a spider web.

Lewis Rockwell pounded on the brakes, sending the Mercedes into a partial spin, and it joined with a bark of tires.

The Tourist comically observed Lewis Rockwell step from the car in a panic. In horror movie fashion, he slowly circled to the front of the car and stared disbelievingly at the crumpled figure that had pitched off the hood when he hammered the brakes.

"Hey, hey, buddy, are you all right?" Lewis asked the lifeless decoy.

The Tourist quietly walked toward the Mercedes.

"Oh, my God. This is just fucking great. This is all I need right now. I can't believe I just ran over a fucking bum. Hey, answer me if you're okay. Are you? If I give you some money, could we just forget the whole thing?"

The figure in front of him didn't respond.

"Shit, shit, goddamnit shit!" Lewis screamed.

"Is there a problem here, sir?" the Tourist asked.

When Lewis spun around, the obvious sight of the police uniform sent a terror coursing through him.

"Officer, this guy just stepped out in front of me. I had a green light and everything. Hey, where's your patrol car?" Lewis asked as he studied the deserted street.

The Tourist stopped a few feet from Lewis Rockwell. "I'm foot patrol for this section of the downtown district. Is that alcohol I smell, sir?"

The Tourist had known it was alcohol, and probably a large amount of it. Lewis often spent the late-night hours playing poker with his associates at the office as they did every Tuesday night. It was a night devoted to alcohol, pornographic movies on the big screen, and the raw stench of cigars as the men loaded the pot, hoping to have the best hand. The other four had left nearly an hour ago. If anything, it was Lewis's routine that would cause his death tonight.

"Um, yeah, I guess I had a few beers. I'm completely capable of driving myself home."

"I can tell that your driving skills are in perfect condition tonight," the Tourist said and nodded toward the figure in the street.

Lewis glanced at the body and then turned to the officer and offered a million-dollar smile.

"I'm Lewis Rockwell, you know, I own a lot of the real estate in D.C. I'm sure we can chat. Maybe if you told me something that you'd really like to have, I could make that happen."

"Are you talking about money?"

"Well, money, property, or a new car. Whatever. I'm really good at negotiations," Lewis Rockwell slurred.

The Tourist smiled. "Interesting. Anything I want, you say? How about if you become my number two?"

"Yeah, sure, your number two. Wait, what do you mean? Do you mean like a second in command? A sidekick or something like that?" Lewis asked, confused.

"Not exactly. I was more thinking along the lines of my second victim. Yes, that's what I want. I want you to be the second victim out of five. Can you negotiate that deal?"

Lewis's million-dollar business smile faded, and he quickly replaced it with a look of confusion.

"Huh?"

The Tourist removed his sidearm from the holster and delivered two rapid shots into Lewis Rockwell's chest. The man released a hard gush of air as he stumbled, then collapsed backward onto the centerline of Victor Street. For good measure, the Tourist placed a final round into Lewis's forehead, painting the road in red.

"You're right, Mr. Rockwell, you're one hell of a negotiator."

16

As I stepped into the bright sunlight of Wednesday morning, I felt an eerie calmness as I retrieved the newspaper. I hadn't slept well with the knowledge of Katherine Ryan's death weighing heavily on me. What bothered me even more was the fact that I had no idea how I was going to corner the man known as the Tourist and find Dillon Ryan alive. The Tourist was a ghost, a phantom that rolled away in a faint breeze and left signs of death in his path.

I nearly dropped my coffee as I opened my cell and scrolled through the headlines. An article about Senator Ryan's rebellion against the kidnappers and his wife's murder was the top story. It wasn't just this article that grabbed my attention the most. At least not right now. It was actually the article below that demanded to be read.

Real Estate Mogul Gunned Down in the Streets of D.C.

The article was brief, as the murder had gone down sometime after 1 a.m. The reporter could only insert the smallest details leaked by local police enforcement.

I stormed into the kitchen and startled Clara and Kaylee. They were at the kitchen table eating waffles with strawberries and focusing on the morning news.

"Harper, what's wrong?" Clara asked.

"I just got run down by a steamroller," I said.

"Did you see the news?" she asked.

"I saw it all right." I turned my cell to her.

Clara glanced at the article and said, "No, I was talking about the video of Senator Ryan. They're replaying it now."

I put my cell down and turned toward the television. The video playing had obviously been homemade and had not been shot with the aid of any local news crew. Since I had been in the senator's home the other day, I could verify that it was his furniture in the background. He was shooting the video from his living room.

"My name is Senator Andrew Ryan and I'm speaking to the cowardly men who kidnapped and murdered my wife, Katherine. I know that you're still holding my son, Dillon, captive. You abducted them Sunday night and ordered me to withdraw from the presidential race. I had refused, and as a punishment for my resistance, you murdered Katherine and discarded her in a park like a piece of trash. You've made a terrible mistake to come after my family. We've now reached the crossroads at which I'm going to give you a choice. If I were you, I'd make a quick decision on this option I'm going to hand out to you. I'm proposing that you release Dillon now and I promise that when I eventually find you, and I will find you, I'll show you more mercy than you showed my wife. My resources are great, and I will see to it that the world knows your identity and you will face severe punishment."

Senator Ryan paused for effect and took a long drink of water.

"Here's what I'm offering to every red-blooded American who has grown tired of fearing men like you.

I'm placing a one-million-dollar bounty on your head. You can now understand why I said that my resources are great. Every American that has become enraged with those who choose to destroy and rebel against our way of life will be gunning for you. I will not allow our nation to be terrorized anymore. We will not give in to your destructive forces. We will fight and win against any man or woman who dares to bring forward the ways of evil in our country. To the man who calls himself the Tourist, I am speaking directly to you. Release Dillon now and your death will be swift. If you make an unwise decision and harm my son, I will trail you to the end of the earth and I will bring fierce vengeance upon you."

The video ended and the news reporter, who had probably seen the video several times already, wore an expression of complete shock.

"Holy shit. He's completely lost his mind. He's gone right off the rails, and he doesn't care when or where he'll crash and burn. He's just ruined any chance he had left at getting his son back or winning the White House. He's started a personal war and made it highly public. American voters won't allow a rogue senator to take a presidential position. The men who took his wife and son don't take threats lightly. Now they'll probably kill the kid for sure and then take the senator out," I said.

I quickly stopped talking. I had been caught up in the moment of unsettling events, and completely unaware that we were having an intense adult conversation in front of a twelve-year-old.

I leaned in and kissed the top of Kaylee's head and said, "I'm sorry, honey. We shouldn't be speaking like that in front of you. It's just that this morning has suddenly become an insane migraine."

"Does that mean you'll have to work late, Daddy?"

Those beautiful blue eyes got me every time. I sometimes hated the fact that my position at the FBI formed a wedge between the three of us. I tried to keep as many promises as possible, but often circumstances wouldn't allow it.

"I'll hopefully be home at a sensible time. Kaylee, you've got school tomorrow, so I don't want you attempting to stay up late waiting for me. Understood?"

"Okay, I won't."

I kissed them goodbye. Ever since I saw the photos taken of us, I'd been battling over the idea of sending them to Clara's sister's house on the other side of town to stay until this thing blew over. I'd scratched that idea for a simple purpose. Moving them temporarily across town wouldn't offer much protection from whoever was watching us. I could've probably flown them across the country and those professional men would most likely find them. Besides, I hated the idea of being bullied from our home. I kept several guns in the house for defense, and Clara was one hell of a fine shot.

Of course, Senator Ryan had stood against the threats of these men and the final results gave him a murdered wife and possibly his child's death by the day's end.

My cell rang as I quickly strode to my car. I almost jumped out of my skin as the caller ID announced Director Gill was calling. I figured it was another hammer blow of news completing this morning's trifecta.

I opened my phone and said, "Is it too late to put in a request for the day off?"

"If you find Dillon Ryan alive and apprehend the Tourist and his cronies without anyone getting shot, I'll give you a long weekend," Director Gill said.

"Well, shit, I should have that done by noon."

"I'm going under the assumption that you've seen Senator Ryan's current broadcast?"

"A few minutes ago."

"Then I sincerely hope that you're on your way to speak with our good friend, the senator. Offer whatever words of wisdom you can to get him to remove the one-million-dollar bounty he placed on some seriously dangerous men. Tell him we're going to get his son back, but he has to back off from these guys and let us do our job."

"That sounds more like your job. I actually thought the senator could wait awhile," I said.

"What?" Director Gill asked sharply.

"I'm heading to the crime scene downtown. You know, the one where Lewis Rockwell got spattered with a large-caliber gun near his office."

"That has nothing to do with us. That's local law enforcement's problem."

"Actually, it has everything to do with us, I think. Ms. McNeal and I spoke with Lewis Rockwell earlier yesterday, and now he's dead. There's no way that's a coincidence. I followed a lead, just like I'm doing now," I said and slipped into my worn-down government sedan.

"When the hell were you going to inform me about interviewing the city's largest real estate developer?"

"Sorry, I wasn't even sure the lead had a leg to stand on until now," I said and then delivered the steps Sara and I had followed after we left the park yesterday.

"So, you're telling me the Tourist struck again and Lewis Rockwell was the second victim of five?"

"I believe so, but I won't know for sure until I get down there."

David said, "All right, follow this hunch of yours. Just so you know, the county coroner removed Mr. Rockwell's body a short while ago. Apparently, Captain Rollins of the D.C. police didn't think it would sit well with the commissioner for the entire business workforce to view a body lying in the middle Victor Street during their morning commute. But the rest of the crime scene remains. Don't forget to pick up your partner."

"Got it. Thanks, boss."

17

Despite the hammering blow of the morning news, I chuckled a little when I rolled up to Sara McNeal's quaint home on Xavier Street. It was certainly small, probably only two bedrooms, one bath, and the kitchen and dining area were most likely the same space. What stood out the most about the home was that it was a brilliant pink. She had told me which house to look out for when I came to pick her up. I was sure that even a blind man could have found it.

Sara spotted me pulling up, came out the front door, and hurried to my car. She was wearing a pin-striped suit with a beige blouse. Her stark black hair was pulled back in a ponytail.

"I hope you didn't have any problems finding the place," she said as she slid in.

"No. I noticed it from three blocks down. It's a good thing I was wearing sunglasses when I approached, because I could have permanently damaged my sight. There's a John Mellencamp song popping into my head. Can you guess which one?"

"Oh, piss off. It's not even my house. It's a rental. I tried to strike a deal with the landlord about painting it before I moved in. I told him I'd buy the paint and do the work for free. He wouldn't go for it. What the hell, I'm hardly there, anyway."

"I'll probably need to bring a vomit bag if I pick you up again," I said and smiled.

After a moment of silence, Sara said, "So, how long have you been with the FBI?"

"Twelve glorious and nonstop action years. I went from a local patrol officer to detective in a matter of a few years and eventually decided to take the FBI exam. It's been a thrill ride ever since. What's your story?"

Sara was watching the scenery outside roll by as we headed downtown. "Well, I was born and raised in L.A. After high school, I attended Berkley and kept my focus on behavioral science and psychology. I graduated top of my class and finally decided I wanted to work for the DHS and analyze the hell out of bad guys for the rest of my life. You may have been surfing the thrill ride for a dozen years, but I think mine has just begun. As an added note, I'd also like to say that I want to begin my long career with a solid win. Whoever these guys are, they're going down."

I liked Sara's motivation and enthusiasm to take down a small clan of professional killers, but she was still young and lacked the knowledge that sometimes circumstances were completely out of your hands.

"Why do you think this guy calls himself the Tourist?" she asked.

"I have no idea. Maybe it's because no one knows who he is or where he comes from. Maybe he went with the Tourist because he's a man without a country. The entire world has become foreign land to him, and he has no place to call home," I said.

"I like that, even if you made it up on the spot. In my opinion, the Tourist isn't a name that really strikes fear into the heart of potential victims. It's not a sinister enough name for a professional killer. I would have gone with something like Dr. Raw Pain or something like that," Sara said.

"That sounds more like a professional wrestler or a really bad dentist."

"I'm just spit balling ideas here. I'm sure I could come up with something more menacing if I had the time. I can't believe that we just spoke with Lewis Rockwell yesterday and now he's dead. I guess you just never know when some moron is going to stroll along and punch your ticket. I bet Rockwell thought he had the world by the balls, and then someone came and took it all away in a split second. He was a jerk anyhow, but he probably didn't deserve to go out that way. Poor bastard," Sara said.

"Most people don't deserve the death they receive. It's a cruel world that's rapidly spiraling downhill. The evil that men do seems to double each year. All the good people left in the world are losing the battle against a tidal wave of hatred and greed. I'm one of those good guys, and I feel my sincerity and empathy slip away a little each day. I'm desperately trying to hold on to a greater hope for mankind, but with every morbid crime scene I visit, my grip loosens a little. The only reason I continue to do this is for my wife and daughter. I'm trying to hand down a jigsaw puzzle to my daughter and future generations. So far, the puzzle is missing a bunch of pieces, and I'm trying to get them back in place before my time is up."

"How old is she?"

"Twelve. She was born the same year I started with the Bureau. She's a good kid. Unfortunately, she's reached the age where she believes she must set standards for independence and the incompetent parents that we are should just step out of the way. Of course, we've all been at that point. I gave the same ultimatum to my parents. I quickly learned that self-reliance at that age wasn't necessarily a great thing."

Sara rotated three of the dash vents so that they angled toward her face, and then she cranked the air-conditioner knob to the maximum setting.

"I'm not a big fan of summer. It's the humidity that gets to me. I don't recall L.A. ever being like this," she said.

"Probably because you primarily concerned yourself with finding fresh air to breathe and avoiding the looming smog. I was in L.A. a few times. As long as I never get forced there again to deal with a case, I'll schedule my vacation time elsewhere," I said.

"So now that you know my studies were on human behavior, you're probably concerned that I'm analyzing your every move, right?"

"Actually, I wasn't really worried about that. I think any fifth grader could figure out my simple personality in two minutes flat. I thrive to catch bad guys without boasting to the press about it. I absolutely love spending all of my free time with my family. I love to be challenged to a certain degree, and I hate looking like a complete fool. That's as complex as my life gets."

"I actually analyzed you when we first met. It's nothing personal, just a habit. I believe that was exactly what I read from the way you carried yourself. I'm glad I hit close to the mark. I guess those professors did something right," Sara said.

"You'll make a dynamite DHS officer after all."

"I could be mistaken, but it looks like we're here," Sara said as she studied the row of patrol cars and swirling lights.

18

Police sectioned off Victor Street from 5th to 6th Street. I managed to find a parking spot among the clutter of squad cars.

The bad thing about this crime scene was that it was already over six hours old. There had been countless police officials walking across the scene and damaging any evidence that was overlooked. Lewis Rockwell's body was long ago removed, but I could see his Mercedes parked diagonally across the centerline. The driver's side door was open, and a crime scene tech was processing the interior.

I showed my badge to an officer at the perimeter. Sara showed an award-winning smile, and he allowed us passage.

As we walked to Lewis Rockwell's car, I scanned the area. It was an odd location for the Tourist to plan a murder. If the Tourist was truly behind this unsettling event, he could have executed Mr. Rockwell at any place or time during the day. Why would he make a charge in the late-night hours on a deserted downtown road? Was this location and method of murder some sort of clue that I didn't fully understand yet?

I searched each face of the crime scene unit and realized that they were the same men who processed Katherine Ryan's crime scene just yesterday.

"Well, isn't it a small world after all?" the lead investigator said. I remembered that his name was Charlie King.

"Too small. You guys aren't really the ones behind the killings, are you?" I asked.

"Actually, yeah. We were just cleaning up our mess before making a getaway. Let me guess, since the feds decided to take over the Katherine Ryan case, you already found her killer and figured that you'd help out us lowly investigators?"

"What can I say? We work fast in the FBI. Is everything just about finished up here?"

The man who was processing the vehicle said, "Yeah. It was still dark when we came down here. We began working the scene around three in the morning. We've been running down the area again since the sun came up. We wanted to make sure we didn't miss anything in the dark."

"What time did you get the call?"

"A passerby made the 911 call just before two in the morning. First on the scene were Officer Johnson and his partner, Officer Reyes. They saw the body, recognized the face, and made a panicked call for the rest of us."

I walked to the front of the car and studied the damage to the hood and windshield. The Mercedes had plowed into something heavy and caused Mr. Rockwell to make a hasty stop.

"Any idea what caused the damage?"

"Whatever it was, the unidentified subject who initiated the accident took it with them. If I judged by the impact, I'd say that it probably weighed 150 pounds, or maybe a little more. At first, we thought that it might have been a person, but with an impact like that, there would be blood for sure. As you can see, there isn't. I'm sorry to say that we have little evidence to go on. The person who did this was quick and efficient," Charlie King said.

"This sounds too much like Katherine Ryan's murder scene. There's a body and very little evidence left behind. So, I'm thinking this person waited for Mr. Rockwell to approach the intersection and then heaved a heavy object into the street, which collided with the Mercedes. Mr. Rockwell got out to check the damage and figure out what the hell made quick work of his hood and windshield. Then our suspect fires a couple of rapid shots that land Mr. Rockwell in the county morgue," I speculated.

"That's one way it could have happened," Sara said.

Charlie King was busy with roaming eyes over Sara when I heard a soft chirp. I looked around, trying to figure out the source of the noise. Charlie King didn't seem to notice the sound, or maybe it was part of his equipment, and the sound was a usual one.

"What's with the chirping?" I asked.

Charlie managed to pull his eyes from Sara long enough to look stupidly at me and said, "Huh?"

"The chirping noises. What is it?"

"Oh, it's been doing that for the last four hours. It chirps every ten minutes or so. It's the digital phone in the Mercedes. Probably a client pissed about Mr. Rockwell missing a meeting."

"If it's been chirping for the last four hours, I highly doubt that Mr. Rockwell has scheduled meetings that early in the morning. Especially when he's been partying late at night," I said.

"How do you know he was partying last night, Agent Caster?" Charlie asked.

"Good old-fashioned detective work. The first piece of evidence would be the overwhelming stench of alcohol coming from his car that's detectable from ten yards away. Second, he's known as one of the city's wealthiest, and horniest, bachelors. Third, Ms. McNeal and I saw the party room on his office floor yesterday. He had the room set up for some kind of get-together."

"Ms. McNeal?" Charlie said, while emphasizing the word *Ms*. His eyes immediately seized a new hunger as he took another long gander at Sara's figure.

"Take it easy, Charlie. I have a gun and I'm an excellent shot. I could even bull's-eye those two pathetic raisins between your legs at fifty yards," Sara said, with a hint of playfulness.

I kept the laughter to myself as I went to Charlie's kit and retrieved a pair of latex gloves and snapped them on.

"So, what the hell were you two doing at Lewis Rockwell's office yesterday?" Charlie asked.

Sara said, "Chitchat. He really was a fun-loving kind of guy. Did I mention I told him that if he continued to use terms of endearment on me, I would staple his dick to his forehead?"

"Right. I think you two just moved up to the top of my suspect list. But with all that being said, I think I'm totally in love with you. If I get us tickets to Cancun, is there a chance I get to see you in a very tiny bikini?" Charlie asked Sara.

"Cancun? In that case, I can minus the bikini," Sara offered.

"I wish I could be anywhere else in the world right now," I said.

I walked over to the open car door and then asked the tech if the vehicle processing was complete, which it was. I slid into the front seat and checked out the dashboard and all the sci-fi accessories the German car offered. The interior appeared more like a sophisticated arcade game rather than a method of getting around town. The number of buttons and switches was nearly baffling.

"Christ. Does this thing have a built-in toilet, too?" I asked.

"You bet. Those damn Germans thought of everything," Charlie said.

I turned the ignition key to the *run* position and watched the dashboard instruments come alive. Country music suddenly blared from the speaker system. I punched the knob and killed the music. I studied the eight-inch screen just below the temperature controls. There was a menu listed, offering more options than any team of MIT geniuses could figure out in a lifetime. I pressed the screen to open the phone options. Next, I opened the unanswered voice messages. Three messages were from clients that must have come in only an hour ago.

I backtracked and found an option for text messages. There was only one, and it wasn't intended for Lewis Rockwell. The message was meant for me. It read:

You've got two victims now, Harper. You're overanalyzing the game. Follow your instincts.

"Son of a bitch," I murmured.

Sara leaned in the passenger side and read the screen. "So, we were right to assume the Tourist had made this hit. How exactly are you overanalyzing things, Harper?" she asked with a smirk. She didn't understand the sentences any more than I did.

"Beats me. We followed a damn clue that was as far-fetched as they come and still figured out that this might have been his next move. I think he's trying to get me to second-guess myself. If I start questioning things too often, then I'm going to make a mistake and the Tourist will slip away for good once he's completed his confusing mission."

"So, we have a senator's dead wife, and now a deceased real estate developer who backed the senator's campaign. What commonality do they share besides Senator Ryan?" Sara asked.

I shrugged. I couldn't seem to take my eyes from the spot where Lewis Rockwell's body had laid in the middle of the street. The wheels inside my head were rapidly cranking, but no matter what, my answers failed production inspections and were sent to the reject bin.

"There are hundreds of other men and women in just this metropolitan area alone that are involved with Senator Ryan's presidential campaign. So far, each murder was a person high on the ladder of the campaign. Lewis Rockwell was the bankroll, and Katherine Ryan was the inspirational backboard to the senator's quest for the presidency. Eventually, the Tourist will kill enough people to crumble Senator Ryan's chances. It's like a house of cards. When you take out enough structural cards from any level, there will be catastrophic failure," I said.

"The Tourist has to have some other valid goal besides destroying Senator Ryan's chances at the presidency. Like you said before, the Tourist could have killed the man in his own bed but didn't. There's a reason behind that, besides fucking with your head, I'm sure," Sara said.

"I'm sure," I agreed.

"You're aware that something this large is also being investigated by half a dozen other agencies, right?"

"It had crossed my mind. I didn't think that the government would put only a cranky, worn-out old man and a rookie on the case. There are probably hundreds of people all over this. They're probably watching us from a satellite right now."

Sara looked up and offered her middle finger to the morning sky.

"Now they probably won't want to work with us at all. Way to go," I said.

"You know, I could make a few phone calls. I've made some connections over the years with men and women in the intelligence gathering business. Some of them are the people I partied and studied with in college. I might be able to call in a few favors and acquire certain information from them without risking their jobs."

"I hope they're not DHS."

"No, I work for the DHS. Why would they tell me anything?"

"Good, I don't trust those guys, anyway. I heard they're responsible for the vegan craze."

"Actually, they have no knowledge of such an accusation, and decline to comment further."

I smiled. I enjoyed Sara's charismatic outlook toward her employer and the overview she gave life. She had a way of pressing her thumb on the important matters, while also offering a sadistic sense of humor to it. Of all the people they could have sent to me to assist with the investigation, they gave me a good-looking young woman with a dynamite personality and a flare for stepping into the face of danger with little regard for her own sense of mortality.

"Okay, make your calls before we, unfortunately, stumble over corpse number three," I said.

Sara grabbed her phone and walked away from the crime scene and out of earshot range. Apparently, she wasn't willing to share her informants with either Charlie or me. That was fine. I wouldn't share mine either. If I had any, that is.

19

Sara and I were checking through security of the Hoover Building when my cell rang. The caller ID displayed that Clara was trying to reach me.

"Harper, Harper, can you hear me?"

My cell clicked and buzzed with an annoyance that barely allowed Clara's voice to slip through.

"Yeah. Hang on, the line has a lot of static." I moved down the hallway and stepped back outside. Sara followed close behind my lead. "Okay, is that any better?"

"Yes, I can hear you better now. Harper, our house phone has been ringing off the hook all day. I've been trying to figure out what exactly is going on, but I don't understand any of it," Clara said with trembling panic.

"What happened?"

"Well, shortly after you left this morning, I went to the store, and they denied the bank card I tried to use. The store rejected all of our credit cards due to insufficient funds. I called every credit card company when I got home. They claim we maxed out our credit cards and we haven't made a payment in three months. So, they've frozen the accounts until we get caught up on payments. I know for a fact that we've had less than one thousand on both cards according to the last statements. They wouldn't believe me and said their records show us in default for months and the accounts are being turned over to a collections department. I went to the bank and had them confirm the balance of our checking account. It's completely empty. The bank also shows our savings account at a zero balance. Every dollar we had in savings is gone. Harper, what the hell is going on?" Clara asked.

Clara was crying, and I could imagine her trying to get a handle on things.

I was making random pacing patterns on the sidewalk outside the building. Sara watched me with a hard degree of concern. She could no doubt read the tension in my voice and facial expressions.

"That isn't the worst of it, Harper."

I pinched my eyes shut. I couldn't even anticipate the size of the hammer she was going to hit me with next.

"What else?"

"The bank has our house in the process of foreclosure. The mortgage company called, and the guy on the phone said that we have five back payments to make or they're going to foreclose. We don't even have anything left in any of our accounts. How could we possibly make even a single payment?"

"I don't know. I don't understand any of this either."

"I know for a fact that I've made every credit card and mortgage payment. I even have the canceled checks from the bank, but when I went to the bank, their computer records don't show any of our bills being paid in months. I can't imagine what we're going to do about all this. Every company I call won't bother to listen to me. They think I'm lying to them. They think I'm trying to completely bullshit them about something being seriously wrong."

As if I didn't already have a truckload on my mind, I now had the possibility of losing my home to contend with today. I leaned against the building and slowly lowered myself into a crouched position.

"I promise I'll figure this out. Even though you won't listen, I want you to calm down and trust me that things will work out once we get to the bottom of the problem. I have to go, but I'll call later and let you know when I'll be able to get home. All right? When Kaylee gets home from school, try not to worry her if you can help it," I said.

"I won't say anything to her unless something else unexpected comes along. Please come home soon. I love you."

"I will. I love you, too."

I pocketed my phone and gazed up at Sara. She had only caught my side of the conversation and was in the dark about what Clara had said and my personal anguish that just tripled with a phone call. I told her everything.

Sara stood at the curb, her hands in her pants pockets, and watched the passing cars on Pennsylvania Avenue. She was nodding, perhaps at a thought. I think she was searching for a series of comforting words to offer my distressed outlook for the day.

Instead, Sara said, "He's fucking with you. Do you realize that?"

Of course, I knew exactly who she was talking about. I had already run down every hypothetical possibility about the source of my crumbling situation.

"The Tourist," I said flatly.

"Yeah, the fucking Tourist. This guy is attempting to destroy every aspect of your life. Whoever he is, he's particularly pissed at you. He's targeted you to lead this mind-fuck of a case. If that's not bad enough, now he's crumbling your life outside the FBI walls. Can you think of anyone you've put away that could be back on the streets who would love nothing more than to cripple your existence?" Sara asked.

"I've already gone down that road when this whole thing emerged. I've searched through the criminal databases of all the names I could think of that are wise enough to come up with something this clever. There are only a couple of people released in the last few years that have the intelligence to run something this crooked. But the problem is that none of them have any obvious links to Senator Ryan or reasons to destroy his campaign. I certainly don't believe that any of them contain the skill set to pull off the trick of wiping out my bank accounts and changing other accounts to appear as if I've neglected my bills for the last three or four months. We're looking for someone with a lot of talent and a deep-seated loathing for my insignificant life."

"A person like that could be hard to come across unless you know exactly the purpose behind his madness," Sara said.

"I honestly don't. I don't have a clue what this guy wants from me. I don't know why I've become his entire focus."

"I have a distinct feeling that you're going to obligate your time by uncovering the mystery," Sara said. She offered her hand. I took it and she pulled me up from the sidewalk.

"What can I say? That's what they pay me for. I'm going to find this guy and all of his men. I'm going to ask him to return Senator Ryan's son and offer a sincere apology for all the anguish he has caused. Next, I'm going to ask him politely to correct all of my accounts, and then I'm going to send him to where all bad guys go."

"New Jersey?"

"No, the other bad place."

"Sounds like you've got it all figured out. Do you need my help at all, or should I head home for the remainder of the day?" Sara said.

"I hope this informant of yours gives us something solid to go on. Otherwise, I don't think victim three is going to have a chance in hell," I said.

20

The sun raced across the canopy of trees, and Dillon Ryan desperately tried to follow. One painful step followed another. Rocks and sharp fallen branches on the forest floor had lacerated his bare feet over the last two hours. The wounds had clotted and later reopened as he stumbled through the dense undergrowth. When the forest thickened and forced him to climb over a fallen tree, size-six red footprints trailed across the bark. And now Dillon could feel nothing below his tired and sore knees.

Half an hour passed since he had come upon a bush filled with reddish berries. His father had told him during a previous camping trip that if someone got lost in the woods, they needed to be cautious of the plants, insects and animals they chose to eat for necessary nutrition. There were some plants and insects that could make you very ill, and some could even kill you. His father had also warned him about pools of standing water and what was safe to drink and what wasn't. Still water was a breeding ground for bacteria and his father said that he should stay away. Clear running water from a stream was usually safe.

Dillon had spent ten minutes picking the berries and carefully placing them in the small pouch of his backpack. He couldn't remember if his father had ever told him about these types of berries and if they were safe to eat. He had taken a chance by eating only a few and waiting. The berry juice tasted sweet and didn't give him what his father had once called the runny shits.

The sky began changing colors, from a majestic blue to a rustic orange, and now had given way to a looming gray that was having difficulty breaking through the forest ceiling.

Dillon stopped, retrieved his media player from his backpack, and worked in the earphones. He pressed the play button on the glowing digital screen and continued to chase the sun. The music was an odd mix his mother had collected for him. The songs were from decades before he was even born. His mother claimed that the songs were from a time when life was carefree and pretty groovy. Whatever that meant.

As Dillon listened, the sun had sunk low enough to cause the forest to become overwhelmed with a blanket of blackness.

Dillon thought of the man with the accent. He thought of what the man had told him shortly before they allowed him to leave the cabin.

"I want you to listen to me very closely, Dillon. I've done a great deal of mapping out this area and I've taken considerable time and effort to work this out for you. Do you understand how important it is for you to listen? Your life will depend on what I have to say."

Dillon had nodded but kept his eyes on the rough planked floor of the cabin. There was something evil in the man's eyes and Dillon felt a serious tremor of fear ripple through him when he locked eyes with the man.

"Based on your size, and by that, I primarily mean the length of your legs and the distance of your stride, I've calculated the area of the forest ground you should cover by each hour. I've also taken into consideration the conditions of the forest you'll be traveling. I greatly apologize that none of my associates had a clue to pack a pair of shoes for you when they took you from your bed. They had a simple obligation to grab you, a change of clothes, your music player, and a few other essentials to keep you occupied during your stay. Obviously, they lacked the insight to include a pair of sneakers. It's with my greatest apologies that you will need to travel the forest with no protection for your feet. Walk swiftly but carefully."

Dillon nodded again.

"When I let you go in a little over an hour, I want you to follow the descending sun. You should be able to follow for two hours before the sunrays are gone. You'll get tired and you'll want to stop and rest, but you can't stop. I have a direction marked out for you and there will be no time for rest. When the sun reaches the part of the sky where you can't see the light anymore, you should be able to see the glow of the half-moon through the trees. I want you to shift your direction at this point and follow the moon. Follow the sun, and then follow the moon. Understand?"

He nodded.

"I want you to know that I could drive you to a safe place and release you, but I'm not going to do that. I want you to leave on your own and find safety. I want you to take time during your walk and think about how precious life is to you. We all have to earn our lives one way or another. I want you to earn it, Dillon. It will be completely up to you whether you live or die."

Another nod.

"If you follow my directions, you'll make it out of the forest and then you'll come to a road. At the time of night you reach this road, there probably won't be many vehicles passing. But when one does, I want you to flag it down. I want you to wave your arms and get them to stop. A car will see you and they will be worried about your well-being. Someone will stop, I promise. Just remember that you can't stop walking until you reach the road. That's very important. If you stop, it will throw off the timeline of the falling sun and your path will be completely out of whack and then you'll miss the road altogether. You'll forever be lost in these woods if you stop. Do you understand that Dillon?"

He nodded again.

"Tell me you understand. I want you to say it."

"I understand."

"No, I mean tell me what I want you to do."

"Don't stop walking. Follow the sun until it's gone, and then follow the moon to a road. Stop a car."

"Right. Stop a car and tell them who you are. They'll be sad for you and take you to the authorities. You'll be safe then. That's a good boy."

Dillon *had* stopped. He had become overwhelmed with hunger, and the berries had looked so inviting. He had a hard time understanding what exactly the man had meant by a "timeline" and why it was so important. Dillon understood that the man was serious when he explained he would die in the woods if he didn't follow the directions. Despite his tired legs and the bleeding soles of his feet, Dillon quickened his pace to make up for lost time after he had filled his backpack pouch with berries. After a short while, he figured he must have made up for lost time and slowed his momentum to its earlier progression.

He saw something shift in the darkness to his left. Dillon stopped, quickly removed his earphones, held his breath, and waited for the thing to move again. His heart hammered hard enough that he could feel the beat in the hollows of his eardrums. He narrowed his eyes, and in the night he could see the gentle sway of disturbed undergrowth.

"Who's there?" he called out, and his voice seemed to find an infinite echo in the bleak woods.

Whatever it was halted its movement.

"I have a knife," he said, even though it was a lie.

The statement appeared to give him a little more confidence. He felt his courage surge and he took a few steps toward the thing in the darkness.

The thing took flight from his advancing steps and disappeared through the thick growth.

After Dillon was sure that it had been a forest creature, not a person, and was long gone, he tilted his head to glimpse the looming half-moon and followed it again.

A cramp in his left thigh that had announced itself twenty minutes earlier had steadily gotten worse. The ache rapidly switched to a fierce bolt of lightning that coursed the length of his entire leg, which slowed his pace and gave him an awkward hobble that made it difficult to maneuver the forest grounds.

Dillon tried to focus on the music and words that were playing from the speakers. He couldn't bring himself to stop now, even for a moment, because he was sure that the road was somewhere up ahead and if he stopped, he could possibly miss a passing car.

Something, a branch maybe, bit into the bottom of his right foot, but Dillon felt little pain break through the numbness.

The words played to him, and he tried to follow along, singing out loud the words he could remember.

When Dillon looked up from the bitter night path in front of him to the curtain of black, he saw something that made his heart begin racing.

Ahead of him, a pair of fireflies danced in the blackness. After a moment, he realized they weren't fireflies at all. They were the headlights of a car drifting down a road beyond the trees.

Dillon ignored the cramp and the bleeding soles of his feet. He broke from the edge of the forest, crossed the shoulder of the road, and ran toward the approaching vehicle.

There was a screech of tires and the car spun away as the driver tried to avoid hitting him. Dillon stood watching the vehicle and hoping the person would help him, just like the man at the cabin had promised someone would. A kind-looking man stepped from the car and stared at him in the humid night.

"What in the world have you been doing, young man? I could have run you over. You can't go running into traffic like that, especially when it's dark outside."

As the man stepped closer, his face changed in the red glow of the taillights to a look of deep concern and his voice became gentle.

"Hey, are you all right, young man?"

Dillon Ryan fell to his tired knees, held his head in his hands, and began crying.

21

"This is insane," I said.

Sara was leading me into the stretching shadows of Elmore Park. I had a bad feeling about this whole situation. There was no doubt that I wanted, maybe even needed, to meet Sara's mystery contact.

The evidence of Katherine Ryan and Lewis Rockwell's murder scenes provided us with little to go on. We had the small soil sample taken from beneath Katherine's fingernails that had no distinctive elements we could trace to a specific section of D.C. Also, the deformed 9mm slugs pulled from Rockwell's body didn't match any recovered bullets from databases listed as used in previous crimes. I honestly didn't know where else to turn.

What bothered me the most was that I was walking into a situation I couldn't control. I had no part in setting up the meeting. I certainly wouldn't have suggested the darkness of a park well known for being the popular hangout for one of the local gangs.

"Relax, kiddo. There's no need to get your panties all bunched up. Everything will be fine. Does the dark scare you a little? Would you like me to hold your hand?" Sara said.

"It isn't the dark, but what's hiding in it that puts me on edge. Fortunately, I don't see anyone out here tonight.

Maybe it's too damn muggy for the gangbangers this evening. If they were out here, we'd be short a couple dozen guns for a showdown. I can assure you that they're not very friendly with any type of law enforcement."

Although I couldn't see anyone, my right hand was inside my jacket and resting on the butt of my gun.

"I told you not to worry. I called ahead to my homies and told them to find another place to chill tonight."

The half moonlight offered only a little guidance down the concrete walkway. Ahead of us, I could see someone leaning against one of the few lampposts. It was hard to tell from this distance, but I thought it was a man wearing a trench coat and a fedora. I saw the cherry glow of a cigarette.

"There he is," Sara said.

"Well, well, your informant actually exists. He's not going to request a strip search on me looking for some sort of wire, is he?"

"Probably down to your skivvies, is all."

"It's too bad I'm not wearing any."

"Huh, then it should be interesting," Sara said, and smiled.

As we approached the man, he dropped the cigarette and crushed it under the toe of his shoe. He stepped away from the white glow of the lamp and walked toward us.

"Harper, I'd like you to meet Lucas. We'll just keep it at a first name basis for now," Sara said.

I held out my hand, only to be denied a simple handshake by a new acquaintance.

"I prefer to speak over here. I'd rather stay in the shadows," Lucas said. His head hung low, preventing me from getting a good look at him. He walked to a bench beneath a large oak and sat in the folds of darkness.

"Sure, however you'd like to run this situation is fine with me. I think this whole secret meeting in a dark park has been overplayed in the movies. I'd prefer a Starbucks around lunchtime," I said.

"This isn't a movie. This is real life, and real conversations that matter. If it bothers you, then we could cut the introduction short and part ways. I'm here doing a favor for Sara. Whether you take this seriously is your choice," Lucas said. He patiently waited for my response.

"I'm sorry. I was a little uncomfortable with this whole secret get-together. I'm over it now," I said.

"Good. So, you have questions and I have answers. Shall we get to it then?"

I shrugged, stepped closer, and said, "All right, I'll be professional about this. What kind of career do you have that allows you to see into certain aspects of this case?"

"Perhaps Sara didn't inform you that my career position is not up for discussion. The only thing about me I'll share is my first name. Even information that small makes me somewhat reluctant to disclose. Next question, please," Lucas said while removing a pack of cigarettes, shaking one loose, and lighting it.

I said, "All right. I just figured that you know a lot about me, so it seems reasonable that I know you as well. But if that's the road you want to walk down, then so be it."

"Yes, I know a great deal about you, Agent Caster. It's what I do. I'm a deep well of information about our fine country and its citizens. I also know a great deal about influential people outside of our borders. All of this is beside the point. Please ask your next question."

Although his face fell in shadows, I could tell that Lucas was eyeing me contemptuously over a rolling cloud of smoke.

"Okay, that seems fair. I guess us lowly FBI guys don't deserve to know such things." I waved my hand as a gesture of moving on. "If you're aware of the current case Sara and I are working, and I'm sure you are, do you have any idea why someone would want Senator Ryan removed from the presidential race?"

"No, I don't know why someone would go to such lengths to see him withdraw his candidacy."

"Well, that's great. I'm glad I could meet up with you late at night in a park to find that out," I said.

"Take it easy, Harper. I'm sure there's plenty we can learn here," Sara said.

"Ask the right question and perhaps I'll give you the answer you're searching for."

The guy was so smug that I had an overwhelming desire to hit him. He seemed destined to play games with me at this late hour. I didn't have time for games, but I felt Sara was right and we would learn something helpful tonight.

"Okay. Why would Senator Ryan refuse to meet the demands of the kidnappers? Why would a man risk the lives of his wife and child to test the seriousness of the people who took them?"

"I think Senator Ryan is the only person in the world who can answer that for you. I suppose one could decipher from his broadcast that he's telling the American people he would never give in to terrorist demands. He's not even the president yet, but he's standing on a strong footing where others have failed. Some of our greatest presidents have both publicly and under extreme secrecy given in to those who have threatened the American way of life. Someone in Senator Ryan's position must weigh all options. In the end, he lost his wife, but I believe his purpose will thrive. Senator Ryan is a determined man to find and destroy not only the people who savagely murdered his wife, but to all those who stand against the U.S. Honestly, I admire his courage. Ninety-nine percent of all loving husbands wouldn't have challenged the orders of the kidnappers. I can honestly tell you that I wouldn't have sacrificed any of my loved ones for a career position. Not even to take a presidential role. Terrorism or not, I would have given in to their demands to keep my loved one's safe. Of course, that's just me. Maybe you should ask yourself where you would have stood on that fine line. Would you have given in or stood defiantly?"

I didn't answer his question. Instead, I said, "So does that mean that Senator Ryan didn't love his wife? Does that mean that she was expendable in his cause for something far greater than the support and love of a wife?"

"As I said before, Agent Caster, Senator Ryan is the only one in the world that can answer a question like that." Lucas dropped the cigarette butt and crushed it under his heel.

Even though the sun had long since found its bed, the humidity lingered. I removed a handkerchief from my jacket pocket and wiped the trickle of sweat away from my face.

"If these guys truly wanted to destroy Senator Ryan, they could have easily killed him the night of the abduction. Instead, they later kill his wife. Why not kill the son as well as punishment for the senator's resistance? Have they been taunting me from the beginning? Why are they giving me the opportunity to stop them?" I desperately asked.

"I'm sorry, were those questions directed toward me or were you simply thinking out loud?" he asked.

As I tucked the handkerchief into my pocket, I looked at him. I realized I wasn't sure if I had been asking him or trying to get my brain to somehow magically piece everything together.

I said, "Actually, I couldn't care less who answers the questions as long as I get some sort of answers I can agree with."

"I will tell you this: you're in dangerous territory. Sara told me these people left pictures of your family at Senator Ryan's house. To me, that's a clear indication that your family could be in serious jeopardy if you get too close. They dragged you into this for the single reason of watching you fail. By the end of this chase, you may not have only lost the game itself, but perhaps those you love. They've placed you in an impossible situation that leads to at least one failure after another."

"So, what do I do? Should I play the game by their rules or go after them full force? Any road I go down could put my family in danger. What would you do?" I said irritably.

He didn't answer, only watched my anger build.

The whole situation of being dragged out here in the late-night hours and receiving answers that had no clarity was driving a bad attitude to the surface. I didn't think Lucas was an ally I could count on.

"I was under the assumption that we were meeting out here during the night because you chose to shine a bright light on my troubling case. Was I wrong to assume such things? Is this a stupid game you're playing at my expense? Do you honestly think I have nothing better to do?" My voice was flaring now.

"Harper, calm down," Sara warned.

"I have no reason to calm down. I want some goddamn answers."

"I don't have to tolerate this. Goodbye, Sara," Lucas said and stood.

Lucas's right side turned toward me, and under the glow of the trail lamp, I saw that his face was partially disfigured. The wounds had long since healed, but the effects of whatever disaster befell him would forever remain.

"Christ, what happened to your face?" I asked.

He stared at me in the gloom for a moment, then removed his brimmed hat and stepped toward me. I realized that long ago fire once ate away the right side of his face and the skin never healed the same. The iris of his right eye was a faded blue and eerily noticeable compared to the intensely brown left eye.

He rotated his head so that I could clearly see and then said, "Take a good, long look, Harper. This is one of the rewards I've received from the country I once loved so much. It's the mark of betrayal by someone I once believed was a friend, a partner. This is what happens when someone gets careless and takes things for granted. I can assure you that I will never make the same mistake again." He put his hat on and nodded to Sara and said, "Goodnight. Will you call me tomorrow?"

"Of course. I'm sorry about this, Lucas," Sara said as she apologized for my behavior.

He turned and began walking down the dark trail. Sara and I started heading in the other direction when Lucas said something that halted both of us.

"Remember this, Harper, if you get too close to these people, well, you just might get burned like I once did."

He turned again and disappeared into the shadows of the park.

"What the hell is that supposed to mean?" I asked Sara.

"Nice going, Harper. He's usually a levelheaded kind of guy, but now you pissed off one of the few guys who could have helped us figure something out."

"Sure, I bet," I sarcastically said. "How long have you known him?"

"Lucas?"

"Yeah, who else would I be talking about?"

"Oh, since I was a kid. He's been one of my father's best friends for as long as I can remember. Why?"

"He has an accent. He did a great job of masking it, but I still detected it," I said.

"Accent? I've never known him to have an accent. You're probably mistaken."

"No, I'm not. Because he was able to mask it so well, I couldn't tell if it was maybe a Russian or a German accent for sure. Also, why did he say he received those scars from the country he once loved so much? Doesn't that sound a little strange to you?"

"I don't know why he said it like that. He's from Cleveland, for crying out loud, Harper."

"Yeah, so he says."

22

Something seemed out of whack when I returned home a little after ten o'clock at night. Aside from the rest of the block being lit up in the dark, our house was completely void of lights. I suddenly had a bad feeling creeping up my spine and setting off every nerve ending along the way.

I got out of the sedan and peered through the windows as I approached the front door. There was a faint glowing inside, and I saw a few candles burning within. I saw Clara and Kaylee sitting at the coffee table, playing a board game. I let out a breath of relief and unlocked the door.

"What's this all about? Jesus, it's like a sauna in here," I said as I took off my suit jacket and threw it over the back of an armchair. The temperature inside nearly matched the outside temperature.

"Isn't it neat? We're pretending like it's the 1800s or something," Kaylee said as she rolled the dice.

"I wish I could share her enthusiasm," Clara said. "Luckily, we still have running water at this point, but I can't be sure if that will last much longer."

"They shut off our power?"

"Yep. I think it's going to be a sweaty night, and not in the fun way you're thinking," Clara said and smiled.

"Are you talking about sex?" Kaylee said, as she looked up from the board.

"All right. You know, I'm pretty sure I told you this morning that you wouldn't be waiting up for me since you have school. It's time for you to get ready for bed," I told her.

"It's too hot to sleep," she immediately resisted, and then finally gave into our parental order.

After Kaylee gave hugs and disappeared upstairs, I said, "What did the power company say when you called them?"

"Well, since our house phone went out of operation after I called you earlier, I had to use my cell. The power company said the same thing every other creditor said when I called them. They told me that we were three months behind on payments and that service would be terminated until they received a payment for the entire amount we're behind."

I went to the refrigerator and snagged a slightly chilled beer. I popped the cap and downed half of it. Collapsing on the sofa, I ran the glass bottle across my forehead.

"I have some emergency cash upstairs, and I think this constitutes an emergency. In the morning, one of us will have to go to the power company office and pay them what they want in order to get the electricity back on. Then we'll have to figure out the rest of this mess," I said, and offered the rest of the beer to Clara.

"I guess that would be me since I'm taking a well-deserved week off work and you have a psycho to catch," she said.

I didn't resist, but simply said, "Thanks."

"Do I really want to know what this is about, or should the surprise wait until the end of everything?"

I massaged her neck and shoulders and said, "I think I'm just now figuring out a few things myself. I suppose you'll have to wait until I know. Sorry to disappoint you."

"That's okay, I do enjoy surprises," Clara said with plain sarcasm.

I didn't. In fact, I feared this surprise.

"Good. I'd hate to ruin everything. Besides, there's so many puzzle pieces right now that somewhat fit together, but they're being incredibly stubborn about it," I said.

"At least tell me that everything is going to work out. You better damn well promise me that at the end of this cat-and-mouse chase, we're going to be okay. I hope you understand that by saying *we're,* I also mean our bank accounts."

There was serious doubt. There was the undeniable fact that at this time, I wasn't entirely sure which direction I was supposed to be facing. Even against the mountain of resistance, I thought that just maybe good would prevail again. Just maybe.

"Yeah, *we're* going to be just fine. I also wanted to tell you that Director Gill called me as I was heading home. We found Dillon Ryan," I said.

Clara gave me a look of horror.

"No, not like that. He's alive. He's dehydrated and his feet are cut up pretty bad, but he's alive and doing fine."

"How?" Clara asked.

"He said they let him go. He said they held him in a cabin in the woods and then they decided to let him go. He had to walk through the woods, but the kidnapper gave him guidance that led him to a road. I simply can't believe they did that."

"Whatever the reason is, I'm glad they couldn't bring themselves to hurt him. Hell doesn't have a furnace hot enough for people that kill children," Clara said.

"I agree. Come on, let's go to bed."

Clara and I opened more windows as we made our way upstairs. It was beginning to get uncomfortably stuffy inside and, at least this way, there was a little more airflow moving throughout the house. Having the windows open while we slept made me a little edgy. I knew anyone could slit open a screen door and quietly slip inside while we slept. For some reason, madmen were watching us. Someone had earlier announced intentions of placing my family in harm's way if I got too close to the answers.

I thought of how easily they entered Senator Ryan's house as the family slept. Hell, they even had a key for the front door and the deactivation code for the alarm. I had a simple deadbolt. I didn't think any kind of security would stop these men from getting exactly what they wanted.

I knew I was going to have to sleep with my gun under the pillow and one eye open. Even though I badly needed sleep, I didn't think much would come tonight.

Three hours later, Clara was asleep beside me. The heat bathed my body in a miserable sweat, and I idly watched the curtains flutter in the night breeze. As I had expected, my mind wouldn't settle. Exhausted or not, my mind wanted answers. In the quiet of the house, I had figured that the answers would not come tonight, no matter how much I needed them to.

Besides the electricity being shut off by the power provider tonight, one other thing bothered me. I wasn't sure what I was supposed to learn from the secret meeting Sara and I had attended. Sara's connection with Lucas was unknown to me. More importantly, he had agreed to meet and assist us in figuring out the baffling connection between Senator Ryan's wife, and a D.C. real estate king, and possibly what I had to do with the entire thing. As I had told Sara, I left the meeting more confused than before it began. Lucas seemed more intent on answering my questions with a question.

There was one positive thing I had collected when we walked away from the meeting. Lucas had made the point of Senator Ryan throwing up the defenses and countering the kidnappers with a threat of his own. Lucas had questioned me about my devotion to my family and asked if I would do everything possible to get them back safely should I ever be in such a situation.

I would have given in to the kidnappers. I would have withdrawn my presidential candidacy if it meant that there was even a small chance the kidnappers would own up to their promise of releasing my wife and child if I did exactly as they had ordered.

Senator Ryan hadn't done that. So what exactly did that mean? Did it mean that his wife and child were expendable? Did it mean that he loved the possibility of taking the presidential seat far more than he loved his family? Again, I didn't have answers, and it was frustrating as hell.

Katherine Ryan had paid the ultimate price for her husband's personal war against all threats. For some unknown reason, they released Dillon Ryan. Did that mean that the kidnappers didn't have the stomach to kill a child? Did it mean that they feared the worst things to come after Katherine's death and more bloodshed would be pointless? Was the release of Dillon a way of cutting their losses and hoping beyond all hope that Senator

Ryan would recant his million-dollar bounty? Or was there still a road my mind hadn't gone down?

Yet again, no answers found me at this late hour.

23

The following morning, I called Sara and told her I'd pick her up. Twenty minutes later, I pulled up to the brilliant pink house. Sara came out sporting her typical style suit. Today she hadn't tied her hair back in a ponytail but let it hang loosely. She looked as if she'd had a long night as well.

As she slid in, I pointed to the cup holder and said, "I got you a coffee. I'm not sure how you take it, so I left it black."

"Great, it's nearly a hundred degrees out here already and you bring me a hot beverage. Good thinking."

"I've got a cooler of beers in the back that I'm saving until lunch," I said.

"Like I said, good thinking."

"Did you get any sleep?"

"Not much, but I feel like I'm more focused when I only get a few hours. How about you?"

"I'm also focused, I guess. I was thinking about a couple of things this morning. The first thought I had was about your friend I met last night. There are quite a few things that troubled me about the meeting. First, your friend wasn't really helpful in any way possible. In fact, I think he complicated things a little more for me. That is, until I picked up the slight Russian accent. At least I think it's Russian. He did a great job of trying to cover it, but I still managed to pick up on it. How well do you really know this man?"

"I told you, he worked with my father back in the day. I'll stand by his reputation no matter what. Unfortunately, I can't tell you who he really is or where he works, but I assure you that he's well connected and an admirable man. He was trying to help us in his own quirky sort of way. In some way, he gave us information we can use, but it's up to us to figure out what exactly that is."

"And what about your reputation? It's time to cut through the crap and be honest. What do you get out of all of this?" I asked.

Sara was staring out the window, watching the city go by as she tried to find the words.

She said, "All right, I suppose it's only fair to you. The truth is that Senator Ryan personally asked me to oversee this investigation. Maybe he believes that I have a unique ability to assist in profiling the kidnappers. Maybe he believes that bringing me in will better the chances of capturing these men. I really don't know. To be fair, I haven't been an officer for very long, but this opportunity came along, and I took it. Can you really blame me for that?"

"No, I can't. If a presidential candidate asked me to take the assignment, I would have done the same. The FBI has been here every step of the way to see to it that the senator's wife and son were returned unharmed. It was the senator's actions that led to the murder of his wife. His son being released is a whole other matter I haven't understood yet. So that's it, observe and report?"

"He was never clear about what my assignment was. He said that I was supposed to team up with you and see to it that his wife and son stayed safe should the opportunity come along for me to protect them from their captors. That's all I know. Honest."

"So, what about last night? Was last night an opportunity to string me along, getting me to chase my tail for a while? That's what it felt like," I said.

She stared out the window as if there were some other greater fascinations beyond our conversation. I was suddenly feeling like the relationship Sara and I had formed over the last few days was a sham. I was having a hard time believing that her sole mission was simply to protect the senator's family should the chance arise. It was difficult to tell if and when she was being honest with me.

"Senator Ryan didn't want anyone to know that he was trying to oversee this investigation. I don't mean to sound like a movie here, but there are serious dark forces at work in our city," Sara said while watching me closely.

I shook my head in confusion. What I needed was a partner with a head screwed on tight. I decided to challenge her and see if she could think in a direction I had yet to travel.

"Victim three, who's it going to be?" I asked.

She smiled. I think she understood that I was opening the door for her, and it was up to her to find the intellectual ability to walk through.

"Obviously another man or woman connected to Senator Ryan personally or with a business connection."

"I know that. We need to figure out who else would benefit from Senator Ryan's fall from power," I said.

"That could take all day compiling a list. There must be a hundred names that get something out of Senator Ryan failing to take the presidential seat."

"I know, but who are the people at the top of that list? Whoever your informant is that we met last night, I think you need to call him back. This time I want answers, not more questions. Do you think you can handle that?"

"Well, it's not as easy as ordering a meatball sub, but I'll see what I can do," Sara said as she retrieved her cell.

24

I laughed a little as I saw Lucas walking toward Sara and me while carrying a beverage tray with three cups of Starbucks coffee.

"I take it that this is your form of an apology?" I asked him.

"I never apologize for anything I've ever done. A man in my line of work never does. I would just say that this is one of the rare occasions when I'm being good-natured. Call it a peace offering if you must," Lucas said as he offered the tray and took a seat on the park bench.

I accepted one of the coffee cups and handed Sara the other. I waited until Lucas took a sip of the remaining coffee before I took a drink.

"Thank you," I said.

"You're welcome. Now tell me what sort of developments have come about since our last meeting."

I rolled my eyes. He was already toying with us.

"I'm going to cut to the quick. Someone is tapping into all of my credit and seriously fucking over my way of life seven ways from Sunday. I've had next to nothing for sleep last night. What sleep I got was with a gun within easy reach because I'm not entirely sure who is keeping me under surveillance or which direction they might be coming from next. You've agreed to meet a second time because you have information that you're willing to share. I don't really need to know who you work for or which country you're originally from. It isn't relevant to the case. What I want to know is who the hell the Tourist really is and the purpose behind this stupid game."

"Well, from the information I have about the current case, I wouldn't say that the game is stupid by any means. It's actually quite clever," Lucas said.

"All right, I'll take the bait. In what way is the game clever?" I asked.

Lucas smiled in an all-knowing way. He obviously knew far more about this case than I did.

"In order to appreciate what the Tourist has done, you must look from a completely different perspective. Instead of viewing it from your current perspective as an FBI agent hunting down a criminal, you must focus on the current devastation he has caused. Try looking from the vantage point of the person who has the most to lose from all this."

"You mean Senator Ryan?" I asked.

"No, Senator Ryan certainly has a lot to lose should the Tourist prevail, but there's another that will lose much more."

"I don't see how that could be. Senator Ryan has already lost his wife and possibly the presidential campaign. Who could stand to lose more?"

"Agent Caster, you understand that behind every powerful man, there is someone far more powerful. Senator Ryan has his backing like Mr. Lewis Rockwell. But Lewis Rockwell was possibly one of the smaller fish in the pond. You need to cast a line. You need to run your bait deep and see what kind of bite you get," Lucas said and drank his coffee.

"I've never been a fan of fishing, not even metaphorically. So, Senator Ryan has an ally standing strongly behind him, giving him all the right nudges at all the right times. Are you saying it's someone backing Senator Ryan who the Tourist is really trying to destroy?" I asked.

Lucas didn't respond. He only stared at me as if waiting for me to form an answer to my own question.

I set my half-empty coffee cup on the park bench and stood. I thrust out my hand as a parting handshake.

"As always, Mr. Lucas, you've been no help whatsoever. I'm done communicating by riddles or codes to which I have no key. I've wasted more than enough of my time with this game of yours. I have a lot to figure out and not nearly enough time to do it."

When Lucas didn't accept my offered hand, I turned and headed down the path.

Sara asked for me to stop. I kept going until Lucas called after me in a tone that I read as defeat. Well, maybe not so much defeat, as it was more along the lines of professional courtesy to at last find the surface.

I stopped and turned. It wasn't going to take much for me to start going again.

He motioned for me to come back.

"Please, there are too many curious eyes and ears at this time of day," Lucas said.

As I approached Lucas and Sara, I said, "I may have to deal with the Tourist's games, but yours I could do without. What do you say? Are we done playing coy?"

"All right, I suppose the secrecy isn't helping either of us. I'm going to give you the stepping-stone you desperately need. I believe you can understand my reluctance to disclose confidential information. Even though

I agreed to meet you here for such a discussion, my profession prevents me from spilling out privileged information. I will try to lower my guard for a few moments. I apologize for the games. I owe Sara more than I can say, and it's only fair that I do her this one favor."

"Thank you, Lucas," Sara said, and patted his hand.

I found my seat again and picked up my coffee.

"Okay, I'm listening," I said.

"You understand that everything I'm going to tell you is off the record, right?"

"Agreed," I said.

"Good. The truth is that I work for the CIA as a foreign consultant. I'm Russian, born and raised. I would rather not explain the details of my many careers for the Motherland. As of now, it's unimportant. Like so many others, I was a victim of the Cold War. Also, like many others, I defected and sought refuge in the U.S. I love this country far more than I ever loved my own. I have vast knowledge of the political workings of Russia. I know her strengths and weaknesses. My job, my purpose, is intelligence related to my homeland. This is how I know of your current case," Lucas said and tossed his empty cup into the trashcan.

"What does Russia have to do with Senator Ryan's wife and son being kidnapped? For that matter, what does Russia have to do with Senator Ryan failing to take the presidential seat?" I asked, as now the conversation completely captivated me.

"That part I could not say, but I can tell you a little about the man called the Tourist. At least, who we believe him to be."

"All right, I'll take whatever information you have. At this point, anything small or large could help me more than you know," I said.

"Very well. There's limited information I know about the Tourist. However, I can tell you that his real name is Mikhail Alexandrov, once employed by the Novilov Russian Mafia family. They are currently one of the largest Mafia families in Russia. Their hands are dirty from everything, including weapons distribution, drugs, prostitution, gambling, hired killers, and so on. Over the years, they've found very profitable means in government dealings. Although no one can confirm it, the rumor is the Novilov family owns a great majority of Russian government officials. I'm not sure of all the circumstances behind it, but apparently Mikhail Alexandrov decided to overthrow Kiril Novilov and assume complete control of Novilov's empire. Kiril caught wind of the treachery and had his men rig explosives to Mikhail's vehicle. They thought it finished everything, but apparently Mikhail doesn't die so easily. I understand that the men working for Kiril were truly on Mikhail's side of the war. The men warned Mikhail of Kiril's orders to have him killed. Mikhail went deep into hiding for many years. I have no doubt that he's the one known as the Tourist and that he's resurfaced with a plan to create major chaos for Kiril Novilov and his business here in the states."

I remembered the name Kiril Novilov from the files I collected from the FBI database. We might finally be on the right track.

"Are you saying Kiril Novilov was trying to worm his way into the U.S. government by bribing officials just as he had in Russia?"

"Yes. It's unknown at this time if he has yet established contacts in the U.S. It wouldn't surprise me if he's made bribes to every official that would give him a minute and listen to his proposal," Lucas said as he removed a handkerchief from his jacket pocket and blotted his sweat-streamed face.

"So, is it possible that Kiril made contact with Senator Ryan and the senator turned down his bribe? Maybe Senator Ryan even threatened to go public and expose Kiril Novilov's agenda, and maybe he was even able to expose all of Kiril's current contacts. That could be a reason why the senator's wife and son were taken."

"But remember, Harper, it isn't the Russian Mafia that kidnapped Senator Ryan's family or killed Lewis Rockwell. We know the Tourist did these things because he left a message telling us so. If Kiril Novilov and the Tourist are enemies, then there would be no reason for the Tourist to help Kiril silence possible threats," Sara said.

"Unless we're looking at things the wrong way. Maybe Senator Ryan really is under Kiril Novilov's thumb and the Tourist is determined to destroy everything the Mafia godfather has structured. I don't think we can conclude anything at this point," I said and turned to Lucas, waiting for more insight if there were any to be given.

"I told you I was going to give you a stepping-stone to assist in your investigation. I've told you who we believe the Tourist to be. Now I'm going to help you a little more than I expected to. Here's a bit of information that might help you reach that answer you so desperately desire. Kiril Novilov is currently in the United States. In fact, he's right here in D.C. If you have any more questions, save them. I've already shared more than I should have. The rest of the answers you will have to find on your own, Agent Caster."

As Lucas stood to leave, I said, "You said a few minutes ago that you didn't think the Tourist's games were stupid by any means. That means you either know exactly what he's up to or you have a reasonable clue. So, what is it, Lucas? Sharing time isn't done until I know what you know. If you really do work for the U.S. government, then you must realize that we're on the same team. Together we can bring the Tourist down by the end of the day if we're lucky and more people won't have to die."

"You'll need much more than luck. The end of everything is never written in stone. Questions-and-answers time is over, Agent Caster. Good day and good luck to you both," Lucas said, turning and walking down the park path.

25

There was something about the atmosphere that sickened the Tourist. The aroma filling the restaurant was nauseating, and the endless clank of spoons and forks against plates was nearly enough to drive him mad. But the thing that crept beneath his skin, the thing that released its poison into his bloodstream, was the random blathering from one table to the next. The men and women dressed in overpriced clothing, accompanied by an absurdly snobbish tone that seemed to place them on a pedestal of the most ridiculously soulless human beings of the twenty-first century.

There was an individual that sickened him the most. A man who had crossed half a world to see the finale of his divine plan placed into motion nearly twenty years before. It was humorous that the man couldn't foretell his death in this outrageously overpriced restaurant in one of the city's elite hotels.

"Is the clam chowder to your liking, sir?" the Tourist asked.

"Bitter. Do you honestly expect me to pay for this?" the fat Russian responded.

"Sir, I can see that you've eaten most of the dish. So, I'm afraid we'll have to add the plate to your bill. If you like, I could bring you a fresh batch when the chef has finished preparation."

"No. Bring my main course. I've been waiting," Kiril Novilov said.

"Right away," the Tourist said and turned. He stopped, snapped his fingers, and rotated on his heels to face the fat man and the two bodyguards. "I almost forgot."

The Tourist removed a small silver whistle from the inside pocket of his white waiter blazer, placed it at his lips, and gently blew. The sound was high-pitched and immediately seized the attention of all the restaurant patrons. Most of them offered a look of irritation at the unexpected interruption to their lunchtime dining experience.

"What is this?" Kiril Novilov asked.

The Tourist held up his index finger to the man, informing him that his answer would come in a moment.

"Gentlemen, it's time."

Three men on the restaurant floor sporting matching white blazers each withdrew a silenced Beretta and took position. Three other men came through the kitchen's double doors. One remained at the kitchen doors as the other two found positions at the front entrance.

"Ladies and gentlemen," the Tourist said as he no longer tried to conceal his accent, "I apologize for any inconvenience. I will try to execute the efforts of my plan with great speed. In a moment you will be able to return to your tasteless and overpriced meals."

"I recognize the voice, but not the face," Kiril Novilov said in Russian as he studied the features of the Tourist. "It has to be impossible. The man I'm thinking of has been dead for some time."

"Dead? No. Perhaps a man of exile, some might say."

"Impossible, nonetheless."

The Tourist quickly turned his attention to the men on each side of the Russian cartel leader and said, "Gentlemen, this matter is not your concern. I can read your eyes and your thoughts. It would be unwise to reach for the guns beneath your jackets. I promise that you won't make it. My men will cut you down the moment they see a finger twitch."

The bodyguards glanced at each other and then slowly raised their hands.

"Very good and very smart. Now, Kiril, where were we?"

"I saw your body. I saw the burnt remains," Kiril said.

"Do you know what the problem is with you, Kiril? I'll tell you. Your problem is that you trusted men on your payroll to execute a man they liked better than you. The majority of your men secretly worked for me for many years. I was going to overthrow you. I was going to take control of the cartel. You knew, didn't you? You knew that I wanted more and that's why you tried to execute me. You saw me as a future threat and the only person who could bring your organization down in a heaping, crumbling mess, didn't you?"

"They blew you up. I saw it with my own eyes. I saw your bones blackened!" he said and slammed his large fist on the table, which rattled plates and glasses.

The Tourist took the seat across from the fat man and smiled.

"No, you only saw what I wanted you to see. The only person you killed in that car explosion was a poor village man who had a remarkable resemblance to me, from a distance, of course. That poor man was paid half a dozen loaves of bread to drive my car from your estate. I'm sure he was unaware that the ignition would trigger a bomb and therefore end his life. I obviously knew. I was observing you from the estate perimeter. I watched you watching him. When the car detonated, I witnessed that awful smile of yours. Even with one of those disgusting cigars crammed in your mouth, I saw you smile. You thought the terror had ended. You thought that you were safe again."

"I've never feared you. Never! There wasn't any possibility that your feeble mind could take control of my business. Even now, I'm certainly surprised that you're alive, but I feel no fear."

"Ignorance of the situation at hand was always bliss for you. Always. Even now, as everything crumbles beneath your feet, you remain incompetent. I'm destroying everything you're trying to unfold here in the U.S. The plan for you is falling apart, Kiril. This is my revenge. You've spent twenty years of your pathetic life creating this ideal vision of yours. Now I'm going to unravel everything from your grip in only a matter of days. I'd also like to tell you that the men you instructed to invade Senator Ryan's home and take his wife and child are actually working for me, not you. I also want you to think about Brandon Harris and Kyle Sawyer. You remember them, of course. I want you to know that I've found Brandon Harris and his copy of the stolen file," the Tourist said and offered a genuine smile.

"Rat bastard," Kiril Novilov shouted.

Kiril drew in a stuttering breath, leaned back in the chair, removed a handkerchief from his breast pocket, and blotted his reddening face. He used his right hand to gently massage his throat as his eyes shifted to the squad of armed men scattered throughout the restaurant. He tried to clear his throat with some obvious difficulty, then retrieved his glass and swallowed the remaining wine with a quick motion.

"You shouldn't anger yourself, Kiril. When you add wine to raised blood pressure, it only makes the effects work quicker," the Tourist said.

"What? What are you talking about, traitor?"

"When I approached your table and asked you how the clam chowder was to your liking, what was your response?"

"I said that it was bitter."

"Exactly. A secret ingredient caused the bitterness in the chowder. I know that you're very concerned with your fellow dining patrons, but you shouldn't worry, you're the only one in this establishment that received the added ingredient."

"What have you done, Mikhail?"

"Oh, have I forgotten to tell you? I'm no longer known as Mikhail Alexandrov. He actually perished in an unfortunate car explosion in Russia nearly four years ago. The Tourist is the only identity I go by now, Kiril."

"What have you done to me?" he shouted.

The Tourist held out his hand to comfort the man. "Didn't I warn you about the anger? You see, when the blood flows faster, that increases the absorption of the poison. If you manage to calm your temper, you'll enjoy a few extra minutes of my pleasant company before you choke to death on your own blood."

"You're lying. You never would make such a daring move."

"No, I never lie. I can see that you're feeling an overwhelming irritation at the back of your throat. That is one of the first symptoms. You see, while you were eating the clam chowder, the poison began absorbing into your bloodstream. The lining of your esophagus and stomach are eroding at this moment. This wonderful concoction is also racing through your veins and attacking every vital organ. Sounds delightful, doesn't it?" The Tourist stood and offered a slight bow.

Kiril violently coughed into his handkerchief. As he withdrew the silk cloth from his mouth, his eyes locked on the crimson spatter on the fabric. There was a brief look of confusion, which rapidly transitioned to fear and then a thundering anger.

"Kill him!" Kiril screamed at his bodyguards.

Neither man made the slightest motion for the guns hidden beneath their jackets. They helplessly glanced from Kiril Novilov to each other and back to the Tourist. It was apparent that both men understood that their employer was enduring a painful death and his death did not need to be matched by their own.

"What do I pay you for? I said kill him!"

"Your guards are wiser than you are. It's obvious to everyone here that you are not a person they would give their lives for. You're a pitiful man who has lived far more years than you ever deserved."

They all watched as Kiril cupped his large gut in his arms and released a howl of sobbing cries. His breathing became shallow and labored, followed by a series of fitful coughs that sprayed the tablecloth in red.

Slowly, the bodyguards slid away from Kiril while keeping their hands raised. The armed men in white blazers also shifted position from the once great Russian Mafia leader. The Tourist took three strides back for the single purpose of keeping the man's blood from reaching him.

"Hum, hum, ugh," Kiril exclaimed and then pitched slowly forward. His face found the center of his bowl and the uneaten remains. There was a dull splash, followed by the brief release of red bubbles that rose to the surface of the clam chowder. These would be the final unintelligible words from a man that once held thousands in the grip of fear for decades.

The Tourist turned to his men. "Exit through the kitchen."

As the men obeyed the order, the Tourist turned to the bodyguards who had the look of men coming to terms with a pending death.

"I recommend you travel back to the Motherland and find employment elsewhere. Gentlemen, go home and kiss your wives and children, because today is the luckiest day of your lives," the Tourist said.

26

Despite the runaround about additional information Lucas had provided at the park, Sara and I had done some legwork and as lunchtime passed, we located the hotel Kiril Novilov was staying.

The problem was, so had nearly the entire D.C. police force.

It seemed that our run of bad luck and timing was going to continue. We were rapidly losing the game. The Tourist had three deaths to our zero saves. Two more lives hung in the balance, and I was now having serious doubts that either of them would make it through the week.

"Shit, shit, shit," Sara said, and thrust her fist into the dashboard.

"My thoughts exactly. But let's not get ahead of ourselves. We don't know yet if the authorities are here for Kiril Novilov or for some other reason," I said.

Against my statement, I had already formed a conclusion. I was sure that somewhere inside the hotel, police investigators were hovering over the body of a recently deceased Russian Mafia leader.

As I had the day before, I parked among the clutter of patrol and crime scene unit vehicles. Sara and I moved through the gathering crowd to the police barricades. I showed my badge and went under the yellow crime scene tape. The patrolman held Sara back as she searched her pockets for her identification.

"Actually, I'm with stupid," she said and pointed at me.

I nodded, and they allowed her through.

"With comments like that, I should have left you back there to get trampled by the crowd," I said when she caught up.

"Nah, I would have pulled my piece if one of those airheads even stepped on my shoes. These things cost me a hundred dollars at Macy's."

"You could have fed a small village in the Philippines for that, but, hey, it's your money. Where the hell is your identification?" I asked.

"Shit, I was in such a rush this morning that I think I left it on the kitchen counter."

"Big mistake. Hang on to it like it's a pair of hundred-dollar shoes," I said.

I showed my badge a few more times before we reached the front door of the hotel. With all the security, I was sure that our first hunch was a correct one. Someone murdered Kiril Novilov during the busy lunch hour.

Police escorted us through the lobby to the restaurant near the back of the hotel. It wasn't an average family restaurant, but one that would cost an offer of your firstborn for a five-course meal. I could tell all that just by the attire the patrons were wearing.

The place was a madhouse. The authorities were holding the restaurant patrons and staff until we could verify all identifications. We needed every person's statement, accounting for each moment that transpired during the lunchtime assassination.

Sara and I walked over to the crime scene coordinator. It was good old Charlie King on another baffling murder in our fair city.

"We've got to stop meeting like this," he said as I shook his hand.

"Have you solved the Lewis Rockwell murder yet?" I asked him.

"Shit, I was aiming to ask you the same thing. I'm stumped, which doesn't happen often. Did I mention that you two are still at the top of my suspect list? As a matter of fact, this one isn't looking good for you either."

"I've got a solid alibi. I'm not so sure about her for the Lewis Rockwell case," I said, and nodded toward Sara.

"Actually, I do. Charlie here was at my house, spending the night. There was touching involved," Sara said, and winked.

"I don't need any details," I said and waved my hand.

Charlie flushed and offered an awkward smile. "I might have been there in your dreams. I'm not that easy, unless I'm drunk. Was I drunk? Anyway, according to the passport in his jacket pocket, the victim's name is Kiril Novilov. He entered the U.S. from Russia last Tuesday. You know how we love to welcome our foreigners. The restaurant maître d' said that the two men who were with Mr. Novilov slipped out of here before we could throw a net down on the place. According to the staff, all the other patrons are still here," Charlie said as he moved us to Kiril's table.

I looked down at the fat man for a long, unsettling moment. I knew very little about him, but what I knew certainly wasn't good character-building material. No matter what the man had done during his life, he probably hadn't deserved to go out the way he did.

"None of the patrons or staff touched him, as they were pretty sure he was toast. We found him face down in his clam chowder. It was poisoned. The restaurant patrons overheard Mr. Novilov and the other guy speaking about the ingested poison from the food. He pretty much choked to death on his own blood. Must have hurt like hell," Charlie said as he leaned over the body.

The medical examiner had pulled Kiril Novilov free from his final meal and now his body slumped awkwardly in the chair. Dried clam chowder ran in an oblong circle around his face. The remaining chowder was no longer a pleasant dish to look at as blood had seeped from Kiril's dying breath, mixed with the chowder, and turned it an unappetizing pink.

"Did the patrons get a good look at the man who Kiril was speaking with?" Sara asked.

"Sure did. They also remember most of the faces of his crew, despite having weapons pointed at them."

"He had a crew with him?" I asked.

"Yeah, six others, to be exact. The entire restaurant staff, with the exception of the maître d', we found tied up and locked in the cooler. This guy's men were posing as the staff," Charlie said.

"Do you think Lucas knew the Tourist had a crew tagging along with him?" I asked Sara.

"From what Lucas said, I was sure that our subject worked alone."

Charlie snapped his fingers to get our attention and said, "Whoa, whoa, who's Lucas, and why does he know information that I don't?"

"Sorry, Charlie, it's top secret," Sara said, and winked.

"Top secret, my ass. If you have information that's going to help everyone solve this crime, as well as the

Lewis Rockwell and Katherine Ryan murders, you better start getting in the mood to fill me in before I have to kick someone's balls to get my answers."

I suddenly thought about how oddly things had changed in only a few hours. Earlier, I had been practically begging Lucas to open up and clue me in on information I desperately needed. Now we had the information, and we were unwilling to disclose anything, potentially damaging our progress with the investigation. I now understood the position Lucas was in and his hesitation to share, further protecting the people hiding in the shadows of this case.

"All right, if you want to play it that way, I guess I won't tell you the name the patrons overheard the mystery man call himself," Charlie said.

"It was probably Mikhail Alexandrov," I said.

"Now you're pissing me off," Charlie said and sneered as he watched us.

"Look, I know the position you're in. I've been there myself. I honestly can't tell you anything about the man named Lucas, only because I know little about him. Tell me what the man who spoke with Kiril looked like and the conversation they had," I said to Charlie.

His shoulders sagged a little in defeat. He very well understood that these crime scenes were quickly becoming an FBI high-profile case and there was no way he was going to coax information from us. Whatever perspective he got on the current cases wasn't going to come from us.

"Fine, don't be a team player. I'll probably solve this before you anyhow," he said.

"I really hope so, Charlie. I really do," I said.

"Witnesses said the other man was around six feet tall and about a solid two-hundred pounds. He has short brown hair with some gray in it. Some of these people said he was speaking Russian or maybe German at first and then switched to English. The crew entered from the kitchen and left the same way. There aren't any cameras in the restaurant or in the kitchen. However, there are cameras in the lobby, but not angled enough to capture the faces of the team coming or going. So, we've got a sketch artist coming in to draw up a decent image of the guy based on descriptions of those who saw him best."

Charlie recounted from witness statements the conversation shared between Kiril Novilov and the Tourist. The only thing the conversation confirmed was that Kiril had years before attempted to murder Mikhail Alexandrov. Lucas had shed some light on this matter and now we were positive of the falling-out between the Mafia godfather and his once right-hand man.

Knowing this, we still weren't any closer to any sort of finale, and that was irritating me beyond belief.

"Does anyone have a clue where the hell Kiril's men took off to?" I asked Charlie.

"Like I told you, this guy Alexandrov told Kiril's men that they should head home, kiss their wives and children, and be thankful to be alive, and also to seek employment elsewhere. The patrons said these guys were built like a brick shithouse."

"I think we need to get the word out to local airports, large and small, informing them to hold all passengers destined for Russia until we can identify Kiril's men," Sara said.

"I was thinking the same thing. Thanks, Charlie. Please text me the sketch of Mikhail Alexandrov when your man is done," I said and handed him a business card.

As Sara and I headed for the entrance, Charlie said, "You're a piece of work, Harper. One of these days, the tables will turn, and you'll be begging for my help."

"I appreciate everything that makes you who you are, Charlie. Don't forget, I need that sketch as soon as possible."

27

After we learned of Kiril Novilov's gruesome murder, I made a point to input the description of Kiril's bodyguards into the system that these men were possible threats to national security. Of course, I was sure that there was nothing sinister about them, other than protecting a Russian Mafia warlord. But this way I had a reasonable chance of wrangling them in before they fled this country for their own. We knew they were present during the execution of their boss, and I wanted to get to them while I had my chance to uncover some facts.

"It wasn't easy, but I think we're on the right track again," I said as Sara and I arrived at Dulles International Airport where Nikolai Reikhman and Grigori Piotrovskii were being held.

"I wasn't aware we ever went off the tracks," Sara said as she stepped out of the passenger side.

"Well, maybe not off the tracks, but the train definitely had a few unscheduled stops. I think we're pretty lucky to have your friend Lucas on our side. He's the one that was able to get things rolling again, even if he jerked us around for nearly half a day. If he had come clean from the get-go, Kiril Novilov might still be alive. If we had some sort of knowledge beforehand that the Tourist would go after Kiril, we could have set up a trap and ended this thing earlier today," I said.

We crossed the street that was crowded with shuttle buses and people being dropped off or picked up by family or friends.

"You can't blame Lucas. I told you that he needed to get some kind of feel for you. You have to appreciate the position he's in. Lucas could lose a lot if the government was aware that he disclosed confidential information to us. He could even face prison time or be sent back to Russia."

We squeezed through the crowd of people and went through the revolving door and into the pleasantly cooled airport. With the beating harshness of the sun no longer on me, I felt my mood change for the better. I was actually feeling slightly anxious to interview or maybe even interrogate the bodyguards.

We made our way through the airport and found one of the guard stations. I showed him my badge and explained the reason for our presence. The guard motioned for us to get in the electric car. The guard got behind the wheel, Sara took the empty seat beside him, and I sat on the bench on the back. We motored across the airport relatively quickly as the security guard beeped the horn to move travelers out of the way.

The security guard parked, led us down a corridor, and scanned his ID badge at the door, and then we moved inside the main security station. The guard introduced us to the airport's security manager, Norman Whitfield.

"I'm glad you finally got here. I've been holding these two for no reason that I could see. They haven't been very cooperative so far. I don't know if they can, but both of them refuse to speak English. I think they've been cursing at me in Russian. We don't have anyone to translate, so we just kept them locked away until you arrived. We searched their luggage, but didn't find drugs, weapons, or anything else that would cause alarm. Maybe the FBI would be nice enough now to inform me on why exactly I've detained these gentlemen," Mr. Whitfield asked and politely waited for an answer.

"It's a matter of national security. I've got to speak with them. Which room are they in?"

"National security, huh? All right then don't tell me. I probably don't want to know, anyway. I've kept them in separate rooms so that they couldn't draw up similar stories. Like I said, I wasn't sure why they're here."

"That's good. Thank you," I said.

"Follow me," Mr. Whitfield said and led us across the security area.

Men and women in uniform filled the room, all of them leaning over computers or studying the television monitors that offered a wide view of the airport terminals, baggage claims, and airline ticket counters.

We stopped outside of a white-painted wooden door and Mr. Whitfield said, "I hope you have better luck getting anything out of them than I did."

As my hand went to the doorknob, Sara said, "I'll wait out here, Harper."

I turned and watched her curiously.

"Why? I might need you in there. You might come up with a question I hadn't considered."

"I just think it should be a one-on-one situation. I don't want the guy panicking by thinking we're teaming up on him," she said.

"Well, if you want a one-on-one, then I'll talk to this guy, and you can speak to the other one. We'll get done with this whole thing a lot quicker."

"I don't think that's a good idea either. I think the interrogation should be left up to you. I'm not very good at it and I might foul things up more than they should be."

"All right, if that's the way you feel," I said.

I wasn't sure what Sara's game plan was, if she had one, but I thought her reluctance to hurry through this ordeal was a bit strange.

"If you like, you can join me in the observation room. There's a one-way mirror in there. We can watch them without them knowing we're there," Mr. Whitfield said.

"Sure, I guess that would be better than me sitting out here feeling useless," Sara agreed.

I nodded to the security guard posted beside the door, turned the knob, and went inside. A mountain of a man sat on one of the metal chairs. He wore a blue suit that was a little too small for him as his bulk nearly erupted the seams. He had close-cropped brown hair and gray eyes that intently studied me as I approached. He was leaning with his elbows on the table. His face was that of boredom. This was a man that felt little or no intimidation during his current situation. I figured since he was an assigned bodyguard for one of the biggest Russian Mafia leaders, he'd seen and done things that would have made John Wayne Gacy quiver in disgust.

"I'm Special Agent Harper Caster with the FBI. I trust security has so far treated you well, Mr. Reikhman?"

He spoke something I didn't understand and spat on the floor.

"Do you speak English?"

He said nothing but offered the universal finger.

"Well, that's too bad. Unfortunately, we don't have an interpreter here at the airport. It could very well take several days before we're able to get one in here. I guess we'll talk then," I said and headed for the door.

"I know my rights," he said.

"Oh, I was under the assumption you didn't speak English. I suppose that was my mistake. I think I'm going to boil everything down for you because I don't have the time for a long debate. The problem you currently have is that you have no rights. We believe you're a terrorist in our country illegally. When the U.S. government suspects someone involved in a terrorist activity with plans of harming our citizens, we suspend all legal rights. Besides, you're a Russian citizen, not one of the United States. So as far as I'm concerned, I'll hold you in this room with no restroom breaks and no food or water until Judgment Day. That's unless you'd like to answer my questions, and then we'll let you board your plane and head on back to Russia. What do you say?" I had hoped the lies and empty threats would loosen his tongue.

"Fine, I'll tell you what I know, and you let me go home. Deal?" he said with a heavy accent.

"Good. We can be temporary friends now. All right, let's begin. Why did your boss Kiril Novilov come to the U.S.?"

"Vacation."

"Vacation?"

"Yes. This is a warmer climate."

"Uh-huh. So, your boss comes to our country for vacation and some nutjob decides to poison him during lunch?"

"I suppose. I do not know."

"I thought you said you were going to cooperate. If I don't believe your answers, this situation is going to piss me off and I'll have to bring in the muscle to work you over for a while until you want to play straight with me."

I was bluffing, of course. I figured whatever guys I brought in, this hulking man would probably twist their heads around without even getting up from his chair.

"Bring them in. I am cooperating. I told you I do not know."

"I have witnesses, people from the restaurant who overheard the conversation between your boss and a man who calls himself the Tourist."

"So now you know as much as I do. I have only worked for Mr. Novilov for a little over a year. Whoever this Tourist is, he must have worked for Mr. Novilov before I came in," the Russian said and wiped a bead of sweat from his forehead.

"I didn't say anything about the Tourist once working for Mr. Novilov. I hope I'm not making you nervous with these questions. Or is it the Tourist that's making you sweat? You know, from what I've been able to figure out so far, this Tourist fellow has a funny way of collecting information. It wouldn't surprise me in the least if he's aware that you and your friend are now in our custody. With the way he pulled off the assassination of your boss, I would seriously believe that he could somehow send men into this tiny room in a heavily guarded airport and put a hole right between your eyes before you tell me what I need to know," I said and leaned back in the chair.

"All right. I will tell you. I want to go home. My family needs me. The man who calls himself the Tourist worked for Mr. Novilov years before me. I have heard stories. I think his real name is Mikhail Alexandrov. He was Mr. Novilov's right-hand man. I heard Mikhail had plans to overthrow Mr. Novilov and take over the business. Mr. Novilov found out and ordered to have him killed. I guess it didn't work."

"Okay, I got all of this information from the restaurant patrons who overheard the conversation and also from another informant. I'd like for you to tell me something I don't already know. Maybe then we'll let you fly home. Your plane is waiting."

"All right, I'm getting there. This is what I know before the restaurant. Since Mr. Novilov is dead, what I might tell you does not matter anymore. Mr. Novilov has come to the United States for business, not vacation. I wasn't supposed to know, but when someone is in my position, one cannot help but to learn certain secrets. Mr. Novilov has been investing a great deal of money. I have heard that he has given several millions to see to it that Senator Andrew Ryan wins the presidential election."

My nerves tensed. There it was again. This whole thing just made another clear connection to Senator Ryan. The Tourist and his absurdly confusing plan definitely connected to the death of Kiril Novilov and the presidential race.

"And why would Kiril Novilov care who gets elected president of this country?"

"This I cannot say. I only know of some things, but not everything. It will have to be your job to find out the rest," he said and defiantly crossed his arms over his chest.

"Anything else you'd like to talk about before I have a chat with your friend in the other room?" I asked.

"I have nothing else to say."

"Whether you want to talk anymore is up to you, but I want to know one more thing before you're released. If you give me an answer I like, I'll have airport security get you and your friend on the first plane back to Russia."

His eyes narrowed. "Then ask your question."

"Who are Brandon Harris and Kyle Sawyer? The restaurant patrons said that they overheard those names mentioned by Mr. Alexandrov. He said that he found Brandon Harris."

Nikolai Reikhman broke eye contact with me and looked at his massive hands on the table. After a moment, his eyes found me again, and I lightly tapped my watch, indicating that time was dramatically running out.

"All right. I don't know the full details, but I will tell you what I do know. Mr. Novilov's staff members at his estate have big mouths. They speak secrets when they should not. I overheard a conversation when I first started. They were speaking about two kids in the U.S. that were able to steal files from Senator Ryan's computer a few years ago. It was some big business deal he's been working on with Mr. Novilov for many years. I don't know exactly what. Mr. Novilov paid them a large amount of money to get back the files they stole. They received the money but never sent the files. He offered millions of dollars to anyone who could bring the both of them to him. Many men have been searching for them and the files for years."

"Sounds pretty serious if he's offering millions for their retrieval."

"I suppose so. I've done what you asked. Let me go home."

I nodded and said, "I made a promise. I always keep them. After I speak with your friend, I'll talk to the security manager and work everything out."

I collected my notes and stepped from the room. I spent less than five minutes with the other bodyguard. His English was barely understandable. He repeatedly claimed that he had only been on the job for less than a month. I wasn't able to get additional information from him. I wondered how many bodyguards Kiril Novilov went through in a year. It seemed like one of those professions with an intensely short life expectancy.

"Well, where do we go from here?" Sara asked as we met in the hall.

I said, "Good question. I need to have one of my computer guys run down Senator Ryan's political contributions. I want to know exactly why Kiril Novilov was donating millions of dollars to help Senator Ryan land the presidential seat. I need to know how a Russian mob boss could gain anything from that. I think this entire ordeal goes far deeper than anyone could have imagined."

"And what about the two kids? Apparently, Brandon Harris and Kyle Sawyer could have something major to do with this," Sara said as we walked back through the security office.

"That's going to be our job. Whatever these kids got their hands on years ago could be beneficial to us if we can find them."

28

Back at the Hoover Building, Sara was using one of the computers in the outer office when I hit gold. We'd been doing a massive search through the FBI's database as well as an internet search for anything on Brandon Harris and Kyle Sawyer.

When my eyes could barely stay open and my head began pounding fiercely in frustration, I found the information I wanted. Well, part of it, anyway.

"Sara, come in here. I think I've got it."

She entered my office with a fresh cup of coffee and came around the desk to look over my shoulder.

"While you've been on a coffee break, I'm been working my fingers to the bone. Check this out," I said.

She glanced at the screen and said, "Well, well. Nice job, partner."

"I figured in what the bodyguard told us and narrowed my search. I thought that if these two were able to hack into Senator Ryan's personal computer and retrieve files, then that means they have some considerable computer skills. I searched some of the top schools in the country and found out that MIT had both boys registered from 2002 until 2005. According to the university records, they were at the top of their class, but they left school before graduating. So, in 2005 they did a mysterious cut and run."

"So, in 2005 is when they probably stole Senator Ryan's personal files. Then the mob boss gives them a chunk of money only to be stiffed. So, he offers millions to anyone who can hunt them down."

I opened the articles I had previously been reading.

"Right. I believe he found out exactly who they were. Here are a couple of articles from *The Boston Globe*. Someone murdered the families of Brandon Harris and Kyle Sawyer in 2005. I'm willing to bet that Kiril's men showed up in Boston and interrogated the family to give up the location of both boys. Obviously, the family members didn't know their whereabouts since Brandon and Kyle are still on the run," I said.

"So, you don't think they've been found?" Sara asked.

"Well, we know the Tourist found Brandon Harris, but Kyle Sawyer is still in the wind."

"Ha. You must have thought that I was really on a coffee break. You should know that I offer a lot more than a nice smile," Sara said, and gave me the great smile she claimed.

"I'm listening. What's the scoop?"

"Well, while you've been in here simply reading articles, I've been digging deep. I found Kyle Sawyer," she said.

"How could you find him in a few hours when lots of people have been looking for years?"

"More than a nice smile," she said again.

I watched her with a look of disbelief until she gave up the goods.

"You'll be happy to hear that Kyle Sawyer is alive and well and currently here in D.C. under the protective watch of the CIA."

"Bullshit," I said.

She shook her head and said, "No lie. He turned himself over to the authorities earlier yesterday. I bet if you ask Director Gill nicely, he could probably contact the CIA and get us a location of where they're keeping him. We might be able to speak with Kyle face-to-face and get some decent answers about what's going on. What do you think?" Sara asked.

I was about to pick up the phone to call Director Gill when Simon Matheson walked into my office.

He dropped a stack of papers on my desk and said, "Senator Ryan's financials are clean. I'm sure these political guys are pretty good about hiding money and where it comes from, but as far as I could dig up, I didn't see anything that would raise a red flag."

I leaned back in my desk chair and said, "You couldn't find a money connection to Kiril Novilov?"

"None. I'm sure if there's a connection, then it's buried deeper than anyone here at the FBI could go. Senator Ryan has received a lot of donations slash contributions since his nomination, and many of them are anonymous. However, there are quite a few bigwigs that have coughed up millions, and one of those is a name you already know."

"Lewis Rockwell," I said.

"Right. He pitched in a hell of a chunk and wound up dead for his effort."

"Yeah, but why? The line we're trying to follow is incredibly hazy right now. I've asked this question before, and I'm going to ask it again. Why would the Tourist go through all the trouble of attempting to get Senator Ryan to withdraw from the race when he could have just killed the senator during the home invasion?"

Simon held up his hands and said, "Whoa, dude, that's your department to figure out. My job was just figuring out where all his political backing was coming from. I do all the computer stuff. Remember? I've done my part, so I'll leave you to do yours."

Simon headed out the door without offering us a bit of good luck.

When we were alone, I called Director Gill. I told him about Brandon Harris and Kyle Sawyer and the mess they were in. I told him it was possible that Kyle Sawyer had files downloaded from Senator Ryan's computer that might help put this whole situation into perspective. He told me that he'd contact the CIA and see if he could make some sort of bargain for five minutes of Kyle Sawyer's time.

I turned to Sara after I hung up. She slumped in one of the chairs. She looked completely done in, which was exactly how I felt.

"Director Gill is going to make some calls and get back to me," I said.

"I guess that means we've got time to kill."

"Okay, so let's speculate. Let's put our heads together while we've got some time. Do you have any theories about the Tourist's plan?" I asked.

"None."

"Wonderful," I said.

"Hey, look at the bright side. When he kills off two more people, the chase will be done, and then you can move on to the next case."

"I love how you find that fleeting bright side to every situation, Sara."

"It's how my parents raised me."

I leaned back in my chair, closed my eyes, and forced my tired mind to focus on a single point toward the beginning of the investigation. I linked one confusing clue after another until I reached the ending of the interview with Kiril Novilov's bodyguards.

Something sparked in the recess of my mind. It wasn't much, but there was a small flicker of light in that expanding darkness.

"I was always told that if I couldn't figure something out, then I should step back and gain a better perspective. What if, and believe me, this is a huge what if, Senator Ryan is behind it all?"

"Are you seriously blaming a presidential candidate for the deaths of three people?" Sara asked, astonished.

"I'm just trying a different view. What if Katherine Ryan and Lewis Rockwell learned something devastating about the good Senator Ryan that would corrupt his chances of being president and possibly get him jail time? What if Katherine and Lewis learned about the contents of that file? Maybe this file contains information about Senator Ryan accepting money from a Russian Mafia leader. Maybe it's something even bigger."

"You're honestly claiming that Senator Ryan had his own wife killed and his son kidnapped? Then he has his biggest financial supporter wiped out? Then what would be his motivation for killing Kiril Novilov if he were receiving a bunch of money from the guy? I think you're reaching out in desperation, Harper."

"I'm not saying he killed them, but maybe he paid someone to do it. Bear with me for a minute. Everyone has secrets. Of course, like mine, they are minor secrets that most people wouldn't give a hoot about. But some people, especially politicians, in my opinion, have a chest full of secrets that are both great and small. People will go to extreme lengths to hide important stuff, and I don't think Senator Ryan is an exception."

"None of that makes any sense. We know the Tourist killed those three people. If Senator Ryan and Kiril Novilov had something major planned, then the Tourist is destroying this plan as revenge for Kiril trying to kill him off years ago. We just don't know what is in this mysterious file, if it does exist after all," Sara said.

I shrugged. "You never can tell these days. It's a twisted, wicked world. Just because someone has a kind face and gentle words doesn't mean he's a saint. In our line of work, you've got to expect the unexpected. I prepare myself for the worst possible outcome every day. Maybe that's why I'm still alive. I've been able to outwit or outmaneuver all of my adversaries so far."

"Except this time. I think the Tourist has you by the balls, and I guess that means that he also has me by my unmentionables."

"As of right now, I'm not sure if we can get ahead of him, but we might be able to keep even until we eventually overtake him. He's the craftiest son of a bitch I've faced yet. I think I might have underestimated the power of the dark side," I said.

"I don't think it's too late to switch teams," she shot back.

"I honestly don't know how the Tourist thinks I can figure out in advance who he's going to kill next. In the beginning, it could have been anyone in the entire world. But when he sent me the video of Senator Ryan's home invasion, it became clear that it would be five people revolving around the senator's life. I couldn't tell you how many people, great and small, are involved with the senator's presidential campaign and his personal life. Are we supposed to have around-the-clock protection on hundreds or thousands of people?" I asked.

"I don't know. We're not going to sit on our thumbs, are we? Once we find Kyle Sawyer's location, we're going to speak with him, right? He could help answer a great deal of these questions," she said.

"No, I thought I'd go see a movie or something. You want to go?"

"Only if it's a romantic comedy. I've had enough of this action shit for a while," Sara said, and drank half of her coffee.

My computer beeped as a new email came in. When I opened it, I saw who had sent it and a cold spike ran across my nerves.

After I read the email, I knew the only option I now had was to move Clara and Kaylee to a secured location.

"You've got to see this," I told Sara.

29

-----Original Message-----
From: thetourist@wildmail.com
To: hcaster@fbi.gov
Sent: Thursday, September 3rd, 2020 3:22 PM
Subject: Falling behind

Special Agent Caster,

    I'm beginning to worry about you. At first, I thought I was going to have a challenge on my hands. I honestly believed that out of all the countless articles I've read on your victory cases over the course of the last twelve years, I thought that this was simply an open and shut case for your high intellect. I wonder if I've made the game far too complex for you. Perhaps it isn't me at all. Perhaps your mind has grown tired and the fire for the chase isn't there anymore. In any case, I'm greatly disappointed. I hate being disappointed. You see, by your inability to triumph, I also feel like a failure.
    I also wonder if perhaps you've been working an angle of your own. I'm very curious to know if you've somehow managed to calculate the direction I'm heading and if you have a grand finale of your own. Do you? No, don't tell me. I really do enjoy surprises. If you had the pieces properly put together, old Kiril Novilov wouldn't

have drowned in his clam chowder. How unfortunate for him, but beneficial for you. It's another jigsaw piece fitting perfectly in place. His death has opened another door for you, Harper. Are you brave enough to walk through that door and see what's on the other side? I believe you are. Of course, I could be wrong. In the end, we both might be surprised.

You looked uncomfortable last night. It doesn't seem as if you slept well. I'm sure that trying to find comfortable sleep in the balmy humidity of your home was difficult to do. You were worried about leaving the windows open all night. I can tell you were. The gun on the nightstand told me so.

Your wife really is quite lovely. I kissed her precious lips in the darkness.

I also kissed your daughter as she ran down the ever-expanding fields of dreams. She twitched a little when I kissed her. Do you think she believed I was you? Maybe she thought that Daddy needed to offer another sweet kiss goodnight. Do you sometimes do that? I think you should. You never know when everything you love will be gone the next moment.

Do you think Senator Ryan believed that he would see his wife again when I took her away? Do you think that he wished he had kissed her just one more time before bed? I bet he does now.

Time is fleeting, Harper. Love every moment of it, whether good or bad. That's what living is really all about. People survive even the worst of heartaches. Believe me, I know.

I'm going to let you in on a little secret. Of course, I'm sure you've figured out this part. I was going to kill Katherine Ryan, no matter what her ignorant husband did. Never in my wildest imagination did I think he would go to such extremes. What was he thinking when he went public? What did he hope to gain by placing a one-million-dollar bounty on my head? Whether he realized it at the time, it gave him a dead wife.

How can someone expect the American public to catch a shadow? Or maybe I'm more like the wind. I'm always there in front of everyone's face, but I go completely unnoticed until I bring on the destruction.

I have much destruction to bring forth, Harper. People are starting to pay closer attention now that everything is beginning to crumble. The walls around your American borders, your hopes and dreams have been infected with an incurable virus. I've injected the disease that will bring mankind down to its knees.

Then I'm going to disappear in the chaos as the willing survivors desperately try to make sense of everything. Some of them will overcome. Most of them will not.

Which one will you be? How strong is your will to live, Harper?

Sincerely,
The Tourist

30

The CIA had goddamn found him. The little bastard was now in protective custody in an unknown secure location. After all this time, after all the efforts to find him before the authorities did, had gone up in smoke.

After the worst possible scenario had come into play, the Tourist smiled to himself. The CIA could use any and all means necessary to protect this man, but there was a surefire trick still left in his box of magic. The Tourist had Brandon Harris, the king of super hackers, and he had a gun. With these two things, he could own the world.

The Tourist had one shot only. The CIA was going to transport Kyle Sawyer in the next hour, but the Tourist still hadn't acquired the important information of where the CIA transport officers were going to switch Kyle from one protective hand to the other. Once the officers made the trade, the Tourist would forever lose his opportunity.

— —— —

Brandon had been vigorously working his fingers over the keyboard for the last three hours. He was desperately trying to attain this information and spare himself a bullet to the back of the head. Brandon was well aware that his life had so far been spared not only to discover the whereabouts of his old friend and fellow conspirator, but for a purpose that his abductors had yet to reveal. He didn't like his current situation, and as he worked in a frantic search, he subconsciously pieced together a way out of this entire mess.

"The clock is ticking, Mr. Harris," the Tourist said as he tapped his watch.

"I'm trying. I'm just not finding what you need."

"It's been three hours now. I think in five more minutes my patience will find its limit. I hope for your sake that you're not delaying the inevitable to save your friend. Your life or his, it makes no difference to me. I need one of you, but not both."

"I'm sorry. The information just isn't in here."

The Tourist turned to face Brandon and said, "Then I suppose I have no more use for you. Time's up."

"I can't find the information. Wherever they're moving him to, it's not in any government computer system," Brandon said as beads of sweat rapidly trickled from his forehead.

The Tourist removed the Beretta from his beltline, drew back the slide to chamber a round, flicked off the safety, and placed the barrel against Brandon's left temple.

"I want that information. You've had enough time. You're stalling to save your friend, but it won't get you anything but dead. I'm going to count to ten and then the hammer falls."

Brandon's fingers quickly found the keyboard and became a blur as his desperation to find the privileged information became dire. There had been no stalling about it. He had used his gift of computer knowledge to search everywhere for Kyle Sawyer. Brandon feared death. He feared the mighty punishment that would befall him as his life ceased and his spirit moved toward whatever destination lay ahead. His level of self-preservation was great, but the situation was completely out of his hands.

As he worked, he subconsciously counted the seconds. When the tenth second clicked by in his mind, and the information was nowhere to be found, he removed his fingers from the keyboard, leaned back in the chair, and closed his eyes. He didn't want to witness the final terrifying second of his life. He didn't want to see part of his head come apart and spray the room wall microseconds before his body even knew it was dead. He took another breath and waited.

"Too bad, I was beginning to like you Mr. Harris," the Tourist said.

Mr. Smith sat on one of the double beds and watched with interest.

Agonizing seconds ticked by as Brandon waited. His mind hadn't stopped counting. Twenty seconds went by, and death still hadn't found him. After half a minute passed, he was about to open his mouth to beg, to plea for more time when the sound of a ringing cell phone sounded and almost made him wet his pants.

The barrel left his temple as the Tourist stepped back, dug in his pants pocket, retrieved his phone, and studied the caller ID. A wicked smile found his face. He winked at Brandon and held up a finger to indicate that the execution would resume momentarily.

"Sasha, so good to hear from you. I trust all is well?"

Brandon could hear a female voice but couldn't understand the words from this distance. He shifted his sight to Mr. Smith and saw that the man was now lying on the bed, his legs crossed, and his hands laced behind his head. His distasteful smile hadn't vanished since Brandon had run out of time.

"I see. Very good, I'm proud of you, Sasha. I'll take care of everything. Yes, continue with the plan. We will see you soon."

The Tourist disconnected the call and placed his phone back in his pants pocket.

"Saved by the ringtone, Mr. Harris. I have the information about Kyle Sawyer's next destination. If the information I've acquired is correct, that means that the CIA is temporarily moving your friend from a safe house on Douglas Street to a secured facility at 1441 Kasson Street in just over an hour. It's a three-story building disguised as a typical office building. I'm told that this secured facility is where they hold those who will testify in a court of law against men of corruption. Just like the man I happen to work for. Unfortunately, I don't have a mental layout of the entire area. I have to prepare. I want you to bring up a layout of the surrounding buildings at the 1400 block of Kasson Street," he said.

Brandon went to work by hacking into the city's central development department and brought up the blueprint of the area. As he worked, he could hear the man who called himself the Tourist unzip one of his cases and begin constructing a rifle with extreme precision. Brandon's attention went from the laptop to the man who professionally assembled a dozen pieces into a menacing-looking rifle in less than a minute. He watched the man fold the stock, sling the rifle strap around his shoulder, then remove his trench coat from the hanger and put it on. When he finished, the rifle was unnoticeable beneath the material.

"Here it is," Brandon said.

The Tourist grabbed the laptop from the motel room desk and studied the screen as he walked to the bed. As he sat on the edge of the bed, a small smile danced on his lips.

"Are you satisfied?" Brandon asked.

"Yes. Very satisfied. This time, you've found exactly what I need. Thank you."

"Does this mean you'll release me now?"

The Tourist raised the Beretta, pointed it at Brandon's right eye, and this time squeezed the trigger. The hammer fell with a dry clack on an empty chamber and silence followed.

"Mr. Harris, I believe you know the answer to that. Your work is far from over. The next time you disappoint me, the gun won't be empty," the Tourist said.

He rammed a clip into the gun, chambered a round, tucked it at his beltline again, and shifted his sight back to the laptop screen.

When Brandon could find his breath again, he quickly rotated his eyes to the floor. He had damn well known what the answer was going to be. He had asked as a simple method of measuring their next move. They had more work for him, and that meant that he was going to live for a little while longer, anyway.

31

The mark, Kyle Sawyer, was playing the game, and he was going to lose. Kyle would, unfortunately and unknowingly, find himself labeled as an additional target to the original five. The Tourist hadn't suspected that he would find Kyle Sawyer so soon. He hadn't expected to uncover the whereabouts of the kid this early in the game. Granted, Kyle Sawyer had done a superb job hiding all these years, far greater than Brandon Harris, but death was closing in on him.

Kyle Sawyer had probably never suspected that three years ago, when he assisted in hacking the wrong computer, he would eventually find himself in the crosshairs of a professional hitman.

No one paid attention to the man with the average appearance, dressed in simple attire as he entered the elevator of the Parkman Hotel and rode it to the top floor. Even the heavy, floor-length trench coat he was wearing in the blistering August heat hadn't received much more than a second glance.

On the twelfth floor, the Tourist quickly found the locked door of the roof access. He removed his pick set and in less than a minute, the door was open. As he traveled up the steel steps, he withdrew the assembled rifle from under his coat. The blinding sunlight struck him as he calmly strode across the pebble-topped roof to the west side of the hotel. From this position, he had a nearly perfect viewpoint. The vent shafts that emerged from the roof gave him reasonable coverage from anyone looking out one of the neighboring buildings.

He retrieved the range finder from his pocket and fixed the sight on a light pole directly in front of the facility. There wasn't an underground parking structure at this facility, which would give the Tourist his one chance. The CIA operations officers who were transporting Kyle Sawyer would have no choice but to walk the man right through the front door. The Tourist would have no more than ten seconds to take a perfect shot.

The range finder made a soft beep, and an image appeared on the screen. According to the highly sensitive instrument, he was currently facing a shot of just over three hundred yards with an eight-mile-an-hour crosswind. It certainly wasn't an impossible shot, even with a moving target. It was difficult, sure, but not impossible.

He settled into a crouched position that would minimize leg cramping if he had to maintain the posture for a long period. According to the CIA agenda that Sasha uncovered, the company should arrive in less than fifteen minutes.

The Tourist calculated the distance with a series of careful modifications to the scope. He slowly dialed the crosshairs up, which would compensate for the slight loss in velocity. Next, he dialed to the right to adjust the shot affected by the wind. Unfortunately, he wasn't able to test his adjustments. Even though the rifle had a custom suppressor, the streets below were moderately active. A shot, even one directed into the wood of the light pole, could alert someone enough to bring the police around and ruin any chance he had.

The Tourist thought of the chain reaction that would follow a missed shot. If he simply wounded Kyle Sawyer or missed altogether, the course of hellish events afterward would warrant international headlines. It astounded him that a single bullet could make or break the men of a brave new world. Their reliance fell on his abilities to do exactly as he claimed. If he missed, he would walk away from this operation with little personal loss. However, his employer would crumble both financially and socially. His employer would become a wanted man by international government agencies. In turn, his employer would use the last of his resources to hire other professional men to hunt the Tourist beyond all borders. He would become a man forever on the run.

The world was balancing on a second of precision and skill.

Very interesting, he thought and smiled.

The heat of the day had almost become unbearable when he spotted a black sedan with government plates approaching the front of the facility. As he spied the vehicle through the scope, he could see three individuals inside. Two men were in the front, and he was sure that his target was the third man in the rear seat. The sedan drew to a stop in the front of the building and both men, dressed in typical CIA attire and dark shades, stepped from the car and casually glanced up and down the street. They momentarily observed each face that walked toward them on the sidewalk.

The Tourist had thought that the men had actually expected an ambush at street level. Even though their destination and time had been strictly concealed from unauthorized personnel, these men were preparing for a worst-case scenario. Even though they were supposed to be professional government employees, he was humored by the fact that neither of them had glanced higher than the first floor of any of the surrounding buildings.

Carefully, the Tourist placed the crosshairs just above and to the right of the rear passenger door. When Kyle Sawyer stepped from the car, the bright, sunny D.C. day and the passing faces would be the last things he saw in his miserable life.

The driver rounded the vehicle and pulled open the rear door. The Tourist could see that he was saying something to the target. As the crown of Kyle Sawyer's head came into view, another sedan screeched to a halt next to the other. The CIA officer shoved Kyle back into the car and quickly reached for his sidearm. He was holding out his hand, apparently ordering the unexpected guest to remain in the car.

When the Tourist rotated his sight to the other car, two people he recognized stepped out. He smiled at what he saw. It was FBI Special Agent Harper Caster and his temporary sidekick.

"I knew you'd be coming, Harper. You're a little early. Did you hurry because you wanted to witness the gruesome execution of Mr. Sawyer?" he whispered.

Have you figured it out yet, Harper? Is that what you're doing here? No, I don't think so. But you're certainly on to something. You must have reached the conclusion that Kyle Sawyer has valuable information that he's going to bring forward. How crafty of you. I'm terribly sorry to inform you, Harper, that the information he was going to share will be scattered across the sidewalk momentarily.

Although the Tourist couldn't be positive, he thought that Kyle Sawyer wouldn't have the information with him. He would have thought far in advance before turning himself over to the authorities and hidden the information in a safe place until he could bargain with the CIA about his long list of cybercrimes that spanned at least the last three years.

If the information was with him or if the CIA already had possession of the file, the plan would crumble. In any case, Kyle Sawyer's death was inevitable.

There was a degree of agitation between the groups, but the escorting officers relaxed as Harper showed his identification.

The driver rounded the car again and ordered Kyle to exit the vehicle.

As the curly brown hair came into view again, the Tourist set his aim and gently squeezed the trigger. The gun released a gentle cough and slight recoil.

Kyle Sawyer's head had no longer been at the point where the Tourist's bullet zipped by. Instead, Kyle had tripped a moment after stepping from the car and was now sprawled across the curb.

"You stumbling motherfucker!" the Tourist shouted.

He could see the agents turn their sight in the direction of where the bullet had sailed over the open door and connected with the sidewalk. A moment after the fierce whine of the ricochet, all four agents registered the reasons behind the disruption.

They withdrew their guns, frantically turned in every possible direction, and looked for the shooter.

The Tourist didn't have a clear shot until the escorting CIA officer grabbed Kyle by the shirt collar and hauled him to his feet and shoved him toward the entrance of the facility. The officer apparently understood that the car was no longer a safe zone under fire and getting the man into the building was the only option.

A walking target was one thing, but now he was facing an extremely long-distance shot at a man in a full-bore run.

He was sure that the next shot would give away his position. The risk had to be made. Kyle had information that must never find the light of day.

Kyle charged up the steps and as he yanked open the front right door, the crosshairs found him through the pane of glass. There was a moment of hesitation as Kyle looked through the glass. Whatever the reason that possessed him to momentarily glance down the street toward the hotel, the result was death.

32

With the new information that placed us on the confusing trail of Kyle Sawyer, I thought that just maybe we would find ourselves one step ahead of the Tourist. I would have taken any kind of lead at this point.

When the bullet sliced through the window of the front door and into Kyle Sawyer's right eye, I knew that any type of gain I had made during the investigation was immediately lost.

I was looking in Kyle's direction when someone fired the shot. I had been mentally urging him forward, praying that he would make it through the front door and into the safety of the building. Kyle had information I desperately wanted. Whatever he stumbled across years ago had brought one of the world's worst trained killers after him.

The information he once had was quickly lost as the bullet began to fragment from the impact with the glass. The mass of that high-speed, fragmenting bullet entered his right eye, gathered brain matter, and made a hasty exit through the back of his skull. His head made a vicious snap backward and the rest of his body followed. The light-colored brick of the building was sprayed in bright red. His body collapsed to the steps and lifelessly tumbled down toward us.

A woman in a dark blue suit dropped her purse and began screaming as she witnessed the finale to Kyle Sawyer's life.

"Take cover!" I yelled at all the pedestrians on the sidewalk. They were staring dumbfounded at the empty socket of Kyle's eye. As the realization of the cause and effect of that empty socket finally hit them, they scrambled for any type of cover.

I was crouching at my front bumper. Sara had quickly taken position next to me. Our guns were pointing over the front edge of the hood as we cautiously searched for the sniper.

"I think it came from the hotel," I told her.

"From a room window or the roof?" she asked.

"I'm not sure. I think it was the roof. He's already on the move. He has his fourth victim now, so he probably won't shoot at us. Neither one of us is number five."

I chanced a look at the hotel. I couldn't see anyone positioned on the rooftop, but I caught a quick reflective glimmer of something that was there one second and gone the next.

We slowly stood and quickly studied the other buildings. I didn't see anyone. The Tourist was most likely on the run. He had what he came for, and now it was time to do a vanishing act.

"Call in for backup. We need to lock this area down as quickly as possible," I yelled to the CIA officers as I began running toward the hotel.

I couldn't be for certain that the hotel had been the sharpshooter's position, but if I combined the brief glimmering reflection, and the vantage point of the rooftop, it would have been the mostly likely place to take down a target.

Sara was matching my pace as we ran with drawn guns down Kasson Street. Pedestrians on the crosswalk quickly moved aside as they saw us approaching. Cars screeched to a halt as we entered the intersection. We had almost taken a full-force impact from a semi that braked moments after the other vehicles. I gave Sara a gentle shove and spun myself away from the hovering semi-grill.

We hit the revolving door of the hotel and made for the customer service desk. The hotel guests rapidly parted as we halted at the counter out of breath.

"FBI. Where are the elevators?" I asked.

The man's face was a mask of terror as he saw our guns. He pointed to the right. "Down the hallway."

"Call the police and get these people the hell out of here," I said.

As Sara and I went down the short hallway and stood before the two elevators, she said, "I'll guard the lobby in case he comes down."

"Good idea. He's on the move, and we don't want him slipping by us. I'm going to the roof first, and if he's not there, then I'll have to stop on each floor and clear them in case he's hiding out." I pressed the elevator call button.

"I'll be here. Hopefully, the backup gets here soon."

"Be careful," I said as I stepped into the elevator and hit the top floor button.

As I rode the elevator, I prepared myself for the worst encounter. I was skilled in my own way, but the man I might face was an expert killer. The FBI trained me to use my mind and decrypt confusing puzzles. I'd had my share of hand-to-hand combat, and an even greater share of shoot-outs, but this one scared me. How could I compete with someone trained in the art of death?

Whoever the Tourist really was, his true identity and upbringing no longer mattered. He had grown and molded into the professional killer who feared nothing. He had become a man of action.

The elevator chime announcing the arrival to the top floor was the only sound I heard. I placed my foot next to the open door to keep it retracted as I drew in a few stout breaths and worked up my nerves. I slowly pivoted out of the elevator. An empty hallway greeted me.

Then I heard an unmistakable sound. From somewhere far below, echoing through the elevator shaft, a rumble of gunshots.

I quickly jumped back in the elevator and punched the lobby button. The elevator car's descent was painstakingly dragging. I couldn't imagine what kind of mayhem I would find when I reached the lobby floor. With no idea of who fired the shots, I suddenly had a deep fear of the situation Sara was in.

Finally, the elevator landed, and the doors parted. The desk clerk must have immediately taken action, as I had asked. Except for Sara McNeal, the entire lobby was deserted. She was lying on the floor. Her eyes were closed. Two large holes bore through the FBI jacket I had loaned her.

"Oh my God," I whispered.

When I kneeled beside her and gently placed my fingers to her neck, she jolted with a hard, raspy breath. Her eyes fluttered open, closed, and open again. She momentarily stared wide-eyed at me as if from a lack of understanding of the previous events.

I unzipped her jacket to survey the damage. She had done exactly what I had hoped for. She was wearing a Kevlar vest. Two disfigured slugs had molded into the vest. One would have punctured her right lung and the other would have pierced her heart if the protective gear hadn't been there.

"Just take it easy. You're going to be all right. I'm glad at least someone listens to me. This vest just saved your life," I said.

Sara sat up and moved against the wall.

"Son of a bitch, that hurts. That bastard came from behind me. I was watching the elevators and the lobby. I didn't even pay attention to the stairwell door behind me until I heard it open. I turned and faced a handgun staring me down. He was packing more than the rifle he used to take out Kyle Sawyer. He didn't even say anything to me, he just started shooting. I don't know if it was from the impact of the bullets or from knocking my head on the floor, but I must have blacked out. Christ, it feels like my sternum got shoved out my spine."

Sara pulled the Velcro straps loose, removed the vest, unbuttoned her shirt, and inspected her skin at the impact points. There was an ugly redness and swelling, but thankfully no blood.

"It looks like you're going to have some hellish bruising. Maybe even some broken or fractured ribs. You'll need to have a doctor look at that. I don't think he wanted to kill you. That's why they were chest shots. He probably suspected that you were wearing a vest. He's an expert and he could have easily put one between your eyes. The Tourist is determined to kill only the original five they contracted him for. He's avoiding unnecessary casualties. He only wants five perfect murders and then he'll vanish just as he claimed he would. But he's wrong about one thing; I won't allow him safe passage to freedom. We'll get him one way or another."

33

"Tell me," I said as Sara and I stormed up to the CIA officers.

"What?" the one with the crew cut said. He backed off a little, apparently reading hostile intensions in my approach.

A massive crowd had gathered on Kasson Street. Teams of business people were leaving their offices to take in the full show of horror that had gone down moments ago. The two CIA men had been trying to keep the crowd clear from the body of Kyle Sawyer.

After a precise shot to the head, Kyle Sawyer had propelled against the left entrance door and then tumbled down the front steps, all the while leaving a horrifying trail of red. Kyle had come to rest with the lower half of his body on the sidewalk and his upper body cocked awkwardly on the first step.

Several men had left the private facility to assist the CIA team in holding back the surging onlookers until the police arrived. I couldn't believe that these people could fixate on a man shot dead only moments ago and not think once about their personal safety.

"What did this man die for? That's what I'm asking. What information did he have that was so important that it was worth his life?" I asked.

"This is certainly not the place or time for this," the CIA officer said.

"The man who did this shot my partner. If she hadn't been wearing a vest, she'd be dead as well. I want fucking answers right now!" I shouted.

The man with the crew cut held up his hands in surrender. "All right. I'll have to clear any information with my boss. I don't know if I can tell you anything, but if you want a chance at information, then you can wait for us inside. After we contain the area, I'll make several calls, and then I'll come and talk to you."

A screaming match in public wouldn't help ease my temperament, and rarely resulted in mutual satisfaction. Sara and I passed the body of Kyle Sawyer as we went up the steps and into the building.

For forty-five minutes, I paced the small break room near the front offices. The man at the front desk, Neil Flynn, according to the nameplate, resisted my every argument to allow our passage into the back offices. He had pointed to the break room and claimed that someone would be with us shortly.

I purchased a soda and a small bag of peanuts from the machines as I impatiently waited for one of the CIA officers to pull us into a private area and unload their secrets. I didn't think it would go down like that, but I was flying on a little hope. I offered the bag of peanuts to Sara, who declined, and then I threw a fistful in my mouth and ground them irritably.

"You're a good-looking woman, can't you talk to these guys? If you use a little sexual charm, you might grease the wheels into motion."

"Sure, I bet these guys would give up confidential information just because I showed them some cleavage.

These guys don't give a crap who I am or what I have to say. These guys are professionals," Sara said.

"Yeah, I can tell that by the dead body on the front steps. These guys are the best the government can churn out. Seriously," I said with hard sarcasm.

"So do you think the guy behind the shooting today was the one we've been chasing, the one that calls himself the Tourist?"

"I can't think of anyone else who would be ballsy enough to take a risk like that. Whatever information Kyle Sawyer had, I'm afraid it was finally brought to the light of day when the back of his head opened. Of course, I don't know what that was because I'm not a mind reader," I said.

Sara gave a little chuckle to my twisted joke. "Only someone like you could find humor in a situation like this. When was the last time you scheduled a therapy session?"

"I had one last night when I went off the clock and spent time with my family. That's the only therapy I need. By the way, don't be too quick to judge me. We've only known each other for a few invigorating days. I still might bombard you with an unexpected surprise."

"I know. Of course, I might do the same," Sara offered.

"Agent Caster? Could I get the both of you to follow me?" the crew cut CIA officer asked as he stepped into the room.

As instructed, we followed him to a room near the back of the facility. There was a metal table and four metal chairs. There was also a two-way mirror on the wall to our right as we entered. This was some kind of interrogation room. I briefly wondered if he was going to interrogate us or the other way around.

"Who's behind the glass?" Sara asked.

"No one. You have my word. This isn't being recorded either. This information I'm going to share with you is strictly off the books. No one will ever know this information came from the CIA. Understood?"

Sara and I agreed.

"Good. Well, for starters, my name is Mitch Reynolds. As you know, I'm an operations officer with the CIA. My detail is handling special projects that are of the highest national security. Let me straighten this out for you the best I can. We're not, by any means, obligated to share information with other agencies. I've cleared the request with my superiors and your director for the sole purpose of locking down the killer as quickly as possible. We believe that if we include the both of you in this particular case, we can acquire the information Kyle Sawyer contained."

"And what the hell kind of information did he have?" I asked.

Officer Reynolds scratched his head and eyed us carefully. He slid a thick manila envelope across the table. I cautiously watched the envelope as if it were crawling with a deadly virus specially designed by the U.S. government. Finally, virus be damned, my curiosity got the better of me and I removed the contents.

"I think I already know the answer to this, but I'm going to ask it, anyway. Have you ever heard of the Blackstone File?" Officer Reynolds asked.

34

I laughed a little. "The Blackstone File is a myth. It isn't real."

"Isn't it? How can you be so sure, Agent Caster? No one knows all the sinister secrets the governments of the world have been concealing for centuries. Don't reach the wrong conclusion until you've looked into the deepest, darkest hole of the human heart," Officer Reynolds said.

"I'm missing something. What the hell is the Blackstone File?" Sara asked.

I was smiling a little. I figured Mitch Reynolds was having a bit of fun with us.

I said, "It's a hypothetical scenario the big brains of the U.S. government conjured up as a way of anticipating a secret invasion by other world governments. Primarily, it's a method of dominating another country under the radar. Instead of a full-frontal attack, the Blackstone File speculates that if a country were to implement some of their members into a government position or even manage to buy off officials already in good standing, then they could seemingly control the governmental institution without the international attention."

"You're wrong. The U.S. didn't construct the Blackstone File, Agent Caster."

"I've never seen this so-called Blackstone File, but I've heard rumors of it over the years. I've even heard that several U.S. governors and senators were accused of following the Blackstone guidelines by accepting bribes from other world governments, but there wasn't enough concrete evidence to force them from their positions. Since then, I haven't heard much about it," I said.

"Wait a minute. I'm trying to get everything in some order of clarity. So, you're saying that this Blackstone File is an instructional manual for impure government officials as a way of undermining the American way for personal profit? That they're not really working for the American people, but instead, they're really in cahoots with other governments?" Sara said.

"Not just the American way, but all nationalities, Ms. McNeal," Officer Reynolds said.

"Hypothetically, it's exactly what Hitler, Stalin, and many others attempted. Well, without blowing everything up and killing everyone, of course," I said.

"It's the idea of a single government controlling nearly every executive order in the world. What you don't know is that the Chinese government first implemented the plan. They were raising Caucasian, English-speaking children and taught them all the necessary knowledge any civilian of Great Britain would know. But they also instilled a deeper knowledge and understanding of how the British government system worked. These children were born and raised to slip into the British government offices, all the while keeping their home country in heart and mind. They believed that once these men and women moved up the social and economic ladder, the Chinese could manipulate the ways of the British law without the British fully realizing everything," Reynolds said.

"So, all of this really happened?" Sara asked.

"Yes. In 1939, as Hitler was gaining enormous power in Europe, the Chinese saw their opportunity as the world held focus elsewhere. They initiated the plan for the first time. A man that went by the name John Blackstone left China for Great Britain. He had all of the necessary documents that claimed he was a born and bred man of England. He joined the military force right away and quickly became a noticed soldier. Because of his high intellect and talent for devising military strategies that baffled those above his ranking, he shot up the military ladder and became one of the youngest generals the British ever produced," Reynolds said.

"So, Blackstone joined the military and kept the important people awestruck during his service period as a method of gaining trust and building his future allies in the way of the government?" I asked as I scanned the files while keeping a sharp tune to everything Reynolds was churning out.

"That's exactly what he did. When Hitler was later defeated, Blackstone took office as an advisor to the council of King George VI. During the years that followed, Blackstone constantly urged the king to pass specific liberties that would benefit the Chinese over the course of time. In the end, the Chinese plan would later crumble and Blackstone's true identity was revealed. Of course, this entire deception was kept under wraps from the public," Reynolds said.

"So, are you telling us that the Blackstone plan has been reinvented and put into action in America?" I asked.

"Yes. Only it isn't the Chinese this time around. It's the Russians."

"I kind of thought they were allies to the U.S. I didn't think we were the best of friends, but certainly not enemies," Sara said.

Reynolds said, "I could go on for days without end about this whole thing. As far as we know, it isn't the Russian government that made the plan happen. There's a powerful Russian cartel known as the Gueztel. The man behind it was Kiril Novilov. As you're well aware, your friend who calls himself the Tourist took care of Novilov's fifty-eight years of breathing. We think that the Tourist might be secretly working for another Russian cartel that decided to overthrow Novilov and seize control of his worldwide connections and business deals. We've only been able to speculate on that part after he killed his former boss for a purpose unknown."

Sara and I thought we knew the purpose, but I wasn't in the mood to share.

I leaned back in the uncomfortable metal chair and studied the file before me. I was trying to take in everything Reynolds had unloaded on us. Was it really possible to inject a man into a country who would eventually gain reasonable control of the executive decisions of that government? In the age of paranoia plus high levels of security, could a person slip through the cracks with little effort and eventually take a prominent seat in office?

A second later, I understood what Officer Reynolds was trying to get across to us.

"Are you trying to tell us that Senator Ryan is one of these Blackstone members?" I asked.

"We have reasons to believe that Senator Andrew Ryan is not the individual he claims to be. Although he's done a superior job at covering his history," Reynolds said.

"What does that mean?" Sara asked.

"According to records, Andrew Ryan attended Richmond Elementary and then Haven Ridge High School in

Pittsburgh. We've spoken with some of his former classmates. Andrew Ryan back then was a completely different person when compared to the one they've seen on television. His current ambition doesn't compare to his outlook during high school. Most of the people we've spoken with told us Andrew Ryan was a pot-smoking kid who couldn't have given a shit about becoming a well-adjusted man with an ideology to change the world for the better. After Andrew Ryan barely graduated from high school, he disappeared off the map. He was a foster kid, no family, no real friends, and no one to care whether he lived or died. Truth be told, I think the real Andrew Ryan is dead. I think Kiril Novilov found a subject here in the U.S. and had him killed off. No one even noticed the kid was gone. A few years later, Andrew Ryan pops up again. Despite his high school grades, he was accepted to Brown University and got high marks. He walked away from college with a master's degree in Political Science and became the man the world now sees. He never held down a job during his college years, and no one can say for sure how he paid for school and room and board during that time. The money came from somewhere. My guess is that Kiril Novilov secretly donated the money. The CIA believes that Andrew Ryan, the one you know, was surgically altered to look just like this kid and took on his identity and then this kid disappeared for good. Of course, we can't prove anything. Like I said, all of this information was going to be delivered to us once we signed an agreement with Kyle Sawyer. He wanted immunity for all of his computer crimes. Now we have nothing but theories."

Sara said, "So? All of that doesn't mean a thing. Everyone was like that. Well, maybe not everyone, but most kids are completely different compared to the way they were in high school. I could tell you about some serious run-ins with the law I had during that time. Now look at me, I'm on the side of the law. Just because someone was a slacker back then doesn't mean they didn't finally get their head on straight, and figure shit out."

"I'm just giving you what I know. We were investigating Senator Ryan long before Kyle Sawyer turned himself in and unraveled one hell of a story with a promise that he had all the necessary files to back up his claim. I believed him. Kyle's been on the list of wanted criminals for a very long time. There would be no other reason for a kid like Kyle to turn himself in after years on the run. Especially when he faced countless years in prison for all of his cybercrimes that we know about," Reynolds said.

"So, you're claiming that the man who will most likely become the President of the United States has a false identity carefully constructed by a Russian cartel to control important aspects of our country?" I asked him.

"I can't think of a better way to dominate an entire country than by secretly placing one of your men on the top pedestal. It appears that the Russian cartel has their inside man placed within the most powerful and technologically advanced country in the world. Once they complete the final move, the rest is just icing on the cake."

It was hard to accept all that was said. This was on the verge of a nightmarish testimony to the death of the U.S. Even though it was difficult to swallow all the private conversation unloaded here, I believed Officer Reynolds for the simple purpose of knowing that a tall-tale delivered in the wake of an assassination would be borderline insane.

"You realize the information I've shared here will never see the light of day, even after we incarcerate Senator Ryan, right?" Reynolds asked.

"You're going to arrest him?" Sara said.

"You're damn straight we are. The only problem is that our perfect witness just got his brains splattered all over this building. No matter what it takes, I'll pin Senator Ryan to a fucking cross at the end of this."

"Kyle Sawyer was going to testify as a witness in the case against Senator Ryan?" I asked.

"A witness of sorts. Kyle Sawyer had exceptional talent as one of the world's most superb computer hackers. Actually, there's another man named Brandon Harris who was good friends with Mr. Sawyer. They were roommates at MIT. They worked and learned from each other over the years. Together, they've hacked some of the most secure databases around the world. They've also heisted millions of dollars from the wrong men. They have a sizable bounty on their heads, dead or alive. When Kyle and Brandon parted ways years ago, it was Brandon that kept the Blackstone File. Kyle said he wanted nothing more to do with it. Then two days ago, Kyle received an email from Brandon that contained the file. Brandon was in big trouble and needed a way out. Kyle said that a man who refers to himself as the Tourist abducted Brandon. So, Kyle hopped a plane from Brazil and handed himself over to us," Reynolds said.

"Yeah, we researched the both of them. That's how we ended up here. If Brandon and his talent are now under control of the Tourist, that might explain my recent financial crisis. So, what do two computer super geeks from MIT have to do with Senator Ryan?" I asked.

"Therein lies the secret, Agent Caster."

35

CIA Officer Mitch Reynolds stood from the metal chair, cracked his back, and slowly paced the small room.

"I really need a cigarette, but I'll hold out until I finish. I wouldn't want the suspense to kill you while I was outside. All right, Kyle Sawyer and Brandon Harris had set up an elaborate network that oversaw key subjects on the internet. As Kyle tried to explain to me before his death, he said that they had created a sort of super virus. Now this virus roams the internet, searching all computers. The virus doesn't destroy personal files but collects them and automatically downloads specific information to their computers."

"Sounds like they're a little brighter than me. I just figured out that there weren't actually evil little men inside my computer making the thing operate," I joked.

Reynolds continued as if I had said nothing. "I understand that the system was a spectacular operation. They observed the world closely from a simple laptop. They had no interest in stealing from average citizens like us, but they went after the big fish that would land them hefty paychecks. They plucked information and used it as blackmail. These kids had their fingers twirling in a large kettle of corruption. There's a long list of people they blackmailed dating back six years. Unofficially, they were two of the most wanted men in the world. Then in 2005 they went after the wrong man. They came across the information that is the basis of the Blackstone File. They pulled it straight from Senator Ryan's personal computer. After realizing the plot within the file and the man behind it all, they blackmailed Kiril Novilov. They offered him the return of the file and their silence for five million dollars. Reluctantly, Novilov paid the two their blackmail rate only to be stiffed on the agreement made. Novilov placed a five-million-dollar bounty granted to the one who brought the two hackers to him. Since then, there have been hundreds of bounty hunters and the all-out desperate trying to pin these two down."

"So, Kyle Sawyer and Brandon Harris went deep into hiding?" I asked.

"Very deep. With a price like that on your head, no place is safe. They wished each other good luck, divided all assets, and parted ways. Both of them continued to constantly move around the world. They changed identities and appearances on a regular cycle. We were fortunate enough to finally get our hands on Kyle Sawyer. Like I said, Kyle got scared after he learned the Tourist had snatched Brandon Harris. We had everything set up until that motherfucker came along and killed our one and only chance to destroy Senator Ryan."

"Bad luck for Kyle. He probably thought he was going to get a sweet deal from you guys in exchange for the Blackstone File. Instead, he got a high caliber shot through the head," Sara said.

"We hadn't made a deal yet. I have no idea where he's keeping the file. It could be anywhere," Reynolds said.

"So, if you want to make a solid case against Senator Ryan, you're going to have to uncover the whereabouts of Brandon Harris," I said.

"Right. When we find Brandon, we'll find the Tourist or vice versa."

"So, in what standing does that currently put you?" I asked.

"Up that famous creek," Reynolds replied and then slumped in the chair.

Sara said, "All right, I have a question. Why would the Tourist kill the kid who can blow the top off the whole thing with Senator Ryan and Kiril Novilov's grand plan? Why is he trying to destroy any chance Senator Ryan has at the presidency? Why wouldn't the Tourist just kill Senator Ryan and Kiril Novilov and have his revenge done with? Does that make sense to either of you?"

"That's four questions," Reynolds said with a smile. "Like I said before, we believe the Tourist has either taken employment with another cartel that wants to destroy Novilov's plan or it's all about revenge. Maybe this other cartel, if it exists, didn't like the idea that Kiril Novilov would have one of the most powerful allies in the world. We honestly don't know the genuine reasons behind the kidnapping of the senator's wife and son and the demand to step down from the race. We don't know why Senator Ryan is alive. With all the Tourist's skills, he could have easily killed Senator Ryan ten times over. Maybe he has another plan that we're not seeing yet. I think he must, otherwise he wouldn't have bothered to risk capture in order to kill Kyle Sawyer and destroy the information he had," Reynolds offered.

I was sensing the fierce rumble of a headache coming on. All of this information was interesting as well as confusing. The whole thing was a series of interlocking nerve endings, and the Tourist was trying his best to sever all the connections behind his true purpose of the five murders.

"Is there any possible chance that you might have an inkling of an idea of who the fifth victim will be?" I asked.

"Fifth victim?" Reynolds asked with an amusing look of confusion.

I suddenly realized that he didn't know about the emails the Tourist sent at the beginning of this horrific week. He didn't know that Lewis Rockwell was one of the Tourist's victims as well. I took a moment to explain the events leading to this point. Reynolds didn't interrupt. He only fixed a look of mild interest. I suspected he was a man who had heard and seen things far worse than the plan the Tourist had set in motion.

"So, you're chasing a wicked trail of death, which caused the three of us to collide?" Reynolds asked.

"I suppose so," I said.

"You said that Katherine Ryan was the Tourist's first victim. Lewis Rockwell was victim two. Kiril Novilov became victim three. Now Kyle Sawyer has sadly taken the position of victim four. The obvious connection is Senator Ryan and the presidential campaign. The Tourist was once a supporter of Kiril Novilov and his plan for an inside man in the United States, but now he's gone insane and he's desperately trying to undo what Kiril put into action," Reynolds said.

There were so many unanswered questions that I was trying to wrap my mind around. I could take an uneducated guess at the motivation behind the entire ordeal, but I felt I'd be wrong, regardless. What I knew for sure was that the Tourist had something huge in the works and he was going to steamroll any effort we could put forth. Damn, I hated this guy.

Who the hell could the Tourist have marked as victim five?

36

"I really hate to be the one to ruin the invigorating afternoon we've had, but I believe we're being followed. Don't turn around, just use the rearview mirror," I said.

Sara was watching me closely, perhaps expecting me to crack an uncontrolled smile and give away the secrets of a playful game.

"Seriously?"

"Yeah. There's a blue four-door sedan three car lengths back that's been following us ever since we left the CIA facility."

Sara leaned to the left, grabbed the rearview mirror, and rotated it as if she were inspecting her appearance. Her eyes were investigating the row of vehicles behind us as her hands casually pulled at the black curls of her hair. She shifted back into her seat and finished out her performance with a simple flip of her hair.

"Nice going. I think you fooled them for sure," I said with a chuckle.

I rotated the mirror back into position. The blue sedan was still there. Although I couldn't see it clearly, I was sure there were three men inside. I had spotted the figures at the last corner I took.

"I can barely even see the car. How can you tell it's the same one that has been following us?"

"It's one of those FBI gut instincts. Should we play a game and see if these guys really are following us or if I'm just being completely paranoid?"

"I like games," Sara said and clapped like a child expecting a present.

"Games it is."

I eased on the brakes until I dropped my speed by half. For this action, I received annoyed bursts of the horn from the driver behind us. The red Thunderbird ripped into the right lane and nearly peeled off the bumper of the car that previously held the position. The Thunderbird roared by us with a squeal of tires, and a bulky arm jutted from the driver's window, offering us a long glimpse of his middle finger.

"Hey, I think I dated that guy once," Sara said.

"Too bad it didn't work out. He seems pleasant enough to bring home to your parents."

"Who said it didn't work out? I've been meaning to call him back, but I've just been so terribly busy."

I watched in the mirror as the green sports car in front of our guys opted out of trailing my snail's pace, signaled the lane change, and carefully passed us at the posted speed limit.

"You see, now that guy would be more for you. He followed all the driving laws."

"I can't get into guys who won't take a risk. I need the show of some big brass balls. What's Mr. Blue Sedan doing now?" Sara asked.

"He's slowing down as well. Maybe I'm not being paranoid after all. Is your seat belt tightly secured?"

Sara gave the seat belt a firm tug and said, "As secure as it's going to get. Are we going to have some fun now, or can I nap for a little while?"

"It's going to be difficult to nap at Mach three, but if you think you can, then by all means."

"Mach three in this thing?"

"It's all in the driving skills. Watch and learn what an old man like me can teach the young and naïve."

I could tell that Sara was about to protest my last remark but didn't get the chance. There was no signal, no indication that I was going to take flight in a separate direction. I stomped the accelerator as I quickly calculated the forward motion of the vehicles to my right. With precise timing, I cut through the narrow gap in traffic and tore off down Stilton Street. I checked the mirror and saw that the blue sedan quickly braked and took a chance at pissing off a long line of traffic as the sedan stalled the entire lane. Somehow, the vehicle slid through and quickly began pursuit.

"I think they realized they blew their cover." After a moment of watching over her shoulder, Sara said, "Um, I hate to further ruin your leisure afternoon drive, but our friends brought their friends to the party."

I glanced in the mirror and discovered that there wasn't one blue sedan, but there were actually four. I wasn't having fun anymore. I suddenly felt a cold ripple travel the length of my spine. I had a bad feeling these guys meant bone-breaking action.

"What is this, a new D.C. street gang? The Blue Sedan Hell Raisers? They can't be serious," Sara said.

"Somehow, I think they're being very serious. I'm honestly not curious about what they want, are you?" I asked.

"Absolutely not. Put the pedal to the metal and don't look back."

I did exactly that and went on the offensive, making every daring maneuver possible as I hammered down the busy D.C. streets. I avoided half a dozen collisions that would have either been a long hospitalization or perhaps a quick trip to the county morgue. I couldn't shake them. Whoever these guys were, their skills exceeded my own.

"I thought you were going to impress me? I'm still waiting for that. In the meantime, I'm getting worried as hell."

"I'm desperately trying not to kill us."

"Maybe we should just see who they are and what they want. Maybe it's not as bad as we think," Sara said.

"No, I think it would be far worse than we think. I think they want us dead."

I wasn't going to play this game of terror anymore. I grabbed the mike of the CB radio, and I was about to request help from local law enforcement when the rear of our car exploded.

One of the blue sedans thundered forward and delivered one hell of a punch to the rear end. I momentarily lost control as the steering wheel spun wildly in my grip. I slammed the brakes just short of sliding into a parked car, took a hard left, and gunned the accelerator.

"Jesus. I think you're right. I don't think they want us to see tomorrow. Get us the hell out of here, Harper."

"I'm trying. These guys are stuck right on my ass." A series of signs flashed by, which gave me an idea. I wasn't sure if the idea was a good one or a definite suicide. "I'm going to hit the highway. I might not be able to outmaneuver these guys, but I'm certain that I've got more horses under the hood than they do. Hang on."

"Yep, still hanging on."

A moment later, we raced up the on-ramp. I pressed the pedal to the floor and my car gave me every last piece of itself. The engine quivered as my speed topped out at just nearly one hundred miles an hour. I had hoped for more, but graciously took what I got, as I dangerously weaved between traffic. I chanced another glance in the mirror and couldn't believe what I saw. I hadn't left them far behind. In fact, the gap between us hadn't changed the slightest since the pursuit began.

"Use the CB and get some help out to us. Quickly."

When Sara grabbed the mike from the floorboard, they offered another jarring hit to the left side. We shot straight ahead but thankfully didn't waver on the road as before. If we took another shot like that, I had no doubt that I'd lose control, possibly killing commuters as well as ourselves.

One of the blue sedans somehow had enough power under the hood to keep pace with us in the left lane. The vehicle's windows were darkly tinted, but I could see three shadows within. Each face turned to us and watched intently for my next daring move.

I was desperately trying to think of what to do next when the car to our left rolled down the rear window. I couldn't immediately recognize the type of gun that jutted from the vehicle, but I knew that seconds from now, we were going to be riddled with holes.

"I'm about to do something incredibly stupid," I frantically said.

Sara watched my eyes and said, "No, Harper."

I saw an exit rapidly approaching. Our speed was suicidal, and I honestly didn't think I'd make the sharp, curving off-ramp. I hammered the brakes, cut a hard right, and angled the best I could toward the off-ramp and away from the squad of killers. Cars spun out from my sudden action, followed by a crush of metal.

As we took the off-ramp, I realized I was right. I couldn't make the curve after all.

37

In the back of my thoughts, I realized that I had heard sirens from somewhere far behind us. I had also heard the undeniable crunch of cars colliding at death-defying speeds. I had glimpsed three of the blue sedans steer into one another as they each miscalculated a safe maneuver against my unexpected action.

All of that was at the very back of my mind as my government-issued vehicle screeched along the guardrail of the off-ramp. The left fender peeled like a can and delivered a shower of sparks as the impacting force removed any kind of control I momentarily had. Both airbags deployed, which snapped both of us into a temporary position of safety and then deflated just as quickly.

The guardrail kept us following the downgrade at insane speeds. That was until the fourth blue sedan clipped the rear end with enough force to heave our car over the rail and into the rugged grass terrain beyond.

My driver's window shattered, spraying tempered glass into my face. The door crumpled in and dug fiercely into my left side. My head jolted a hard left and then right as the vehicle spun onto the roof. The roof then caved in, followed by the entire passenger side. Before I knew it, my door was groaning under pressure again.

I wasn't entirely sure how many times the vehicle had flipped, but when we finally came to rest, we were upside down.

When my eyes fluttered open, my vision offered the same sight multiplied by three. I felt a dull thunder of pain tracing a path throughout my entire body. My left side was especially tender and offered a sinister shock with each breath. Even though I knew it was going to hurt, I pressed the seat belt latch and dropped in a heap onto the roof. My head screamed, my side screamed, and I probably would have screamed if I wasn't focused on Sara's condition.

Sara was still upside down, still firmly wedged in the passenger seat. I thought she was unconscious, or perhaps dead, until I heard her moan softly. Her arms and hair were hanging, her legs folded to her chest as the seat belt kept her awkwardly stuck.

"Sara, can you hear me?"

"Mmm, great driving, boss."

"I'm going to release your seat belt. I'm going to catch you when you fall. Does anything hurt bad enough that it makes you think that I shouldn't move you?" I asked.

"Everything hurts but get me down anyhow."

I reached for the seat belt release and popped Sara free. She dropped smoothly into my tired arms. We were huddled together on the wreckage of the roof when I heard the first of many distant gunshots.

I crouched lower in reflex at the all too familiar sound. I didn't hear the metallic whine of a bullet clunking into my car. I didn't feel anything pierce my flesh. After a brief moment of added terror, I understood what was happening. The men from the three blue sedans that were a mangled mess on the highway were having an unexpected showdown with local law enforcement that rushed to the crash scene. The police probably thought they were responding to an unfortunate highway accident, but instead found themselves involved in a massive gunfight with highly prepared mercenaries.

I heard what I thought were returning gunshots.

"We've got to get out of this car," I said.

I could smell gas fumes from the ruptured tank. A simple spark from the damaged electrical could ignite the gas and catch the vehicle on fire, trapping us inside.

I maneuvered through the shattered passenger window and dragged Sara by her arms from the wreckage. When I felt we were clear from a potential fire, I released my grip. Immediately, the hammering pain on my left side returned. I carefully probed the area with my fingertips and winced when I pressed several ribs. I was pretty sure my ribs didn't break during the crash but jostled enough that hellish bruising would follow. Just to make sure it wasn't more severe, I coughed gently into my fist and thankfully didn't see any blood.

Sara was lying still, maybe taking a long mental survey of possible bodily damage. She wiggled her feet, then legs, and worked her way up like she was softly dancing to music only she could hear.

"Is everything in working order?" I asked.

"Check. I don't think I broke anything. I really wish you wouldn't have done that. It could have been a lot worse," Sara said.

There were more sirens, followed by endless sounds of gunfire. I was about to tell Sara that I was going to check on the guy in the blue sedan that sent us pinwheeling, but when I saw a small group of men charging down the hill toward us, I rapidly changed my mind.

I grabbed Sara's arm, yanked her to her feet, and propelled us down the embankment. The mercenaries were 150 yards behind us and quickly gaining. There had been seven men in tow until a well-placed shot from a patrolman caught one of them in the back and sent him face-first into the gritty slope. I witnessed all of that in the split second after a glance back. Strangely enough, I was sure that the patrolmen still in position on the highway were firing rounds not only at the mercenaries but also at Sara and me. As far as they knew, we were fugitives intending to slaughter anyone who kept us from a clean getaway.

Step after painful step, Sara and I crossed the street below the highway and headed for the cover of the crowded parking lots and office buildings. We needed to find a place to hide out until the local police enforcement, with tactical gear, could pin these men down and overpower their defenses.

I still had my Glock secured in my shoulder holster, but my gun couldn't match the automatic weapons these men were carrying. They would shred us apart and keep on running for freedom without even slowing down. Finding a reliable cover was the only thing on my mind. I think it was on Sara's mind, too. She had shaken off the horrific effects of the crash and kept a good ten-pace lead.

"Over there," I said.

We were crouching as we weaved a path between parked cars. To our right was an office building that had gone up in flames in late July, which resulted in four people burning to death on the third floor.

"The condemned building?" Sara asked.

"We have to stay away from civilians if possible. These guys are going to kill anyone to get to us. I don't like the idea that innocent people might die if I lead these men to them on purpose."

I was sure the mercenaries knew our location. I could still hear the close shuffle of their feet as they trailed our lead.

"Why the hell aren't they firing? They could flush us out with a couple of random shots. They could have cut us down on that slope and didn't," I whispered as I rounded a red sports car.

"They could have killed us ten times over by now. I'm leaning toward the assumption that they want us alive. Well, they want you alive anyhow," Sara said.

We crossed the yellow and orange barricades and the posted warnings. I was pretty sure that the building was structurally secure enough to accommodate our brief stay. The rubble from the collapsed three floors in addition to the office equipment offered unlimited spaces for hiding.

"We need to find some sort of stronghold until the cavalry can get to us. I think we might be able to hold them off for a short while. I only have two clips. That's twenty shots, but I always make them count," I said.

"I'm good with negotiations," Sara offered.

"Dynamite. Now we're unstoppable."

We followed a narrow path through the front entrance. It was evident that the removal of the debris had begun some time ago. There was a front-end loader, other mechanical equipment, and high-powered work lights that were currently turned off throughout the cleanup area. Thankfully, no men were working today. We were alone.

I pointed to a corner of the charred interior and said, "I think that's the best place I can spot. If it gets too heated, we can always bail out that door and run again."

I overheard a conversation I didn't understand. The Russians were coming, and they didn't want to ruin their strategic attack by speaking in English and giving away the surprise.

As we quietly shuffled toward our selected position, I noticed that at least two of the men had parted with their company. I glimpsed them through part of the ruined walls. They were rounding the building toward the rear. They were trying to pin us down.

When I turned from the partially collapsed wall in which I spotted the men, I found myself alone. I shifted my sight to the area I had claimed would be our temporary fortress. I didn't see Sara anywhere in the shadows.

"Psst. Sara?" I whispered.

The rear door creaked on scorched hinges. There was a brief flood of daylight, and then darkness again as the door closed. I could hear stumbling footfalls in the front and the rear. I suddenly felt like a terrified caged rat.

"Sara?" I whispered again.

I rotated to my left. That was when I heard something slice through the air. Whatever the object was, it connected across my shoulders with enough force to drop me to my knees. My gun spilled from my grip as I tried to keep myself from going face-first into a pile of jagged concrete.

Another blow caught me at the back of the skull. The blackness surrounding me only intensified as my thoughts and focus swam toward the murky seas of unconsciousness.

38

"Mmm. Mmm. Hmm."

Through the haze, I could hear these sounds. The noise moved across the dreary blackness of my mind like slow, rippling waves. Whatever had been the source of the sound, it began pulling me back to consciousness.

My eyes fluttered open and closed. I briefly glimpsed a dim light to my left before I pinched my eyes closed again. My head was spinning in rapid circles when I focused on anything in the room, and the only way to counter this effect was to keep my eyes shut. Even in the confusion, I felt something strapped around my mouth and if the dizziness became overwhelming, I would vomit and probably choke to death.

Thinking straight was a marathon race away from my current brain activity. I was having a difficult time trying to even focus on the last thing that had happened to me. Someone had blindsided me, and then I felt the gentle prick of a needle to the back of my neck as I lay face down, trying to get an understanding of the situation.

How the hell did someone maneuver behind me? I had a stronghold on my position. Is the Tourist holding me hostage?

A million other questions coursed through my mind, but I didn't think I'd get the answers to any of them. I was certain the Tourist was behind my current circumstances. If he was lingering somewhere in the darkness, he had yet to reveal himself.

The swirling from the head blow had finally subsided, and the drug's nauseating effect faded a bit, too. I let my eyes open a little. I could see a lamp with a low-wattage bulb a few dozen feet from me. Someone had thrown a red shirt over the lampshade, giving the area a sinister, blood-like appearance.

I was in a wooden chair. My wrists were bound to the armrests and my feet secured to the chair legs with gray tape. Someone had removed my suit jacket as well as my shoes and socks. I felt the smooth, cold concrete.

I couldn't have guessed where the hell they'd taken me. It was a large empty room with only minimal lighting. The place could have been as vast as an airplane hangar.

I pulled my sight from the lamp and to my right. My heart stuttered momentarily at what I saw. Sara was mostly clouded in shadows, but even in the gloom, I saw blood staining the front of her blouse. Bound to a chair, her head hung and lulled from side to side.

"Mmm. Mmm," Sara muttered.

I tried to speak, but my mouth couldn't form any kind of response.

Sara managed to pull her head back, and her eyes immediately alarmed as her sight shifted around the room, trying to make sense of where she was. When she gazed down at her restrained arms and feet, she quickly panicked and started thrashing.

"Calm yourself, my dear," someone said from the shadows.

We both turned our heads. Something moved to the left of the shaded lamp. I squinted to get a better idea of who it was I was looking at. The figure stood and slowly pulled the red cloth from the lamp. The deep redness that had consumed the area was gone and replaced with a soft glow, offering more visibility. Although I still couldn't see any of the building's interior walls, I guessed that we were being held in a deserted warehouse. There was an endless concrete floor, steel pillars that ran from the floor to the high ceiling, and little else.

I looked long and hard at the man beside the lamp. Even though it was August, and the warehouse was unbearably stifling, the man was wearing black jeans, a button-up denim shirt, a full-length black trench coat, and tan hiking boots. I judged him to be in his early forties, or maybe a little older. He kept his brown hair closely cropped. Stepping beside me, he leaned in close. His eyes were a pale blue, which nearly matched my own. What was in those eyes was an entirely different story.

His right hand disappeared beneath the inside folds of his coat and then produced a hunting knife. He slid the blade next to my face. I suddenly thought that this was a shitty way to walk out the door of life and to that mysterious place beyond. I thought of Clara and Kaylee and regretted all things left unsaid.

"Hold still, Harper. I don't want to cut you. Not yet anyway."

He carefully slipped the blade between the gray tape and the skin of my cheek. He rotated the sharp edge and cut the tape. After he painfully peeled the tape from my face and hair, he stepped to Sara and repeated the action.

"There, now we can comfortably speak to each other."

"Are you all right?" I asked Sara.

As I had suspected moments ago, it was blood on the front of her shirt. They'd broken her nose sometime during our capture. I hoped she had given the mercenaries one hell of a fight.

"My head is pulsing from when this asshole broke my nose, but other than that, I think I'm okay. How about you?"

"I'm good. Just give me a few seconds and I'll figure a way out of this." I wanted my cockiness to show through. I didn't want him to know I was completely terrified.

His perfect white teeth gleamed as he crossed his arms over his chest and watched me with fascination.

I rapidly shifted my position as I violently tried to flail my arms and legs. The binding tape did little more than pinch the skin of my wrists.

"Nope, that didn't work," I said.

"Your attitude is simply astounding, Harper. Even when you've come to the finale of your life, you manage to maintain a sense of humor. I applaud you for that. I don't think you'll be able to break free, but I'll touch my generous side and cut your partner free," he said.

"I suppose you're Mikhail Alexandrov, the one who calls himself the Tourist?" I asked.

He didn't answer, only offered a smile. He used the knife to unbind Sara. Her face drew with horror as he pulled her from the chair and casually placed the blade at her throat. Her chest heaved in terror as her eyes pleaded for me to help.

"You can step closer now," he called over his shoulder.

I heard the hollow clack of footsteps as a man walked toward us. The person who stepped into the light was little more than a kid. His face was young and smooth, and his dirty blonde hair was brushed meticulously to the right. He was probably in his early twenties. He wore a long-sleeved green shirt, tan Dockers, and white sneakers. He was carrying a face drawn with fear. Just like Sara and me, I didn't think the kid had a choice of being here. This kid certainly wasn't a professional killer. After a long moment, I realized who he was.

"You're Brandon Harris, aren't you?"

He nodded as he accepted the small camcorder the man held out to him. Brandon took the camcorder, flipped open the view screen, and began recording.

"I don't understand any of this. Why have you brought us here? Why did you involve me in your plans to kill five people and expose the plot Kiril Novilov had set into action so many years ago?" I asked.

"Even though you're one of the best agents the FBI has to offer, I must say that I'm greatly disappointed right now, Harper. I would have thought that you had things figured out a long time ago," he said.

Brandon Harris was circling my chair. The camera drew in close to my face and pulled away as he recorded my fixed posture. Next, he turned his view to the Tourist and Sara, and zoomed in close to the blade pressed tightly against Sara's neck. The Tourist watched me as I studied Brandon, my mind taking in every horrifying moment.

"There's no need to concern yourself with Mr. Harris. He's only documenting my memoirs."

"What I understand is that you wanted to destroy everything Kiril Novilov worked so feverishly hard at preparing. I'm sure you have your reasons for killing Kiril and the other people that were connected one way or another to his plan. What I don't understand is why you singled out me to play your games of cat and mouse," I said.

"Death will carry away all whom you care about," he said.

"What exactly does that mean?" I asked.

"Since Ms. McNeal is here now, I'll start with her. I'll eventually find your wife and daughter. You can't hide them from me forever. I'm going to bring down on you what you delivered to me all those years ago. I'm going to take away everything you've ever loved. After you've suffered long and hard from the loss of your family, then I'm going to slowly strip away your life. I think you will suffer more than I've ever made anyone suffer before."

With sudden quickness, the Tourist removed the knife from Sara's throat, drew his arm back and thrust the blade deep into the belly of my partner. Sara's eyes shot open wide, and a tiny whimper slipped from her. Her trembling hands went to the wound when the blade pulled free. Her fingers carefully probed the blossoming red in her abdomen.

"No," I heard myself whisper.

I could only watch with helpless torment as Sara's eyes found mine. Her knees slowly buckled, and she went face down on the bare concrete warehouse floor.

39

"It's a plain shame. She's so young and pretty, only to die a terrible and agonizing death at your feet," the Tourist said.

Sara pulled herself across the concrete floor closer to me. Her blood-covered hands clawed the floor, as her shoes tried to find purchase to push forward. I could see her whole body shaking.

Sara secured a hold on my bound right leg as she drew her weak body up against mine. A path of red followed her gripping fingers up my pants and then across my shirt.

The cameraman, Brandon Harris, stepped in for a close shot as the lens focused on my reaction. I hardly noticed the camera light drawing in close to me. What I did notice was a single word Brandon slyly whispered to me as he recorded the events. Whatever he had meant to convey to me by speaking that single word, I immediately pushed all possible comprehension I could have put forth on the thought to the back of my mind. My partner was dying in front of me.

Sara's face turned up and her terrified eyes found me again. Her breath was stuttering wetly as she pulled in air. She grasped the front of my shirt, and we came face-to-face.

I could feel tears slipping. My heart hammered as I tried to think of a quick escape from the situation and get Sara some immediate medical help. With all my years of experience, with all the knowledge I had learned in the classroom and on the streets, I couldn't think my way out of this.

"Oh, Harper. Oh, God. God, it hurts so much," Sara said in a voice that broke my heart.

"Sara, I'm so sorry. I'm so sorry I got you into this. I want you to hang on. I'm going to get you some help. Okay?"

"I'm so cold, Harper. It's so cold in here."

Sara's blood-slicked hand gently caressed my face. Brandon pulled in for a tighter, more gruesome and heart-wrecking shot.

"Help her, please," I said to Brandon.

When Sara looked into my eyes again, there was a strange twinkle in her look. Her breathing slowly returned to normal. She was able to get her feet under her as her face bowed closer to me. A wicked little smile crossed her lips.

"Oh, Harper. Oh, can't you feel the drama, baby?" Sara McNeal whispered and then offered a soft chuckle.

She slowly stood while using her thumb to swipe the trail of blood from the corner of her mouth and then licked it from her finger.

"It tastes like pancake syrup from back home," Sara said in a heavily accented voice I didn't recognize as her own.

The voice of Sara McNeal now had a considerable Russian inflection that mimicked the Tourist's tone. I quickly turned to Brandon and then the Tourist, desperately looking for some sort of explanation to the madness.

The Tourist began applauding as he stepped to Sara, wrapped his arms around her, and pressed his mouth to hers. There was no resistance on her part. Instead, she circled her arms around his neck in a loving gesture.

"Quite right. Now that was drama!" the Tourist said with such enthusiasm that it echoed throughout the entire warehouse.

Sara glanced at me and said, "Oh, the poor FBI guy looks a little confused."

"I should expect so." He turned his attention to me and said, "I apologize for the added confusion, Harper. My lovely wife decided she needed a large part in this production. You were an absolutely priceless audience and I thank you for the heartfelt sincerity in your reaction," the Tourist said.

Brandon turned off the camera and walked to the small folding table and opened a laptop I hadn't noticed earlier during the chaos.

"I'll copy the recording to your private files, sir," Brandon said to the Tourist as he removed the camera memory chip and inserted it into the computer.

"That one should land in the greatest hits. A stunning performance, Sasha," the Tourist said and kissed Sara again.

"Sasha? Wife?" I asked, stupefied.

No one answered. They only watched me with amusement.

"Will someone tell me what the hell is going on?" I shouted.

The Tourist stepped in front of my chair, crouched, and placed his hands on my arms. Sara took position beside him. This suddenly felt like a full-frontal attack, and I had nothing in my arsenal other than any vulgar words.

"Where shall I begin? There's so much to unfold from this complex work of art that I believe I'd probably leave you more confused than you are right now. I'm certainly not going to ruin the end. I've seen so many of your silly American movies that leave the bad guys dead or in prison, all because they spilled secrets. Although I don't think this is usually a reality, but I'll stay on the side of caution."

"Then at least tell me what the hell this has to do with me? You didn't give me a straight answer before. What did you mean when you said that you were going to bring on what I delivered to you years ago? What does that mean?"

"Life has its little bonuses, Harper. What did you do before joining the FBI?"

"I was a D.C. detective."

"How about before that?"

"I worked as a D.C. police officer."

"Do you remember the year 1998?"

"I do. You'll need to be a little more specific about which month. I think I had a lot going on that year."

"I'm sure you did. How about a chilly November afternoon in a small deli on Walnut Street? Is that more specific to you?"

A cold, hard ripple moved through my body. I remembered every detail about one specific day that month. No matter how much I wanted to forget it, I never would. Even now, those images came flooding back in a relentless force.

"Yeah, I remember. What about it?" I said sourly.

A great deal of things suddenly fell into place in my mind. I knew the name Alexandrov. I had known that name from so many years back.

"Tell me about that afternoon. I know what happened, of course, but I'd like to hear it from one of the men who suffered the experience," the Tourist said.

Although I didn't feel up to reliving the memory, I said, "My partner, Tim Vargas, and I responded to a call involving a robbery in progress. Someone outside the deli saw what was going on and called from a nearby pay phone. We were the first on the scene."

"What action did you take?"

"We moved in. From where we were outside, we couldn't tell for sure if anything illegal was going on inside. As far as we knew, it could have been a crank call. We saw people inside, but no mad gunmen demanding money. We went in the front door. There was a bell above the door. I still remember the tinkling sound it made before the gunshot went off. A perpetrator had rotated around a rack of potato chips and began firing. We had our guns drawn, but we honestly didn't think something that severe would happen on a Tuesday afternoon. Tim took the shot in the throat. One second he was beside me and the next he collapsed against the front windows, grasping his neck as blood poured from between his fingers. Why are you doing this?" I suddenly asked, as past images of my partner's death flooded my mind. I believe I already knew the answer.

My stomach churned. I didn't want to speak of this, not here with this man who desperately wanted to destroy me mentally.

"Please, continue," he urged.

"I went down on my knees, grabbed Tim by his uniform shirt, and pulled him in closer to the store shelves and out of firing range. I held my hand to his throat, trying to stifle the bleeding until backup came. The blood was coming so fast, and I knew he wouldn't be able to hold on long enough. I heard two perpetrators taunting me, saying that they'd got one pig and soon they'd get the other. It took less than a minute for my partner to die in my arms. I went fucking insane. I got up and circled around the racks, finding a small group of terrified faces of customers and two young men with guns. There was something immediately wrong with their look. They seemed to enjoy what they were doing."

"Did you shoot them?" Sara said.

I eyed her with contempt and betrayal. I couldn't believe this woman had been playing me from the beginning of this twisted mind game.

"No, I took aim, but I didn't have a shot. The two men were obviously strung out on drugs. Maybe that's what they had to do to build up enough courage to rob a place of business in the mid-afternoon. They wouldn't stop from getting what they wanted. I didn't even have time to make a move. They started shooting people before I could even react. There were four rapid shots. I never knew for sure what happened between them speaking to me and when the shooting started. Maybe one hostage made a move, or the two gunmen desired a *Butch Cassidy and the Sundance Kid* blaze-of-glory ending. They quickly shot four people before I could fire. I took them both down," I said and shook my head as if it would help brush away the images forever.

"Do you remember the victims?" the Tourist asked.

"I won't ever forget their names or faces. There were actually six victims in all. Maria Lopez was pregnant. They also killed my partner Tim Vargas, the deli owner, Hank Jorgensen, Alyona Alexandrov, and her daughter Anna. But Anna didn't die right away. She suffered a chest wound and medics took her straight to the hospital when emergency crews arrived. She was a strong-willed little girl and lasted nearly a full day before her body gave out. At the end of the whole mess, Anna became the last victim. I suppose now is the time when you tell me that Alyona and Anna were your wife and daughter."

The Tourist stood, slowly pacing around my chair while keeping the palm of his hand sliding from my left shoulder to my right. The only sounds in the warehouse were my unsteady breathing, the ticking of Brandon's fingers on the laptop, and the Tourist's boot soles clacking on concrete.

"I came to America for the first time in 1998. I didn't come here for a vacation or business. I came because I'd received word that my wife and child had been involved in a horrific crime in your country's capital. I came too late. My daughter had passed away during my flight to the U.S. I could not accompany them on their tour of your country. I like to believe that they enjoyed every place they visited across this nation before their deaths. My wife and daughter died because you and your partner stepped into that store and gave those men no choice but to take hostile action. Now, I'm going to retrieve your wife and daughter and return the heartbreak. I'm pretty sure that I know where you're hiding them, and I will enjoy watching the pain fill your face as you observe their slow deaths."

"The only people I killed in that store were the two men who murdered innocent people, your wife and daughter included. I'm not responsible for their deaths," I said.

"Is that what you've been telling yourself for the last sixteen years, Harper?"

I had nothing to respond with to that. In truth, I did partially blame myself. Even in my dreams I regretted my lack of actions before the shooting started. I had been a naïve cop with only a few years on the force. I had never faced personal torment like that before or after that day.

"My new wife will keep you company while I'm away. Have fun with him, Sasha, but not too much fun. Remember that he needs to live."

40

When the Tourist exited stage left, I said to Sara, "So, what's up, doc? I have to admit that I'm impressed with your English. Not once did I catch the hint of a foreign accent. Unlike I did with Lucas. Who is that guy, by the way? No, I suppose it doesn't matter. I'm guessing that you really don't work for the DHS. That figures, I'm always the last to know these things. So, when Mikhail shot you in the hotel lobby, he obviously knew you were wearing a vest. Was that an idea you made up so that I'd believe you were really on my side? So, you figured you'd take a couple of shots to the chest so that your man could make a clean getaway without me suspecting anything foul. You had to make sure that I'd trust you enough to accompany me into the CIA facility so that you could learn if Kyle Sawyer had already given up the Blackstone File, right?"

A sinister smile danced across her lips as she paced the concrete in front of me.

"Like my husband said, you're disappointing. You figured out important details far too late. You know, I still can't figure out what I'm going to do with you. Don't worry, I will not inflict a great deal of pain, only a little. I want you in fit condition for when my husband arrives with your family, and he'll show you the true meaning of anguish."

"Why would you really care what happened to his wife and child so many years ago?" I asked.

"Alyona was my sister and Anna was my niece. Mikhail's family was my own. We found comfort in each other after their murders. Eventually, we grew close enough to fall in love. I wouldn't call it a storybook romance. A certain tragedy occurred that later made us realize what it meant for us."

"What can I say? I think I'm truly happy for the both of you. I'm glad that the mass murder in that grocery store brought the two of you lovebirds closer together," I said and rolled my eyes.

Sara stepped forward and delivered a brain-jarring rap across the right side of my head and another to the left side with her open hand.

"That's for almost killing me on the highway," Sara said, as she removed a knife from her hip pocket and unfolded the blade. "This is for my sister and niece."

I winced as she leaned closer, and the blade moved toward my face. I knew the blade would begin slicing and disfiguring everything but my eyes. They wanted me to witness Clara and Kaylee's moment of suffering.

When Sara suddenly lunged at me in an uncontrolled rush, I thought she had completely lost her mind and had decided to finish my life without Mikhail's approval. She offered a single exclamation of surprise as her body fell against mine, colliding hard enough to steal my breath. Sara rolled to the right, and when her body parted from the chair, gravity grabbed her. She hit the floor with her arms held in front of her. Her left hand still clutched the knife.

When my breath returned, my eyes shifted to Brandon Harris. He was standing a few feet in front of me, grasping a closed laptop computer like a shield. He was staring wildly at Sara as if she would suddenly spring from the floor.

I leaned to the left and gazed down at Sara's crumpled body. If I hadn't known any better, I could have sworn at this point that she was replaying the twisted scene from earlier. Only this time, I knew the blade of the knife had actually punctured flesh. I could see the handle of the knife jutting from her sternum as she rotated onto her back. Her eyes rapidly switched from mine to Brandon's. There was no sense of deception in her breathing this time. It gurgled and hitched in labor.

With no final words, my partner, the imposter, died in that drab warehouse. There was a simple release of breath before her body went slack and she was gone.

"Is she dead?" Brandon asked as he leaned closer, watching for signs of movement.

"I believe so. Get me loose from this chair, please."

Brandon cautiously placed the laptop at my feet and began pulling at the binding duct tape.

"The knife, Brandon. Take the knife from her and cut the tape," I said.

His scared eyes found mine. "Uh-uh. I'm not going to pull it from her. I can rip the tape."

"There are too many layers of tape. It'll take too long. Just remove the knife and cut the damn tape. The Tourist is going after my wife and daughter, and we need to stop him. There's no time to waste, Brandon."

He didn't look at me, his focus devoted to his task. His hands fumbled, fingers desperately trying to start a tear on the tape.

I was about to begin another plea for him to seize the knife when I noticed that he had given up the act of tearing the tape and was now working at unraveling the end. After more than a half dozen revolutions, Brandon thankfully freed my right leg from the chair. Moments later, he made quick work of the remaining restraints.

"Please tell me that there's another car outside we can use," I said.

"Yeah, we came here in two cars."

"Where is here? Where the hell are we, Brandon? Tell me what the hell is going on."

"We're still in D.C. I don't know the city at all, so I can't say for sure. Maybe you'll recognize the area once we get outside. I only wish I could tell you what's happened so far. I don't even know everything myself. There are only pieces of information I have picked up on this guy's plan."

I kneeled and checked Sara's pulse. There was nothing. She was dead and not even a Shakespearian trained actor could fake that. I searched through all of her pockets and her waistband. I was hoping my gun was in her possession, but it wasn't. Instead, I removed a ring of car keys and her Glock and tucked it into my holster.

"I think the Tourist is going to be really pissed now that he's twice widowed," I said.

"That wasn't the Tourist."

"Huh?"

"The guy who was just here, he isn't the man who calls himself the Tourist."

"Then who was that?"

"His name is Mr. Smith. That's the name he goes by anyhow. From what I've been able to piece together so far, Mr. Smith and Sasha are really husband and wife. A psycho love team, I guess. From what he told you, I really think the Tourist's wife and daughter died like he said. I think Mr. Smith was playing out this scene because the Tourist is on some sort of busy hunt and couldn't be here to mess with your head even more."

"While you were filming, you whispered the word *deception* to me. Were you trying to tell me that he wasn't the Tourist? Is that what you meant?" I asked as we exited the rear of the warehouse.

The sunlight came down in a blistering and blinding wave. I looked around, trying to find a recognizable point that I could fix my bearings on and figure out where the hell the two of us were. I'd spent most of my life in the D.C. area, but nothing from this viewpoint seemed even vaguely familiar.

"When I said that to you, I was trying to tell you several things. I was trying to convey that the man wasn't the Tourist, and that the girl wasn't who you thought she was."

"I didn't get any of that from a single word, Brandon. Of course, I was never very good at reading between the lines. Come on."

I started running toward the front of the warehouse. I hoped that I would spot a street sign or another building that would reveal our current location. The only thing I saw that was helpful was a battered Dodge that was our transportation. I pointed for Brandon to get in as I ran around to the driver's side. I slid inside and cranked the engine.

"So, the girl's real name is Sasha?" I asked.

"Yeah. I think they were putting on a bizarre play or something. Apparently, seeing you and your family suffer is something he added to the plan to spice things up. The Tourist is completely whacked out of his goddamn mind."

As I began driving out of the area to a more familiar one, Brandon popped open the glove box and removed my gun, badge, and cell phone.

"I saw them throw your things in here. You might need them," he said.

I pulled Sara's gun from my holster, handed it to Brandon, and replaced it with my gun. Next, I tucked my badge into my jacket pocket and opened my phone.

"I don't want this," Brandon said as he held the gun as if it were crawling with a deadly virus.

"Hold on to it. You might need it."

I had an email. I opened it and saw that Charlie King sent it a half hour ago. There was a quick note letting me know that the attachment was the sketch done of Mikhail Alexandrov. I opened the attachment. Before my phone shut down because of a low battery, I saw the sketch of the man who assassinated Kiril Novilov during lunch. It was the same man that had run me exhausted all week.

Although I only had a moment to see the sketch before the cell screen went blank, there was no denying the fact that I knew the face.

"Son of a bitch, Charlie. I could have used this sketch earlier," I cursed to myself.

"It wasn't his fault. He did send it a while ago. I was told to intercept the email. That woman knew it would be coming and didn't want you to see it. While they were occupying themselves with setting up that strange play for you, I re-sent the email."

"Well, at least now I know who the hell I'm dealing with," I said.

"There's something else you need to know. I want to apologize before I tell you, but they made me get a GPS location on your wife's cell phone."

A vast wave of dread traveled throughout my body.

"I think that's where Mikhail went earlier. I busted my laptop when I hit Sasha over the head, so I'll need another computer to trace your wife's current GPS location. It shouldn't be a problem as long as she still has her phone turned on. You need to understand that I didn't have a choice about everything I've done," Brandon said.

"He won't harm them until he has me there to witness. Just so we're clear, I might have to shoot you when this is finished."

41

Brandon said, "The guy has completely stepped off the deep end of sanity. First, the Tourist and his friend Mr. Smith captured me at a rental house along the Australian coastline. After they rudely awakened me, the Tourist wanted me to decrypt one of my files called Blackstone. I was sure that he was working for a Russian cartel who were behind a conspiracy plot unlike any you've never heard before."

"Actually, I have heard about it. Your friend Kyle Sawyer spilled some of his knowledge about the subject before the Tourist took him out earlier today. The CIA disclosed quite a bit of information to me. Unfortunately, the CIA doesn't currently have possession of the file," I said.

"Okay. So, you know the basics. I'm thinking someone hired them to retrieve those files before it completely screws all chances of Senator Ryan becoming the next U.S. president. On the plane ride back from Australia, he told me that the kidnapping of Senator Ryan's wife and son was supposed to be part of Kiril Novilov's plan of action after Senator Ryan discovered his wife had somehow come across the Blackstone File. The information she uncovered would destroy the election and ignite major chaos between the U.S. and the Russians behind the plot."

"Do you think she found out Senator Ryan's true identity and his secret purpose in those files?" I asked.

"I don't know for sure. All I can say is that it cost her a pretty good life. Senator Ryan told Kiril Novilov that the plan was in serious jeopardy, and they needed an immediate solution. They decided on the kidnap approach and his resistance to withdraw from the race, which resulted in her death. These men were sure that his prepared speech about not giving into threats of terrorism would clinch the presidency. They were positive that the voting American party would view the action as that of a strong-willed man who would dominate a presidency term by trying any and all means necessary to destroy those who attempted to confront the United States with hostile intent. The death of the senator's wife will seize the presidency for him. That's their theory, anyhow. After the media announced Mrs. Ryan's murder, and the personal video of Senator Ryan's final threat aired, his supporters would skyrocket," Brandon said.

"So, then the Tourist comes along and makes up a plan of his own. He took over where Kiril started. His men kidnapped the wife and kid and made the demand to step down. Only I think he was serious about the order. Then he kills Lewis Rockwell because this guy is the bank behind Senator Ryan's campaign. Next, he takes out Kiril to finally get his long-awaited revenge. So, he then kills Kyle because the kid had copies of the file. Why is it that he's trying to destroy Senator Ryan, but also desperately trying to conceal the truth inside the Blackstone File?" I asked.

"He never explained the purpose behind the murders. I think they were simply pieces of the puzzle."

"What puzzle?"

"The one that kept you jumping through hoops all week long. I believe that the murders were nothing more than a method of driving you stir-crazy before he killed you and your family. He told me that he was playing a game of revenge before the curtain parted and the big show began," Brandon said as he slumped on the leather seat.

"All of the murders are linked to Senator Ryan. He didn't do all this just to mess with me. There's a good reason behind it all."

Brandon was staring off into the scenery beyond the window. His arms were crossed over his chest and his entire body was still except for his fidgety feet. I took several glances from the road to watch him. He suddenly looked so incredibly young and innocent. He seemed like a kid who stumbled down the wrong direction in life and couldn't find his way back.

"It's my fault, you know?" Brandon said.

"What is?"

"It's my fault Kyle got killed."

"What makes you say that? The Tourist was the man behind it. It wasn't your fault that your friend died."

"The Tourist wasn't even planning on killing Kyle until I screwed it up."

"What do you mean?" I asked.

"I had a brief opportunity a few days ago when the Tourist and Mr. Smith left me unguarded in the hotel room. They went into the hallway to quietly discuss a part of their plan. Whatever it was about, it was one of the few things they didn't want me to know about. Anyway, I seized the few precious moments I had to get the word out to the only person I could trust. Before we parted years ago, Kyle and I set up an email address to where we could get ahold of each other in case of an emergency. I used my laptop to email Kyle a quick paragraph about my kidnapping and the plan surrounding it. I even sent him an attachment containing the Blackstone File. My instructions told him to contact the authorities and give them the information I sent."

"So, you don't think he planned Kyle's murder?"

"No. After I sent the email, they came back into the room. I was incredibly nervous, and I couldn't calm down. The Tourist watched me for a few minutes, and he must have decided that I had been up to no good when they weren't looking. He took my laptop from me. I wasn't given enough time to cover my tracks. He discovered the email I sent to Kyle. He told me that if he didn't need me so bad, he'd kill me on the spot. I believed him. Instead, he tried to get me to give up Kyle's location. I told him that I didn't know. I truly had no idea. I haven't seen Kyle in almost three years. But I knew I could track him down easy enough if I wanted to. I could have even accessed the account and completely wiped out the email I just sent, but the Tourist hadn't thought of that. The guy's brilliant, but not when it comes to computers."

"Then Kyle took the files to the authorities just like you asked."

"Yeah. They put him in protective custody. I think he held all the cards until the moment he died. He must have given the CIA part of the files I sent him and was in the process of striking some sort of deal for immunity for the crimes he's committed over the years. His list of cybercrimes is longer than mine."

"The CIA officers told us that Kyle withheld the information until they made a final deal," I said.

"I would have done the same thing. If he told them about the information within the Blackstone file and promised to back up his claim with the real thing, I have no doubt that they'd love to wheel and deal and forgive all of his computer crimes," Brandon said.

"Because of Sara, the Tourist knows that Kyle hadn't yet handed over the file you sent. If the Tourist is still planning to go through with everything, then he must be confident that we don't know his real purpose."

"I suppose we're all in the dark about what he's up to," Brandon said.

My mind was buzzing. It was such a large amount to take in during such a short period.

I told Brandon about the first email the Tourist sent and the plans for five deaths and a mysterious getaway.

"Then if Kyle wasn't meant to be one of the five victims, then maybe Senator Ryan is the fourth or fifth victim after all," he said.

"Maybe."

"If Senator Ryan isn't one of the next victims, then who would you take a guess at?" Brandon asked.

I didn't want to answer that. The Tourist and his unquenched thirst for revenge over the untimely death of his wife and child gave me bad images. This man wanted to mentally destroy me. He wanted to punish my existence by taking away everything good in my life and leaving me in a suicidal depression.

I said, "I couldn't even hazard a guess. I honestly think that Senator Ryan might very well be the fifth and final victim. It started with him and seemed like it is making a full circle and ending with him. Just because the Tourist promised he would only murder five people, that doesn't mean he won't get one of his cronies to kill my wife and daughter."

"Maybe that's Mr. Smith's assignment. Maybe it's his duty to track down you wife and daughter and bring them back to the warehouse to wait for the return of the

Tourist. I think you're right. I think the senator's death makes a complete circle," he said.

"Can you be positive that Kyle's murder wasn't part of the Tourist's plan?"

"I don't think it was, but I can't say for sure," he answered.

"Because I believed his letter when he said that there would be only five victims. So, if Kyle wasn't written into the plan before you pulled him in, then I believe the Tourist would have sent a group of his men to take out Kyle and his armed CIA escorts at the secured facility."

"I don't know. It's possible. Maybe the Tourist didn't rely on the intelligence or ability of one of his men to take out Kyle. I bet Kyle spent seventeen hours a day hunched over a computer screen. He had his fingers twirling in a lot of crooked plans devised by men who would dish out a ton of money to keep hidden. Kyle had so much dirt on a lot of big names around the world. It's amazing he lasted as long as he did." Brandon said.

"What about you?"

"I blackballed my hacking talents a long time ago. In fact, I quit right after they slaughtered my family. When I learned about the Blackstone File and ripped off the Russian Mafia for millions, I went on the run and tried a vanishing trick that I failed miserably at. Every time I stayed in one place for too long, I became incredibly paranoid and quickly found a different corner of the world to hide in. Somehow the Tourist tracked me to the ends of the earth. I have half a dozen false passports, but he found me anyway. I probably could have been living in a bubble dome at the bottom of the Atlantic and eventually he would have come knocking."

"If he found you hiding on the other side of the world, then there's no chance of my wife and daughter simply disappearing in a city of a few million. He'll find them, too."

"That leaves you with only one option, Agent Caster. You've got to find him first and place a bullet through his black heart and maybe a couple in the head for good measure. That's the only way the terror will find an end," Brandon said.

"I completely agree. Not to jump off the subject, but I suppose you're the one I can thank for altering my entire financial history?" I said while eyeing Brandon.

"Yeah, sorry about that. With a gun stuck at the back of my head, I would have done anything he told me to do. I'm not proud of the way I've lived my life, but that doesn't mean that I deserve to die by the Tourist's hand. I promise that when this is done, I'll fix every account I've changed. If you like, I could even clear all your debts. You could walk out of this whole thing without owing a single penny."

I waved my hand at the offer. "No, no, I'm too honest to even consider something like that. All I ask is for you to repair everything to its original amount. I don't deserve special privileges simply because I know someone who can work that kind of magic. Please promise me that you'll restore everything as it was," I said.

"Uh, sure. Yeah, I promise," Brandon said.

42

Brandon and I didn't have a clue whether Kyle Sawyer was intended to be victim four. If the Tourist hadn't meant for Kyle to take that position, then whoever was in the crosshairs would be on their own for now. There wasn't much I could anticipate about the Tourist, but one way or another I knew that he'd eventually be gunning for Senator Ryan.

We pulled up to the curb in front of the Russell Senate Office Building. I studied the busy street and the sidewalks. Maybe part of me expected to see a man matching the identity of the Tourist. I was hoping it would finish that easily.

"I'm sorry, Brandon, but I've got to do this," I said as I removed my handcuffs. I secured one end to Brandon's left wrist and the other to the steering wheel.

"Do you honestly believe I'm going to take off running? Where would I go? If you don't stop this guy today, then he'll find me again. I believe he's planning on killing me, no matter what. So that means that I want this thing done as much as you do."

"I know you do. But I need you more than he does. I just don't want you panicking and getting the idea to do a rabbit run."

"Then let me go in with you. I might be able to help somehow," Brandon said.

I thought briefly about it and said, "No, it's too dangerous. You're far better off alive than dead."

I stepped outside into the merciless heat of the sun and ran for the front doors. When I checked through security, I took an elevator to the third floor and hurried down the hall to Senator Ryan's office.

"Where is he?" I asked the secretary. We had been at this point before.

"He doesn't want to see you, Agent Caster. He gave me specific instructions not to talk to you and to send you on your way if you were bold enough to come around again."

"I need to see him now. Not later or tomorrow, but now!" I yelled.

"I'm going to have to call security," she said as a distressed look came to her face, and she reached for the desk phone.

"If you do that, Senator Ryan is going to die. I'm the only one that can help him right now. There's a man after him, and I'm probably the only one in the world who knows what he looks like. You need to tell me where he is."

As far as she understood, I was a deranged FBI agent who invented bizarre scenarios of chaos in my free time in order to feel needed.

"Yes, this is Mrs. Weston, Mr. Ryan's secretary. I need security sent to his office right away. There's an FBI agent here who claims—"

I pressed my thumb on the disconnect button.

"Lady, I told you that I don't have the time to explain everything. The man Senator Ryan placed a million-dollar bounty on is now hunting him. This is the same man who has done a series of other terrible things in D.C. over the last few days. Give me a chance to help Senator Ryan."

The phone rang. There was no way to know if it was just a normal business phone call or if it was security calling back to ask if Mrs. Weston was all right.

"Please, lives are on the line," I said.

She took a deep breath. I could see the wheels of her mind rapidly moving as she tried to anticipate what would be the outcome of telling me or not telling me. She had decided to trust me a little but had also prepared for the possibility that I had full intensions of harming her boss.

"He's in conference room two. I'll call security back and have them meet you there," she said and picked up the phone again.

With a mutter of thanks, I headed out the door and sprinted like a frightened animal down the corridor. I thundered past the elevators, hit the stairs door, and was quickly bounding down the stairwell three steps at a time. I passed several people who eyed me suspiciously.

As I came down the hallway heading for the conference room, three security men stepped in front of me. As I ran to them, I reached for my badge. In turn they reached for their guns.

"Hold on! I'm FBI Special Agent Harper Caster. I'm going to need your help. Are there any more of you?"

All three of them took a long, hard look at my badge and seemed to ease up.

"What's the problem here?" one that had buzz-cut brown hair asked.

Despite the tension of the moment, I almost laughed. Where the hell would I begin if this guy really wanted all of the details leading up to this point?

"There's a man planning to assassinate Senator Ryan. I think he's here. He might be in the conference room right now. Come on!" I said and began running down the hallway again.

I had no idea what I was going to find when the four of us tore open the conference room doors and barged inside.

What I found was something unexpected.

The room was chaos free. It was almost identical to the first time I had been in here and witnessed Senator Ryan telling the world that men entered his home, took his wife and son, and demanded that he withdraw from the presidential race.

Senator Ryan was standing at the podium. There was a large cast of reporters and cameras. They had been a captivated audience to what Senator Ryan was saying until the four of us made a hasty intrusion.

When Senator Andrew Ryan halted his speech and eyed us suspiciously, the entire room took notice and turned to observe us.

One of the security guards must have felt uncomfortably out of place, because I felt a hand grasping my elbow.

"I think this has been a big mistake on your part. We need to leave now, Agent Caster," one guard said.

Reluctantly, I slid my Glock back in the holster. I hadn't thought that I had made a big mistake. What I was actually feeling, perhaps hoping, was that we had somehow beaten the Tourist to the conference room. Then again, there were a lot of faces in this crowd and the Tourist could very well be one of them.

I pulled my arm free from the grip of the security guard and started walking down the narrow aisle.

"Senator Ryan, I need you to leave with me right now," I said loud enough that the entire crowd heard.

Two Secret Service agents assigned to Senator Ryan came forward from the rear of the podium and positioned themselves, just as protocol dictated. Both of them were situated between Senator Ryan and possible threats.

"Just take it easy. I'm FBI Special Agent Harper Caster. I'm going to reach for my badge inside my coat," I said.

I slowly withdrew my hand and showed them my identification.

All the cameras rotated toward me and then back to Senator Ryan. It was almost like spectators watching a tennis match.

"Agent Caster, this is certainly not the time or place. As you can see, I'm in the middle of a press conference and I don't think anyone here appreciates your inconsiderate actions of interrupting. I'll need you to leave now and I will speak with you in my office when I'm finished," Senator Ryan said.

I continued forward, not out of defiance to Senator Ryan's wishes, but more out of the fear of what could happen if I left the conference room. It seemed like a million eyes were on me. I carefully studied each face. I was looking for one face in particular.

"What's he doing?" one reporter asked another.

"Please, remain calm," I told them.

"Hey, security, stop standing around looking stupid and remove this man from the building. Right now!" Senator Ryan bellowed.

The guards gathered common sense and began moving toward me.

A man with short brown hair spotted with gray was pointing his bulky camera at me. The camera concealed the left side of his face, but the right side of his face was all too visible and very familiar. His finger touched a button, and the camera zoomed on my features. I pulled my Glock again and started for him.

The entire crowd gasped, and nervous chatter filled the room.

A smile curled the right side of his mouth. He lowered the camera to his waist and winked at me. The left side of his face that had appeared burnt during our two earlier meetings was now smooth and void of any disfigurement. This was the man I had been within arm's reach of on several occasions over the past few days. I had trusted his judgment and guidance because I had trusted Sara's faith in him. They'd deceived me on both fronts. The master of the game had played me from the beginning of the chase.

I raised my gun and said, "Mikhail Alexandrov, drop the camera and raise your hands. You're under arrest for the murder of four people, computer hacking, financial corruption, and for being an all-around prick."

In the room's stillness, I thought I could actually hear the buzz of cameras as they recorded the event.

He released the camera and slowly raised his hands. The smile never left his face.

"Agent Caster, you played wonderfully."

When the Tourist had assumed the part of Lucas, he had spoken with nearly flawless English. During our first meeting, I had detected only the slightest touch of a foreign accent. Now he made no effort to conceal the Russian inflections in his speech.

"Not well enough. Of course, you didn't give me much to go on in the beginning. Place your hands behind your head and drop to your knees. I need all of you people to step back," I said to the crowd that was much too close to the man.

"I am not resisting arrest. I do not deny the accusations this FBI agent has made against me. I am guilty of many things and murder is my favorite," Mikhail Alexandrov said and offered another smile that gave me a cold shiver.

Something wasn't sitting right in my mind. Something felt terribly out of place. I couldn't believe the Tourist would allow himself to be captured so easily in the end, especially since he hadn't finished what he started.

"Be prepared. It's the Boy Scouts' motto, is it not? How do you think I would let you slap handcuffs on me and take me to prison? Remember what I told you before, during our meeting at the park, Harper? The end is never written in stone."

A gunshot went off to my right and the entire crowd became a moving mass of panic.

43

Before the crowd became a blur of moving bodies, I had just enough time to whip my head around and glimpse the shooter and his victim.

A man wearing a dark blue suit, who I had seen moments ago holding an audio recorder, was now easily holding a smoking Beretta instead. The security guard who gripped my arm, holding me back from making a big mistake, took a shot in the left shoulder. He spun hard and went down, with no one reflexively reaching out to catch him. The two other security guards had already pulled their service pieces and were trying to find their aim among the shuffling bodies.

Three more unknown men in the crowd pulled guns, took aim, and brought down the Secret Service men assigned to Senator Ryan's detail.

Then the room became the definition of chaos.

The screams became more intense, almost eardrum shattering. There were over a hundred bodies trying to go anywhere else other than where they currently were. A mob of people who had no problem trampling someone to death in order to save their own skin hit me. I shoved my way through them, while desperately trying to get to where I'd last seen the Tourist standing. When I finally made my way to the location, the Tourist was gone.

The sea of people had thinned out some and the security guards had their opportunity and seized it. Two of the strangers in the crowd that were rapidly firing went down. Another security guard took a shot to the leg, screamed, and somehow returned fire accurately enough to bore a hole above the gunman's left eyebrow.

A bullet whined over my head and drilled into the wall. I crouched, found a small gap in the remaining people, and fired three times. One bullet caught the man in the stomach, the second shot landed beside his cornflower tie, and the third punched a hole in his throat above the collar. All three shots happened so fast that the man had no time to realize he was hit until his body gave out and crumbled to the carpet with a final gasping breath.

I turned my attention to the podium and saw that Senator Ryan was gone. It looked as if he had simply vanished from the spot in which he was standing, while leaving behind the collapsed remains of his security detail. At some point, Senator Ryan either had taken flight with the rest of the crowd or was taken by the Tourist.

I knelt beside the security guard, removed my belt, and forcefully wrapped it around his leg as a tourniquet. The other guard came over, crouched, and quickly withdrew his radio and called for immediate backup and a building lockdown.

"You stay with him. I've got to go after the Tourist," I told the security guard and suddenly realized that he'd have no idea who the Tourist was.

I ran for the door at the back of the podium where I was sure Senator Ryan and probably the Tourist had gone.

Several injured people asked for help as I ran by. I felt guilty about not stopping or even slowing down. I simply told them that help was on the way.

Full bore, I ran from the conference room carnage. I didn't know how many were dead. I didn't know how many were injured. All I knew for sure was that the Tourist was responsible for the disaster this entire week and he was going to pay the ultimate price for creating such terror.

I bounded up the stage steps and hammered through the rear door. The corridor was empty, but I heard distant footsteps clacking on the tile floor. The door slammed shut behind me and I suddenly felt alone. I was battling against the worst nemesis I'd ever encountered, and I was having an uncomfortable feeling that I was walking into a cleverly designed trap with the end resulting in my death.

I peered down each bisecting corridor as I ran. The hallways were empty except for a maintenance man that was changing an overhead light. He was older than the Tourist and nowhere near resembled the face I pursued. I had intended to keep going forward, but at the last second, I had a quick thought. I came to a sliding halt and ran back a few steps.

"Hey, did a couple of people come down this way?"

"Sure did. They almost knocked me right off my ladder. I could have sworn one of them was Senator Ryan."

I took off after them and nearly knocked the man off his ladder again. I yelled out an apology as I regained my balance.

I reached the door at the end of the hallway and went though. Two greatly agitated security guards were standing there. When I broke through the doorway, their guns swiftly came out and centered on my chest.

"Whoa, whoa, it's all right. I'm FBI Special Agent Harper Caster. My badge is in the inside left pocket."

"Let's see the hands," one demanded.

I reached for the ceiling and said, "Go ahead and check my ID. Senator Ryan and a known terrorist just came out this door. I was right behind them."

The security guard with short, curly black hair stepped forward and reached inside my pocket to retrieve my badge.

"No one came out this door," the other guard said.

"No one came out?"

"Only you," he said.

"Yeah, he is who he says he is," the guard said as he lowered his gun and handed back my badge.

"You haven't seen Senator Ryan?"

"The entire building is on lockdown, man. No one gets in and no one goes out. We've got guys crawling all over this building looking for the senator. We've got the local police coming in to help with the search."

"The maintenance man told me they came out this door," I said.

"What maintenance man?"

"The guy in that hallway fixing a light. He said the senator and the other guy almost knocked him off the ladder."

The security guard unclipped his badge from his breast pocket and waved it in front of the scanner until there was a signal that the door was now unlocked.

"Let's go talk to him. If this guy you're after brought the senator this way, then he knows how to turn himself invisible and slide right by us. We didn't see anyone."

In a sort of sprint-jog, the three of us went down the hallway to speak to the maintenance man, only to find an abandoned ladder and utility belt.

"Shit! He was just here!" I yelled.

"Relax, maybe he went to get more light bulbs," one of them said.

"More light bulbs, my ass. He had to be one of them, maybe a sentry or something. He sent me the wrong way on purpose. There were four shooters in the conference room. The maintenance man must be working with the Tourist as well," I said, more to myself and not the security guards.

I took off in a run down the hallway in the direction I had originally headed before being misled.

"Hey, we can't go on a wild goose chase with you, man. We've got to get back to our posts."

I waved my hand at them in a way of saying that their next move didn't concern me. I had something far more interesting to do.

I bolted down the corridor, ending at several locked doors. After a moment rapping on the doors to get anyone's attention and being disappointed, I went back down the hallway. It was possible that the man posing as building maintenance had access cards to these doors and the group had made a clean getaway or they had gone a separate direction other than the one I had originally thought.

I skidded to a halt when I took the next right turn. There was a large steel door. To the left of the door was a chart hanging on the wall. When I stepped closer, I realized it was actually a map of the subterranean workings of the building. It was the place that became a primary network of plumbing, furnaces, boilers, electrical, phone lines, and God knows whatever else that started down there and branched out to the entire building.

This door didn't require a scan card. It was a simple silver doorknob that reflectively distorted my features as

I peered into it. I tried my luck and, surprisingly, found it unlocked.

With my gun in hand, I shoved the door open. The only thing greeting me was a dimly lit stairwell leading into the bowels of the building.

I reached up and tore the framed map from the wall.

I had remembered what one of the security guards had said. *The entire building is on lockdown, man. No one gets in and no one goes out.*

I couldn't tell from the map, but I wondered if there was a passageway out of the building that security didn't even know existed. I figured there was only one way to find out.

44

The metal door clanged shut behind me as I slowly eased down the staircase. Although there were dim fluorescent lights overhead, the darkness was like an invisible hand curling around me, squeezing tightly until I could barely breathe. It was suffocating, to say the least.

I hit the concrete landing, leaned forward, and swiveled my head to the left and right in order to get an idea of the structure of the basement. There were a series of pipe works along the wall and ceiling that ran parallel from one end of the hallway and disappeared around the first corner. I looked at the map I had torn off the wall. My eyes traveled the layout of the map. It was like one of those mazes in the Saturday morning paper I had often done as a kid. I had found the start, traced with my eyes instead of a pencil as I tried to find the finish. The problem was that there was no clear indication of a finish point. There were hallways that I assumed ended at a foundation wall, but I couldn't be sure.

As my eyes stayed focused on the map, my ears kept finely tuned to everything around me. I was constantly listening to the pops, hisses, and low whistles of the basement. I was actually listening for something more telling. I was maybe waiting for the gentle footfalls of someone approaching from behind or a sudden voice in my ear or even the locking back of a gun's hammer. I was trying to remain prepared for anything that was about to be thrown at me.

After a long, precious few minutes I determined which direction I was going to go. It had seemed to me, by looking at the map, that if there was some sort of escape route from this maze of concrete, plumbing, and electrical lines.

I followed the trail of pipes, pausing briefly to peer around the corners before proceeding on. I stopped midway in one of the hallways to look at the map again. There was something on the map I hadn't spotted earlier. There was a square drawing that was labeled as an elevator. I suddenly felt stupid. Of course, there had to be some sort of maintenance elevator to get furnaces, boilers and everything else down here.

I ran down several more corridors, turning half a dozen directions until I reached the elevator. As I pushed the button to call the elevator down, I had an interesting thought. Why would the Tourist go down only to go back up? Of all people, the Tourist knew they'd lock down the entire building and to go back upstairs meant entrapping himself. There was no possible way for him to get Senator Ryan out the main level doors.

I left the elevator unoccupied and continued in my initial heading. I hit a dead end at the west wall, turned, and followed the corridor south. I found a steel door at the end of this corridor. The security device was disabled, and the door left partially open. I was sure that tampering with the security unit had set off some sort of alarm in the main security office. I hoped that meant that soon I'd be receiving backup, even though I knew I couldn't wait for them.

Pulling the heavy steel door open, I found myself staring down another dimly lit corridor.

I was sure that this wall was the southern end of the building and what lay down this corridor must be a passageway under 5th Street. I suppose, much like me, no one outside of the building's security force would be aware of this door and the passage beyond it. Except for the Tourist, always the Tourist. The son of a bitch had methods of attaining information that astounded me.

With my gun poised in front of me, I carefully made my way down the shadowed corridor. I could immediately tell people rarely used the corridor. There were streams of lightly dusted cobwebs high in the corners. Most of the lights were out or attempting to flicker out for good. There were small cracks in the walls and ceiling, surrounded by rust stains from decades of rainwater bleeding through.

I tried to prevent my shoes from clacking on the concrete floor as I moved down the corridor, but with the tight, bare walls, it was impossible to even prevent my breath from echoing. I moved incredibly slow, maybe waiting for something to jump out at me from the shadows, but nothing did.

I suspected this chase was a simple misdirection the Tourist had planned all along. The Tourist probably figured I would nip at his heels as he tried to make a getaway, and that was the reason he had one of his guys sitting in the hallway acting like building maintenance. I figured that doors being conveniently left open were also another way of throwing someone off his trail.

I considered doubling back when a blinding light flooded the corridor. A welcoming fresh air blew into my face, accompanied by the unbearable heat and humidity of August evening.

When my eyes adjusted to the sunlight, I could see the way ahead. I moved toward the light in a frantic run as door quickly closed with a powerful boom, making the corridor vibrate. Mechanical squealing and the grinding of a machine awaking from a long sleep followed.

I was sure that this door wouldn't remain open. I'd be forced to take the long way back to the street. It wasn't the strangest feeling in the world as I approached the metal door and discovered the green light on the security pad was lit, which meant the door remained unlocked. The knob turned easily. I prepared for an eruption of gunfire as I pulled the door open.

There was a small room with an elevator system that carried a metal cart to the street surface. It was one of those strange things that I thought only existed in the movies. Of course, I've walked over the steel doors on the sidewalks before, but I never put much thought into their purpose. The cart was now at street level. I looked at the wall on my left and then right and found the elevator controls. I pushed the call button and impatiently waited as the cart descended and the steel doors on the sidewalk pulled back down. The elevator groaned as if the thing hadn't been used in a decade, which it probably hadn't. The steel doors fell flush with the street again and cut off the light. When the cart hit bottom, I jumped in and pushed the *Up* button until the thing finally got moving.

It seemed like an eternity until the doors opened again. The sunlight broke through and the elevator cart rose out of the earth. I received a dozen puzzled glances as I pulled the gate open and stepped from the cart and onto the sidewalk.

When I rotated my body to glimpse everything and everyone around me, I spotted one of the most baffling things I'd seen during the last week.

Mikhail Alexandrov, the Tourist, stood thirty feet from me. He was just over six feet tall, with short brown hair spotted with gray and eyes like emeralds. It was those eyes I noticed most of all. There was something cold and devious making those eyes unforgettable. On the previous two occasions we met, he modified the left side of his face to an appearance badly scarred by a fire. He made this alteration for the greater purpose of concealing his identity to play mind games with me. Now the fake scarring was gone, and the left side of his face was smooth and unmarked. This was the man I had known as Lucas. This was Sara's mystery informant, who claimed to be working for the CIA as a foreign consultant.

"Bravo, Harper. Absolutely splendid," he said and clapped.

"Get your hands up," I shouted as I raised my gun and found aim in the center of his chest.

The crowd on the sidewalk took in the moment of action.

"Oh, I don't think you'll be wanting to do that, not just yet anyhow. The fun is far from over. Get in the car," he said and stepped to the black limousine at the curb and opened the rear door.

"Put your hands up or I swear to God I'm going to put three holes through your goddamn black heart," I said, hoping for the man to do something foolish.

"Before you pull the trigger and end my wonderful existence, I have something you'll want to see. If you don't want to see it, then it will be a shame. You see, my friend, I have a great deal of leverage at this point."

"I know about the Blackstone file. I know all about Senator Andrew Ryan. I know who he really is and where he comes from and the men who have been backing him this entire time. You can't use a traitor like Senator Ryan as a bargaining chip with me."

"Do you really think you know? Or do you only know what I've led you to believe?"

Mikhail Alexandrov slowly lowered his right hand and began reaching for his trouser pocket.

"It's going to get very unpleasant for you if you continue to move."

"Please don't be stupid, Harper. Don't you think I could have killed you a hundred times over by now if that was what I wanted? Don't be naïve, my friend. I could have killed you in your own bed. Here, I have a video you really must see," he said.

I thought about how right he was. For that matter, Sara could have also taken me out countless times. I nodded for him to proceed carefully.

Mikhail removed his cell phone from his pocket and flipped it open. After punching several buttons, he turned it around so that I could see the screen. A video began playing. I felt insanely icy hands grip my heart and refuse to let go.

I saw the two most precious faces in that video. Clara and Kaylee were bound, gagged, and silently crying with terror. Their faces looked into mine, pleading for me to save them.

"I'll kill you where you stand if you don't let them go right now," I said as I felt the fear rapidly change to rage.

"Come now, Harper. If I die, then surely they will, too."

45

"You could have even hidden them in the vaults at Ft. Knox and I would have found them, Harper," the Tourist said as he turned off his phone and placed it back in his pocket.

"Just let them go now and I'll do whatever it is you want. They have nothing to do with this," I said.

"You're absolutely wrong, Harper. They have so much to do with everything I've set up. I told you I have a great deal of leverage against you. What I want is for you to get in the car. We'll call that step one. Step two will come shortly. You can keep your gun for now. You'll need it for later. Besides, I know very well you won't be stupid enough to use it against me. Unless you don't really care whether your wife and daughter live or die."

Reluctantly, I lowered my gun and slid the Glock back into the holster. I walked toward the Tourist in a state of defeat. I couldn't think my way out of this situation. Not only did I fear for the lives of my family, but also for the surrounding crowd. I was terrified of what the man would do to a crowd of innocent people if I continued to resist his demands.

While keeping my attention mostly fixed on Mikhail Alexandrov, I took a quick glance in the car before I slid in. Inside the back of the limousine was Senator Andrew

Ryan, the maintenance man I had briefly spoken with in the hallway, and beyond the lowered partition in the driver's seat was the man who had earlier played his own crazy game by proclaiming himself the Tourist while holding me hostage in the warehouse. I remembered Brandon had said his name was Mr. Smith.

Mr. Smith and the maintenance man were holding guns, but neither pointed at the senator or me. They were simply holding them to let us know they weren't messing around. It seemed like playtime was over for them, and now it was time to crack knuckles and get down to the bare bones of business.

I thought of Sara lying back at the warehouse. Of course, there was no way any of them could have known what had happened and that Sara was recently departed from this world. It hadn't appeared to me during the interaction between Sara and Mr. Smith that they planned on setting me free. I believe that they would have eventually returned to the warehouse with Clara and Kaylee and the Tourist would have finally had his misguided revenge. None of them questioned my presence at the senate building. I thought of Mr. Smith and if Sara was really his wife, as they had claimed. If Mr. Smith were aware of her recent departure from life, he would abruptly turn and put a slug into me. I thought about these things but said nothing.

Slipping inside the limo, I sat on the bench seat beside the senator. The Tourist stepped inside, took the remaining empty seat beside the maintenance man, and closed the door. An eruption of panic tore through me as the door closed and cut off the sunlight. Was my life going to end tragically in the back of this limo? I expected an amusing grin from the Tourist as he raised his gun to deliver a single shot to my forehead, completing the final chapter of my life.

The limo jolted forward as we headed down the busy D.C. streets. Three patrol cars flew by us in the direction of the Capitol.

What the Tourist said next was beyond my comprehension at that place and time.

"I have big plans for you today, Harper. You see that I've kept you alive all this time for a reason. I found and seized your fleeing family for a reason. When I said that your family was my bargaining leverage, I didn't really mean it as simple as getting you into this car, but so much more. In fact, what I'm going to have you do today will not only be challenging for you, but possibly suicidal as well. I want you to assassinate Senator Alan Frost."

"What did you say?" I asked.

I shook my head, trying to get a thousand thoughts in order. Was this man completely serious? Did the Tourist really think I'd kill off Senator Ryan's competition for the sheer hell of it? But the second I thought of how stupid it was, I immediately realized how nearly perfect it was.

The man must have realized that I'd do anything within my power to keep my family safe. When he said he had the perfect leverage, I never would have thought that he would go beyond the limits of sanity to get me to perform murder for him.

"You had me running around the city this week trying to save people so that you could later kidnap my family and use them against me so that I would kill for you?"

"No, I had you running around the city falsely believing that you could make a difference with the outcome. Despite what I promised you, I wasn't going to give you a chance to save those people. Those four people had far too much knowledge about the Blackstone project. We couldn't let them live with the knowledge they held over us. If we hadn't taken the actions that we did, the entire plan could have been jeopardized," Mikhail said.

The word *we* worked into my thoughts and stuck. I suddenly understood everything. In my mind, all the tumblers of the baffling lock fell into place. I now fully understood that Senator Ryan was behind the four murders. He was the mastermind behind the entire ordeal from day one. I knew the story behind his rise to power and the plan Kiril Novilov set in motion decades ago. Senator Ryan wasn't the victim of the Tourist but was his employer. Senator Ryan had played the part as well as or maybe even better than Sara had.

I turned to the senator and said, "So it didn't matter much to you that this man and his team kidnapped your wife and child and later kills your wife and dumps her body in a park like some goddamn garbage?"

"My wife would be alive today if it hadn't been for her curiosity getting the better of her. I'm sorry you failed to realize that Agent Caster. You see, my wife, to my reluctance, was able to get into my personal safe. Don't ask me how she did it, because I didn't have the combination written anywhere and I certainly never told her what it was. Perhaps she hired someone to get into it while I was at work. I really don't know, and I suppose it doesn't matter at this point in time. She found my files, you see. I had a ledger containing the names of men and women who have contributed to my success. I had files given to me by Kiril Novilov before I left Russia at the age of nineteen. There were critical documents in that safe containing everything I was desperately trying to hide from the public view. There are important names in those files. These are names that you know, Harper. If the world learned the true identities of these men and women, there would be major chaos that would shake the U.S. governmental system down to the very foundation," Senator Ryan said and folded his hands in his lap.

"You set up the home invasion and kidnapping of your wife and child. You made it appear as if someone were trying to cripple your political career, but all the while, you were trying to conceal your greatest secret. Of course, you couldn't have your own son killed. Not an innocent child, especially since he doesn't know your secret. You might be a monster, but you still love your only son. Dillon knows nothing of who you really are or your big plans, so your friend here released him a few days later. You wanted the world to see that your threat of hunting the kidnappers down was solid and they therefore got scared and let him go," I said and looked from the senator to the Tourist.

"Exactly right, Agent Caster. Unfortunately, Katherine spoke with Lewis Rockwell and showed him the files. It's too bad. I liked Lewis and the boatload of money he sent my way over the years. Did you know Lewis was a full-blooded American through and through? Imagine what someone like that would do if he found out the true identity of a man he was supporting was really Russian? He contacted me, demanded back the millions he'd contributed, and claimed he was going to blow the lid off the whole thing. How could a man that smart really think he was going to live another day knowing what he did? Did he really think I'd send him a refund check, then simply slink away into the night, and never to be heard from again? Of course, it was so much less of a headache to have my associate here take care of Lewis. Sometimes you just have to know when to cut your losses," Senator Ryan said.

I don't know why, but my eyes kept lowering from the senator's deep shaded brown eyes to his hands. It appeared as if his right hand continued to creep from his lap to his beltline.

"What about Kiril Novilov? Did you finally decide to get your revenge when he attempted to blow you up all those years ago?" I asked Mikhail.

Senator Ryan said, "Well, yes and no. You could say that a personal score was settled, but I decided to have Kiril knocked off because I no longer have patience for stupidity. Kiril was brilliant in some respects, but extremely selfish when it came to sharing the well-deserved wealth. If you like, you could even say that I've become too greedy to be controlled by someone like Kiril. I no longer wanted to feel like the puppet but become its master. Now I suppose you could say that the United States will be my puppet and I alone will tug the strings as I see fit. I've devoted my entire life to Kiril's insane idea. I worked with Kiril in Russia for over ten years learning about the U.S. He taught me everything he thought I needed to know. I've spent twenty years in the states working my way up the political ladder. With all of that devotion, shouldn't I be the one to reap the rewards?"

I didn't have an answer for him. Instead, I asked a question of my own.

"Who are the other two? I figured out that Kyle Sawyer wasn't supposed to be victim number four, but he had become an alteration to your plan after Brandon Harris emailed him a copy of the Blackstone file."

"Ah, yes, poor Mr. Sawyer. That was a wonderful shot, considering all the factors I was facing. Wouldn't you agree?" Mikhail asked.

"All I know is that you killed a young man because his friend was in trouble, and he was doing everything possible to help him out. Kyle Sawyer went to the CIA, even with all the computer crimes mounted against him, in order to help Brandon out of a nearly impossible situation," I said, and leaned back in the seat.

I wasn't feeling fear any longer, but instead, I was feeling a rage and loathing toward both men and their secret plans for seizing control of the country.

"Well, Mr. Harris is the only one to blame for the death of his friend. If he hadn't been so bold to send out a desperate email, Mr. Sawyer would be alive and still in hiding."

"You didn't answer my question. Who are victims four and five?"

"We'll get to that later, Harper," Mikhail said.

I felt sick to my stomach when I said, "They're my wife and daughter, aren't they?"

His smile neither confirmed nor denied my suspicion.

I turned to Senator Ryan and said, "For you, it's about absolute power. You've gone through immeasurable lengths to take the seat of the most powerful person on the planet and sacrificed your own wife and political supporters to make it happen. You want no controlling hand other than your own." I looked at Mikhail and said, "And for you, it's all about revenge. Kiril Novilov heard the rumor that you were trying to overthrow him, but you outwitted him and led him to believe you were dead. You remained hidden for years until you had the perfect opportunity to join forces with Senator Ryan and remove Kiril permanently from the picture. But you're not finished there, are you? You decided to get even on two fronts. You figured why not drag me into the picture, make me run around like a chicken without a head, trying to figure out this whole mess of a situation you created. So, what your friend Mr. Smith told me earlier was true, wasn't it? Your wife and daughter were visiting the U.S. when I was nothing more than a patrolman. I remember their names and their faces, Alyona and Anna Alexandrov. They unfortunately got caught at the wrong place and the wrong time and were killed by a couple of gangbangers during a grocery store holdup. According to you, I failed to save them, right? So now you figured it was time to pull me into your plan so that you could take my wife and daughter and exact your revenge. Do you want me to feel the same sadness you experienced when you lost your family? I'm right, aren't I?"

"Very insightful, Harper," Mikhail said.

"What makes you think that I'm going to assassinate Senator Frost when I believe that you're going to kill my wife and daughter, no matter what I do?"

I looked at Senator Ryan again. I saw that his hand had moved up his beltline and now his fingers were hidden under his jacket.

"There is no way you will ever know, Harper. If you don't do what I ask, they will die for sure. If you take out Senator Frost, the possibility of their survival will be much greater," Mikhail said.

I thought about my gun tucked in the shoulder holster. I knew if I yanked it free, I could at least take out two of them before they gunned me down. I desperately wanted to take that chance, but I knew if I did, Clara and Kaylee would never come home again.

"Why do you feel the need to remove Senator Frost, anyway? He certainly isn't a threat to you now. You know very well that when you went public about the kidnapping and offered a reward for the kidnapper's head, your supporters skyrocketed. Senator Frost doesn't have a chance to be president," I said, trying to get a full handle on the plan.

"You're correct, Agent Caster. Senator Frost really isn't much of a threat to my campaign. However, you can never really be so sure how the tide will turn. Can you, Mr. Alexandrov?" Senator Ryan said as his hand easily slipped from his jacket.

At first, I didn't know what to expect. I was looking at a gun gripped in Senator Ryan's right hand. With no hesitation the gun coughed, driving Mikhail Alexandrov back into the seat. The gun's attention quickly shifted to the decoy maintenance man, followed by two muffled reports as red blossoms opened on his shirt. The senator shifted his aim once again and delivered one final shot into Mikhail's chest. His body slightly jolted, as it offered no resistance.

The driver, Mr. Smith, glanced over his shoulder as he maneuvered the limousine through the streets of D.C.

"It's done, Mr. Smith. Please continue as you were," Senator Ryan said.

"Yes, sir," Mr. Smith said as he turned his attention back to the streets.

"It's unfortunate that Mr. Alexandrov believed that Mr. Smith was his friend. I employed Mr. Smith to work with Mr. Alexandrov and not for him. A simple misunderstanding, I suppose. I hope the so-called Tourist doesn't find me at fault for my unexpected actions. Like I said before, my patience has grown thin. I have little desire for stupid games of revenge. It doesn't matter to me that your wife and child are being held against their will, or if they find a gruesome death. I'm sorry, Harper. It doesn't even matter to me that Mikhail wanted you to kill Senator Frost. It was all part of his game, but certainly not mine. I never wanted to play his game. I indulged only until I received exactly what I wanted. I had only asked him to silence those who knew of the Blackstone file. I didn't expect him to bring an additional mess into this situation."

As the gun trained on me, I felt my hands automatically go up in surrender.

"I guess it's a cutthroat kind of business. It's time to keep your enemies close and your friends much closer, huh?" I asked.

"Exactly right. I'm going to be the President of the United States and no one on Earth could possibly stop me now. I'm like a fucking steamroller on a rampage and I'm going to flatten anyone who gets in my way," Senator Ryan said.

I saw two things just then that Senator Ryan hadn't noticed.

I saw that somehow Brandon Harris was driving my government sedan in the left lane beside the limousine.

I also saw that Mikhail Alexandrov's right hand twitched.

46

With careful eyes, I glanced at Brandon. His sight was constantly shifting from the road before him to the tinted back windows of the limousine. He was keeping a steady pace with us. I had no idea how he had undone the handcuffs and started my car, or why he was coming after the men who had snatched him from halfway around the world and at gunpoint forced him to bend to their sadistic will.

I didn't know what he had planned, but his presence gave me a ray of hope when my situation seemed incredibly grim.

"So why the chaos in the conference room? What point did that make?" I asked.

"Oh, that. Well, the world has seen the beginning of this entire ordeal. I thought it seemed fitting that they're given some sort of conclusion to this whole mess. What better way than a presidential candidate overcoming immeasurable odds?"

"Innocent people died for a pointless reason."

"It happens every day, Harper. However, those people will be cherished on this very traumatic day in our nation's history," Senator Ryan said, and smiled.

I wanted to hit him, hard.

"So, what are you going to do now? Are you going to kill a federal agent who knows the truth? I don't think that would look very good on your résumé," I said as I tried to keep Senator Ryan's attention fixed on me and not on the car beside us.

"Yes, but it certainly won't appear that way. Everyone knows that a band of killers took me from the conference room. Luckily, you were there to give chase and assist in my safe release. Unfortunately for you, a gunman fatally wounded you during my rescue. I wish to thank you in advance, Harper. Imagine how big this story is going to be. Everything from the kidnapping of my family to my wife's murder, the attempt to force me to withdraw my campaign, the murder of my biggest financial supporter, and eventually my kidnapping and attempted murder. Holy crap, Harper, the press will write about this until the end of time. I'll have books, television movies, and motion pictures praising the new president who wouldn't back down from any fight. I'll become a goddamn icon for a stronger nation that will no longer give into threats of tyranny and terror."

"You also have the delusion that your plan is without flaws. I think you shot Mikhail a little too soon. You still need him for damage control."

"Whatever issues arise, I'll deal with on my own from now on."

"If you say so," I said and smiled.

"What are you talking about?"

"What you failed to realize during your quest for power and vanity is that Mikhail took out Kyle Sawyer a little too late. Kyle had already spilled the details about you and gave the CIA copies of the Blackstone file stolen from your computer Brandon hacked into all those years ago. I imagine you deleted the files when you figured out someone compromised your computer's security firewall. Then again, information isn't ever really deleted from a hard drive. It must have been when you contacted Mikhail to hunt Brandon and Kyle down. Of course, you still kept a hard copy of your ledger and files in your safe that your wife eventually discovered. The CIA has their hands on everything that was in those files. If I were you, I'd take some of those millions you've acquired from campaign contributions and find an excellent plastic surgeon to alter your features. Then you can find a quiet corner of the world to hide in until your miserable death. I can honestly say that probably all the government agencies and the local police are on the lookout for you."

I was bluffing to the extreme. I was throwing out everything my mind could think of to cause Senator Ryan to panic and rethink his strategy. I was also buying time as I waited for Brandon to make some sort of move.

"Bullshit. If that were true, I'd already be in handcuffs. It takes more skill than that to con a lifelong conman."

"I'm trying to give you an open door to step through. If you don't want to take it, if you'd rather spend the rest of your days in a tiny cell and being gang-raped in the shower, then I suppose that's your business. By the way, do you realize that silencers on guns are illegal? I'll have to remind the authorities to tack that onto your long list of broken laws when they arrest you," I said, and smiled again.

I saw Brandon take a sharp left on 16th Avenue. My hope began draining until I saw him accelerate as he took an immediate right at the next intersection.

Senator Ryan released a heartfelt laugh and said, "I like you, Harper. Even with Death's hands reaching for you now, you manage to keep a level head. You're one calm and collected FBI guy. If you didn't know the things that you do about me, I might have offered a proposal for you to join my staff at the White House."

Mr. Smith braked for a red light.

A block away, my sedan came around the corner in a sideways skid. The car leaped forward under Brandon's command and my government vehicle thundered toward us.

Although Senator Ryan still had the gun pointed at me, I lowered my right hand and reached for the seat belt.

"I'm afraid that seat belt safety can't even save you now, Harper."

"I'd buckle up if I were you because this is going to get ugly," I said as the belt latched.

Senator Ryan followed my gaze. I saw his expression turn from amusement to wonder, and finally to outright terror, as my vehicle hammered into the left side of the limousine.

Tortured metal screamed. The entire limo heaved to the right. The tires jumped the curb, a bus bench disappeared beneath the chassis, and a dozen pedestrians suddenly scattered. Senator Ryan drastically slammed against the left side of the vehicle and quickly rebounded like a pinball to my side of the backseat as our bodies collided. The impact pitched the lifeless maintenance man against the Tourist and the two bodies became one in the chaos.

My head rapped hard enough against the tinted window that the tempered glass shattered into hundreds of tiny pieces. Daylight flooded through the broken window. My fingers fumbled until I found the release of the seat belt. Pulling the door lever, I fell out, collapsing onto the sidewalk.

"Hey, don't move. Help will be on the way. Just stay still," one pedestrian said as he ran to me.

"Harper, are you all right?" Brandon asked as he circled the limo and kneeled beside me.

Brandon's face, lightly powdered in white from the airbag's deployment, watched me. Although obviously shaken up, Brandon appeared unharmed.

I winced when I took a breath. A sharp pain exploded in violent ripples down my left side. The ribs I'd injured during my first car accident today intensified their argument. As Senator Ryan had taken flight inside the car, his broad-framed body crushed against me like a boulder.

Two severe accidents on the same day and somehow I survived them both.

"That was one hell of a game plan," I sarcastically said as I placed my hand on my injured side and gently applied pressure.

"Yeah, I know. Can you believe I just came up with that?" Brandon said excitedly.

I heard a siren close by. Through the gathering crowd of people, I could see several patrol cars weaving their way through the lingering traffic.

"Help me up, Brandon."

"Just sit still. An ambulance will be along in a minute."

"Just help me up damnit."

Brandon moved to my left side, took my arm, and carefully wrapped it over his shoulders. We slowly stood. I immediately felt nauseous, but I managed to hold back the vomit that was working its way up.

Several men and women were huddled at the open rear door. I could hear some of their comments and the change in their tone of voices as they realized that a presidential candidate was inside. I didn't know whether Senator Ryan was alive or dead, and I really didn't care.

My mind felt like I was trying to swim through a maze, and I was rapidly running out of breath.

"All right, folks, let's just back up and give these people some breathing room," a policeman said as he worked his way through the crowd.

I knew that Senator Ryan was alive when I heard the same man who told me to relax make the same comment. Against their better judgment, Senator Ryan was pulling himself from the wreckage of the limousine. A deep gash ran down the left side of his face. Blood was coming out in a steady stream. He held his left arm cradled tightly against his chest. The gun was still in his right hand.

"Oh, my God, he's got a gun!" a woman shrieked.

Three policemen immediately looked up and automatically withdrew their sidearms as their eyes confirmed the woman's statement.

"Just hold it right there!" a policeman said.

Suddenly Senator Ryan had three guns fixed on him.

When Senator Ryan fully removed himself from the backseat, in a half stand, half crouch, he stumbled and fell against the limo.

"I was being held hostage. Call for an ambulance. I need medical help."

"We've got a couple of ambulances on the way. I need you to put the gun down right now, Senator Ryan. Everything is all right now," the blond policeman said.

Senator Ryan looked at me, a thin line of blood went into his left eye, and he hastily wiped at it with the back of his hand. He looked at me again in a strange way, as if he were trying to figure out where he had seen me before.

Senator Ryan pushed himself into a wobbling stance, raised the gun, and said, "He's one of them! He's one of the kidnappers!"

"Drop it," several of the policemen shouted.

"Listen to me, he's one of the kidnappers. He's got a gun," Senator Ryan screeched like a child throwing a tantrum. He fiercely swiped at the blood in his eye again.

Now I had their attention as the policemen instantly accepted Senator Ryan's proclamation. It hadn't surprised me that the police would immediately believe a presidential candidate over someone like me. Hell, the police didn't even know I was with the FBI.

"Hold your fire. I'm Special Agent Harper Caster. My gun is in my shoulder holster and my badge is in my jacket pocket. Senator Ryan isn't who he appears to be. Get him to drop the gun, goddamnit!" I shouted.

I realized how stupid I must have sounded when I told them that the senator wasn't who he appeared to be. I had just confirmed who he was.

"You heard him. Drop the gun and we'll sort this out," one policeman said.

"He's got a gun. I'm ordering you to fire. He's part of the plot to assassinate me!" Senator Ryan bellowed.

Senator Ryan locked back the hammer of his gun.

A deafening shot echoed throughout the downtown area. I recoiled from the sound and glanced down to see the hole in my chest. There wasn't a hole at all. My attention snapped to the three policemen, and I saw they were equally confused.

A crimson bloom rapidly flourished on Senator Ryan's white shirt. He stumbled, regained balance, and rotated to face the limo.

The crowd panicked as another shot rang out. Dozens of bodies scattered in all directions as the chaos accelerated.

I ducked and ran to avoid becoming a static target. I didn't want to reach for my gun and receive a chest full of lead by the police for my actions.

Senator Ryan's throat came open to a river of red. He pitched backward hard onto the sidewalk, the gun spinning from his grip, and he desperately tried to stem the flow of life flooding from him.

Mikhail Alexandrov stepped from the limo in worse condition than Senator Ryan and I combined. The Tourist's body was a mangled mess. His left arm was sickly twisted as if void of all bones. His right foot was rotated the wrong direction, and his nose was horrifically cocked to one side, pouring blood across his mouth.

Before anyone could comprehend exactly what was going on, Mikhail raised the gun and fired three more rounds into the writhing body of Senator Ryan. I couldn't tell where the bullets had struck, but they had completed the job as I saw the senator offer another twitch and then remain still.

Unlike Senator Ryan, Mikhail Alexandrov didn't receive a single warning from the policemen. Guns erupted as the three policemen hammered round after round into Mikhail's chest. He fell against the battered limo and quickly steadied himself. He appeared unfazed, as if they had fired paintballs instead of bullets.

As I reached for my gun, I understood what Senator Ryan hadn't realized before he tried to execute the man. Mikhail Alexandrov was far more prepared than the senator had expected.

"He's got a vest on!" I yelled to the policemen as I pulled my gun free.

Mikhail raised his gun and found me in his sights.

Each of us also raised our aim and fired once.

Four shots tore through the unprotected part of Mikhail Alexandrov's body that offered immediate death.

As his body made a slow descent against the limo, leaving a gruesome trail of blood and brain matter, I thought that the lives of my wife and daughter were dying with him. He had taken them, and I didn't even know where to begin looking.

The limo's driver door opened, and Mr. Smith stepped out. Unlike Senator Ryan and the Tourist, Mr. Smith wasn't going down with a fight. He held up his hands in surrender.

"Please don't shoot. I was being held against my will," he said as he walked toward us.

"Hold it right there," the police demanded as their aim found a new target.

"They took me hostage. I'm an American citizen."

As Mr. Smith stepped onto the curb, something happened that I never would have seen coming.

Brandon Harris balled his fist and delivered a punch to Mr. Smith's right jaw with such velocity and precision that Oscar De La Hoya would have been envious.

Mr. Smith spun, staggered, and went down in an unconscious heap.

"I bet that felt good," I said.

"No, it actually hurt like hell. I might have broken my wrist," Brandon said.

It was then that I saw the police had trained their guns on the two of us, still unaware of exactly how we fit into this mess.

I lowered my gun to the pavement, smiled, and said, "All right, boys, all right. How about if I slowly reach for my badge and then you can put the guns down?"

Brandon laughed a little as he gently flexed his hand and said, "Yep, definitely broken."

47

After Brandon tried and failed at getting another GPS location on Clara's phone, an idea came to mind. I was rapidly pushing my thoughts back to the last few days. My idea was more or less a Hail Mary, but it was the only thing I had to go on right now.

I had finished my part of the three-ring circus that transpired after two people died in front of me with hundreds of horrified witnesses. I gave my statement and promised to follow up every step of the nightmarish journey since Monday by delivering a detailed report to Director Gill sometime tomorrow.

Director David Gill knew my urgency to leave the scene. He even promised that he'd contact me as soon as possible and assist in the search for my family.

After I had hunted down a man named Burt Milton, who was the man that nearly ran down a terrified Dillon Ryan on the dark highway, I received his best guess of the location where he had found the boy on the road before taking him to the nearest hospital. The area was nearly forty miles outside the city limits. The location was rich with Virginia landscape, and I thought it would take more than a miracle to find a cabin in the mass of endless green.

I called up everyone I could think of and asked for help. Volunteers came from everywhere. Friends, family, coworkers, and even people I'd never met before joined in the search. I was glad and thankful to all the people who were taking time away from their families to help in the search for mine.

Two police choppers circled the woods overhead with their spotlights cutting through the night. We were looking for a house or a cabin hiding somewhere in the forest's deepness. Dillon Ryan had spent several days held captive in the house before being turned loose to walk through the woods and find safety. I had a hunch that just maybe Clara and Kaylee had taken Dillon's place. It was a long shot, but like I said, it was the only thing I had to go on. The house, wherever the hell it was, might be the only hope that my wife and daughter were alive.

FBI Director David Gill was at my side. He was one of the best allies I'd had over the years. He'd risked his own career more times than I could count to cover my ass when the ax came down and the politicians wanted someone to be thrown under the bus. I'd had my share of mistakes made during investigations, and it always seemed that David was there to clean up my mess. It didn't surprise me that he was here now. Over the years, his family and mine had become close friends.

"We will find them. You know that don't you, Harper?" David said.

"Yeah, I do. I've got a feeling they're close."

"Good. No matter what, keep the hope alive. We'll find them alive and well. You have my promise on that."

Even though I strongly believed what he had said, there was a painful realization coursing through my mind and heart that brought out the possibility that they were actually in the opposite situation of David's statement. I couldn't help it, but a small part of me thought that just maybe their lives were lost already.

I shook my head, trying to chase away the bad images until I knew for sure my wife and daughter's fate.

During our search, David changed the conversation as he was trying to take my mind off the immediate matters.

"I'm glad you solved the case. It's too bad for Senator Ryan that the Tourist brought you into everything. If it hadn't been for your persistence, the man would have no doubt become president. I only wonder what Senator Ryan would have done with his newly acquired power," David said.

"If things hadn't turned the way they did, it would have been Kiril Novilov who eventually benefited the most. While we were in the limo, Senator Ryan mentioned that there were other important names in the Blackstone file that many of us know. Somehow or someway, these guys had a major plan in the works that would have made Kiril and many others far more powerful. Just imagine what the most powerful man in the world could do," I said.

"You know that after this search is over, you have a mountain of paperwork to do. We still don't have any hard evidence proving who Senator Ryan really is. As far as the public knows, he was a man placed in an unfortunate situation, lost his wife by the hands of the kidnappers, and in the end, he lost his own life. No matter what comes out of the woodwork, that's all the public will ever know. Millions of people will idolize Senator Ryan for his undoubtedly brave actions against the men who tried to crush an American dream. I'm not saying he was brave by any means, not when I know the real story, but that's how the world will see it. That's exactly the way he wanted people to see it, only he wasn't planning on dying in the process," David said.

"In any case, Senator Ryan got what he deserved," I whispered, as there were now several people within earshot.

"Mr. Smith, whose real name is Adam O'Quinn, is sticking to his story about being held captive. He claims that Senator Ryan and Mikhail Alexandrov kept him in fear for his life if he didn't do exactly as they instructed," David said.

"I can counter that statement with the facts. So can Brandon. Mr. Smith and Sara kept us hostage in that warehouse. You guys found her body, didn't you?"

"Yeah, we found her. I can't believe she was able to fool us into believing she worked within DHS."

"Hey, you just got a phone call from someone posing as Secretary Nivens of DHS. I'm the one who worked with her for days and I didn't even pick up on it. She was a world-class actress and con artist. I'll give her that. Even though he said nothing about it, I have a feeling Brandon Harris hacked into several secure government computers and made her claim to be working within the DHS appear legitimate in the beginning. Neither of us disputed her clearance to work on the case, especially when the damn computers told us that she was one of us. It's become a computer age and we believe what the things tell us. It seems to be our downfall for letting technology take over," I said.

I turned my attention to the helicopter hovering above us. The thunder of its blades and the rush of wind made it difficult to hold any kind of conversation.

A crackle sounded over my handheld radio and quickly brought it to my ear. The reception wasn't coming in very clear, but I caught several important words. One of the helicopter pilots was saying something about finding a house buried in the dense woods.

I stopped, closed my eyes, and concentrated on that voice. When I heard the pilot for the second time, I broke into a run. David and the rest of the men and women close by understood that something was happening.

"The house is up ahead, and it's on fire," I yelled to David over my shoulder.

It wasn't long before I could see the orange glow of the fire breaking through the trees.

Only a moment ago I had been feeling the full effects of the week weighing on my tired body, but now my muscles were alive with an energy I'd thought wasn't there. I ran as if Hell was chasing after me or maybe it was Hell I was running to because as I came into a partial clearing, I saw the house engulfed in flames.

A euphoria washed over me as I began screaming Clara and Kaylee's names. I screamed so fiercely that my throat burned in protest. Reaching the front door of the house, I peered through the half-circle window centered on the door. Nearly everything inside the house was on fire.

I didn't pay attention when several gunshots went off to my left. Maybe half a dozen people in the woods were engaged in battle. Only one thing came to mind, and that was how much I needed to be inside that burning house. I knew my family was inside. I knew that someone had purposely set the fire when they heard the helicopters overhead and wanted to destroy all evidence before the manhunt team reached the house. Whoever had set the blaze had not considered Clara and Kaylee as human beings, but as evidence of their crimes that needed to be burned to unidentified remains.

I hoped that whoever had fled the house with the desire of escaping prosecution found justice swiftly delivered from the end of a barrel.

I tried the doorknob, but found the house secured. My right leg went out like a battering ram. The thick wood door gave way under the first strike. A rush of flames blew out the door as my entrance offered the fire much-needed oxygen. A thick cloud of black smoke rolled out, following the flames.

I kept an unsteady balance as I crouched and shuffled inside the house. I used the collar of my jacket to help filter the air, which didn't help much, but it was better than nothing. My watery eyes rapidly shifted around. I was trying to take everything in as I searched for my family. When I yelled out again, over the raging noise of the fire, I could hear something in one of the back rooms. It was a pounding that sounded like someone was trying to break free from a tomb.

I stayed low in an awkward scramble as I went toward the noise. When I reached one of the back rooms, the lowest part of the closet door heaved out but held. There was a latch with a padlock just above the doorknob.

"If you can hear me, get down! Get low!" I yelled.

When the door quit banging, I pulled my gun and fired. I tugged at the damaged lock, but it held. It took two more rounds before the lock came apart. I threw the latch back and yanked open the door.

Clara and Kaylee were huddled together on the floor. Their shirts were pressed over their noses and mouths. Through watery eyes, they looked at me in confusion for a moment before they understood I was here to get them out, to get them safe. I only allowed a snapshot of a second of embrace before I pulled them off me, seized their hands, and made for the front door.

Red embers were coming down in a storm. Smoke had built up so much that we were down on hands and knees and shuffling to the front door. The ceiling crashed down in the room to my right and threw flames directly at us. I urged them forward with words of encouragement delivered with intensity.

I saw hands reaching through the flames of the front door. Large hands were grasping for Kaylee. An instant terror arose in me. I didn't know if the hands were those of someone who had been assisting in the search for the house or if one of the men who fled the house had come back to finish what he started. I almost reached for my gun before I saw David's face. His terrified eyes found us in dense smoke.

With the help of others, we broke free from the burning house and into the blissful fresh air. Even though a coughing fit had overtaken all of us, we came together as a loving family should. My arms wrapped around them. I thanked God we all made it out of the inferno unscathed.

"I can't believe you got us out," Clara said in between each cough.

"You knew I would come for you. You knew I would find you no matter what. You know there's no reason to ever doubt it," I said and hugged them again.

After a few minutes, Clara and Kaylee were looked after by a couple of paramedics that were part of the search team. David had pulled me off to the side to talk. I could tell by the look on his face that it wasn't good. I knew that look pretty well.

"We took two men down that were running from the house. They fired first, we didn't have a choice," he said.

"Sure, I understand. They knew the risks before they made the actions."

"Harper, I also got a call a minute ago. The policemen that were stationed at Brandon Harris's hospital room door went inside after one of the nurses checked on him and found it empty. Somehow, someway Brandon eluded his guards and slipped out of the hospital and has now vanished. They don't know how he did it, because the windows don't open and there wasn't an adjoining room that he could have snuck into."

I was thinking two things at that time. I thought: *Good for him,* and *damnit.* Brandon deserved time served in jail for the computer crimes he'd committed over the years. However, I had no hard feelings against him. The kid saved my life twice. The only thing I dreaded about him making a clean getaway was that he still had all of the information containing the Blackstone File and the mountain of dirt he was holding on Senator Ryan, Kiril Novilov, and Mikhail Alexandrov. All of that information was now in the wind with him.

I didn't know what would become of my career if those files weren't retrieved. As far as anyone knew, besides me, Senator Ryan was exactly who he appeared to be. America saw him as a man with a strong desire to change our nation for the better.

The men of the CIA, who briefly had Kyle Sawyer in protective custody before he died, had their knowledge of the real Senator Ryan. However, like me, the CIA had suspicions, but nothing concrete.

I thought that no matter what, David was right. Regardless of whether we could retrieve the information about Senator Ryan's true identity, the public would never know. Something this sinister would stay hidden deep in the government's secured database and never be whispered again.

The world would see Senator Ryan as an icon who died for his beliefs in making a stronger, even more virtuous country.

It was a pity there were too many damn secrets.

48

"Despite what you think, you're not going to get away with it. I've got you in my sights and I'm coming at you like a freight train. You can stand strong and raise your forces, but I'm going to take you down in the end," I said.

"I beg to differ. I'm smarter, more strategic, and flat-out braver than you could ever hope to be."

"Well, make your move and we'll just see," I said.

"All right, I sure hope you're ready."

"Ready and waiting."

She made her move.

I made mine.

"Oh, come on!" she said.

"I just took Eastern Europe, which means I've conquered the board and won the game. I told you to be ready," I said and laughed.

"Blah, blah, blah. This is a stupid game anyway," Kaylee said, and knocked down her remaining pieces.

"No need to be a sore loser. *Risk* is the game of strategic conquest. It says so right here on the box," I said and pointed.

"Blah, blah, blah," Kaylee said again and began collecting the game pieces.

"You sound exactly like your father when I whip his tail at that game," Clara said as she came into the living room with a tray of assorted cookies and glasses of lemonade.

"Never in a hundred years could you beat me at this game," I said as I folded the board and placed it back in the box.

"I'm up for a game if you don't think so," Clara said and took a seat on the sofa beside me.

"Well, I'm kind of tired right now. Winning the game is no easy feat, even for a smart guy like me. Kaylee, can you put the game back in the closet? Put it way back so that no one remembers it's there," I said and smiled.

"I knew it, big old chicken," Clara said and sipped from her glass.

The doorbell rang, and I raced Kaylee to the door. I said, "Oh, I'll get it. Don't you have chores to do?"

"Whatever," she said, and headed for the kitchen.

"Good evening, sir. I've got a package for you. I just need your signature," the FedEx guy said, and held out the electronic board.

I signed, accepted the package, and said, "Thanks. Have a great day."

He nodded, and I closed the door.

"Who's it for?" Kaylee called from the kitchen.

"Someone who pays the bills around here," I called back.

I heard her tell me, "Whatever," again.

I flipped the large envelope over, gripped the string tab, and opened it. I frowned as I looked inside. There was nothing more than a small black box. I tipped the envelope over and the thing tumbled into my hand. I studied it for a minute before I realized what it was.

"What did you get?" Clara asked.

"I think it's a flash drive."

"Who's it from?"

I looked at the envelope label again and said, "There isn't a return address."

"Oh, the mystery deepens," Clara commented.

"I'll say."

"I want to see what's on it," Kaylee said, as she skipped from the kitchen to my side.

"I'll bet you'd rather play your mom at *Risk*. I don't know what's on here, but I just bet that it has nothing to do with you."

I went to the den and locked the door. At my computer, I slipped the flash drive into the USB port and waited. I had no idea what the hell this was or whom it was from, but I had a feeling I wasn't going to like it.

I was wrong. I smiled when a screen opened and showed the contents of the flash drive memory. There was one folder titled *Blackstone* and a single Word document. I opened the *Blackstone* folder and spent the next hour reading the material Brandon had stolen from Senator Ryan's computer three years ago. Senator Ryan was right. There were names in here I recognized. Some men and women mentioned in the Blackstone file were people who the new president would appoint, pending Senate confirmation. Maybe I was naïve to think that Kiril Novilov had simply placed one man in position. In fact, there were more than a dozen people ready to fill positions of major influence. They had a secret army lying in wait. It was a real-life game of *Risk*. It was a game of strategic conquest.

I finally had the proof, the evidence I needed to show that Senator Ryan wasn't at all who he appeared to be. He was a man who had been wearing a cleverly disguised mask and had almost fooled a nation into making him one of the most powerful men in the world.

I closed the file and was about to remove the flash drive from the computer when I remembered that there was another document. I opened the file and grinned when I saw it was a letter that read:

Dear Harper,

I trust all is well. Sorry about my vanishing act and leaving you in the lurch. I knew that regardless of any deal I could strike with the government agencies that wish to prosecute me for the serious computer crimes I've committed over the years, I would be facing some hard times in prison. I'm not a prison kind of guy. I'm more like a free bird that loves to fly. I hope you can understand that.

I'm glad to learn that your wife and daughter are just fine. I'm truly sorry that I wasn't able to help you uncover their whereabouts. I honestly didn't know. At least everything turned out all right.

As promised, I've let my fingers do their magic and corrected your financial situation back to its previous status as you wished. It was the least I could do.

On this flash drive, you will find all the information I collected from Senator Ryan's computer I used to blackmail Kiril Novilov several years ago. Even though he paid the money I asked for, I just couldn't seem to let the information go and forever keep my silence. Maybe the Boy Scout in me knew that one day I would have to divulge this information and let the world know the big secret. So here it is. Do what you will with it. That file was a burden I lived with for so long and I am no longer its keeper. I leave it up to you to decide the next move.

In case you had a notion to let the world know, I've installed a command on this flash drive. If you press F10, the information on this drive will be downloaded onto twenty-four different public websites. At which point the contents will be unstoppable. Whether the information remains secrets hang in the balance of a simple button being pressed. Again, it's your move.

As for me, I think it's time to fly. The world is my playground and I'm just itching to see what kind of mischief I can get into.

Enjoy everything that you have, Harper. That's what makes you so special. I hope that someday I can get as lucky as you. Maybe one day I'll get married and have a child of my own. I might even invite you to the wedding. Ha-ha.

Brandon

P.S. All right, so I lied. I know I agreed to return your financials exactly as they were. Well, seeing everything that you went through, I couldn't keep that promise. Your bank and credit card balances have returned to the exact amount, but I made some adjustments when I was working on restoring your mortgage. The house is now yours free and clear.

I can hear you scolding me now. I don't want you to worry because the bank got their money courtesy of Kiril Novilov and his blackmail payment. Hey, it isn't like he'll need the money in Hell. Good luck and I wish you all the best.

I read the letter again. When I looked down, I realized my right index finger was hovering over the F10 key. I thought how easy it was that I could just press the key, and all the recent secrets that I had been fighting to uncover would travel across the world at breakneck speeds. A part of me knew that the world deserved to know. But the other part, that moral part, knew that it wasn't really my place to disclose such secrets.

I thought that the world needed a hero as much as it needed a villain. The two balanced each other. Good and evil. Right and wrong. To tell or not to tell, that was really the question.

Could I really keep the silence and let Senator Ryan be the hero?

I thought of Dillon Ryan, and my hand crept away from the keyboard. A wonderful kid like that deserved to think of his father as a hero, a savior. Didn't he? If Dillon discovered the truth about his father and the terrible things he had done to his wife, I didn't think the boy would ever rebound from something like that. I thought that by pressing the button, I would forever condemn the boy to a world he would emotionally spiral away from. He was a boy who would become a man and would forever be emotionally shut in. He would never trust another soul throughout the rest of his days. He would hate the world and its ugliness so much that he would be permanently blinded from its beauty and endless possibilities. Did I have the right to make such a choice?

There were a hundred other reasons running through my head that stayed my hand. But in the end, it was the child that I thought of most.

As much as I wanted to, I knew I couldn't destroy the flash drive and forever banish its existence. I would eventually pick up the phone today and call Director Gill and tell him what was now in my possession.

There was a gentle tap at the den door. I removed the flash drive and placed it in the lockbox in the bottom drawer of my desk. I stood and went to the door. Clara was leaning against the wall, arms clasped across her chest, and she was smiling.

"Is everything all right? You locked yourself in there so long I nearly called the rescue squad to come and break the door down," she said.

"Yep. Everything is just great," I said and gently kissed her.

"Since it's so hot outside, Kaylee worked out a surprise for you."

"Really? I love surprises. Where is she?"

"She's in the backyard waiting for you."

"But if it's so hot outside, why would she be out there with a surprise?"

"I guess you'll have to go investigate the case, Special Agent Caster."

"All right, I'm on it," I said and started for the back door.

Clara followed me in silence. Something was certainly strange with the whole deal, but I went along with it, anyway.

I looked out the back window and said, "I don't see her out there."

"Oh, she's out there. Go on and investigate," Clara said and pushed me outside.

"What is this, hide-and-seek or something?" I said as I studied the layout of the backyard and couldn't find my daughter.

I turned to look back at Clara. She gestured for me to continue the search.

When I took ten more steps, something moved quickly from behind the large elm. I saw a figure and then something the size of a red softball came at me. I didn't have time to dodge out of the way. The red water balloon caught me in the chest and exploded, immediately soaking my blue shirt. I took in a sharp breath as the ice-cold water covered my skin.

"Ha! How's that for strategy?" Kaylee called out as she burst into laughter and did a strange little dance.

"Here's what I think of it," I said as I ran for her.

Before I could get my hands on her, I spotted a yellow bucket hiding behind the tree. Inside the bucket were more than a dozen balloons filled with water. I changed course and went for the prize. Kaylee figured out what I was doing too late. As she tried to get the ammo before I did, I gripped one balloon and popped it over her head.

"Ah! That's cold!" she screeched and ran for her life.

I seized the handle of the bucket and took my newly gained ammo with me as I began pursuit. I launched a round that splashed at Kaylee's feet. The next round caught her on the right shoulder and burst. She screeched again, but I didn't relent in my chase.

My legs almost gave out as the laughter finally took a firm hold of me. My aim got worse while my laughing fit caused the shots to fall short. I came down on my knees to rest, but kept each hand loaded and ready to fire.

A blast of frigid water hit me in the left arm and quickly raced up to my head. I held up my arm to protect my face as I tried to figure out what was going on. Clara was standing beside the air-conditioning unit with the garden hose in her hands and a smile that went from ear to ear.

"Not fair!" I yelled and threw a round at Clara that missed.

Kaylee laughed hysterically as she was far from the reach of the hose's pressure.

"Over here. We'll double-team," I said, and lobbed a balloon to Kaylee.

She easily caught it and together we mounted an offensive attack.

As the three of us engaged in battle, laughing like mental patients, I thought of how much Brandon Harris was right.

The experience during the last week opened my eyes wider than they'd ever been before. I'd always known how lucky I was, but I hadn't appreciated it as I should have with each passing day. What I had right here and right now made me an incredibly fortunate person. I'd never have any doubt about that.

After a while, we collapsed with exhaustion. We forgot about prime time television, and we even skipped dinner. We lay in the soft grass in the elm's shade and talked as we watched the sun find its bed. The temperature fell to a pleasant coolness as night came out to play. The stars came out to play, too, and beneath them the world dreamed of endless possibilities.

Made in the USA
Middletown, DE
22 December 2022